Mary Karras was born in London in 1978 to Greek-Cypriot parents. Growing up she developed a keen interest in the concepts of community, cultural dissonance and belonging, leading her to pursue a degree in English Literature and Language at King's College London. Since graduating, Mary has worked for several national newspapers including the *Telegraph*, the *Guardian* and the *Independent*. *One Night Beneath the Lemon Trees* is her second novel.

Also by Mary Karras

The Making of Mrs Petrakis

First published in Great Britain in 2023 by Two Roads
An imprint of John Murray Press

This paperback edition published in 2024

1

A CIP catalogue record for this title is available from the British Library

Paperback ISBN 978 1 529 34562 9
eBook ISBN 978 1 529 34563 6

Typeset in Albertina MT by
Palimpsest Book Production Ltd, Falkirk, Stirlingshire

Printed and bound in Great Britain by Clays Ltd, Elcograf S.p.A.

John Murray policy is to use papers that are natural, renewable and
recyclable products and made from wood grown in sustainable forests.
The logging and manufacturing processes are expected to conform
to the environmental regulations of the country of origin.

Two Roads
Carmelite House
50 Victoria Embankment
London EC4Y 0DZ

www.tworoadsbooks.com

John Murray Press, part of Hodder & Stoughton Limited
An Hachette UK company

Mary Karras

ONE NIGHT BENEATH
THE LEMON TREES

TWO
ROADS

For L&L, always.

'The buried truth germinates and breaks through to the light'

— George Bernard Shaw

Nico

March 1990

NICO LEMONIADES THUMPS the breakfast table and the boiled eggs quiver in their silver cups like frightened bald heads. He raises his palms to his face with a triumphant 'Aha!' but the bluebottle has made good its escape and is now thrashing hopelessly against the kitchen window.

'Where was I?'

He was in the middle of reciting a beloved anecdote when he became distracted by the trajectory of the moribund fly and lost concentration.

'The English man, Pappa?'

'Ah yes, the English man.'

His wife, Aliki, frowns into her coffee cup while his daughter, Melina, glances down at her watch, the halcyon days when she would hang on to his every word at breakfast a distant memory.

'I'm going to be late for work.'

'Just a minute.' Nico picks up a piece of thickly buttered toast and waves it in front of his audience. 'So, the English man is walking down the street, dressed up in his smart business suit, when he walks into a lamppost. Straight into it. What does he do, do you think, after he has walked into the lamppost?'

Melina pushes her chair back suddenly and the unpleasant sound of metal legs grating against the floor tiles reverberates around the room. 'I've got to go, Noni will kill me!' Her voice is high-pitched and urgent. She still sounds like a child, Nico thinks, as her wet lips press fleetingly against his exposed scalp and her wavy brown hair tickles his ears and nose. Like a little girl hurrying for school. He draws the hair aside as if it were a veil and looks up at her from his seated position.

'He takes his hat off, bows his head regretfully and apologises to the lamppost! How funny is that?'

Her fingers tickle the grey tufts of hair clinging on for dear life behind his ears.

'Do you get it?'

'I get it, Pappa. The Greek man would have kicked the lamppost in frustration but the English man apologises for getting in its way. Cultural differences.'

'It's genius, no?'

'Maybe the first time?' She winks affectionately at him as she dashes out into the hallway to grab her jacket and handbag. The wretched bluebottle, seizing an opportunity to break free from its domestic prison, follows dizzily behind her.

The front door slams shut and, for a brief moment, the ensuing silence rings in his ears. Her absence allows the invisible gossamer that binds them to snap free, and he and Aliki float their separate ways. His wife to the sink to rinse the dirty plates and refill the kettle, and Nico to their bedroom to peer out of the window at the street. In twenty minutes' time, she'll finish the interminable washing-up and ask if he wants another cup of coffee. He'll shout back, 'Yes please, wife,' and he'll sit with her for a bit but there'll be no need for stories about the Englishman. Not without Melina.

He shuffles up the stairs, gathering the dust that has settled along the bannister, and enters the master bedroom with a faint grunt of effort. He pushes the thin net curtain to the side and cleans the misty glass with the palm of his hand, leaving a dirty, rainbow-shaped smear in its wake that obscures rather than clarifies his vision.

Familiarity. The row of soot-stained houses lining Lancaster Gardens, Harringay, execute their usual morning routines, flinging open their doors and spitting their occupants onto the pavement one by one. Mr Williamson, kissing his pretty wife on the lips and hurrying down the steps with his tie flapping behind him – rushing off to his important job, no doubt, in an office in the City. Mrs Richardson dragging two fat, bespectacled children down the street to the school, her own glasses sliding down her large pink nose as she curses motherhood. Mrs Henderson emerging, gazelle-like, from her house to snatch up gold-topped milk bottles before the neighbours can catch a scandalous glimpse of her rollers.

Melina. Heading the wrong way up Lancaster Gardens towards Burleigh Street, instead of left out of their front door and towards the bus stop on Bishop's

Avenue. He stares until the lovely bundle of wavy hair turns the corner and disappears from his view. He wonders where she could be going on a damp Tuesday morning. Why she would be taking a detour today of all days, when she was running late for her job at the hairdressing salon. When she made such a point of it at breakfast.

'Nico! The kettle's boiled. You want another coffee?'

He is about to let go of the curtain when he sees it. The moribund bluebottle. It has finally succumbed to its inevitable fate and expired on its back on the windowsill.

They eat the fish and chips Melina has brought home for their supper. They pass a bottle of ketchup round the table and use the greasy wrappers as convenient plates. It's raining outside and the water drums against the glass like an insistent visitor, impatient to come in – or perhaps to take his leave. Blustery twilight scenes contrast with the steamy, cosy ambience of their little kitchen and, presiding over their meal for the second time that day, Nico feels a twinge of paternal pride.

'Heavy rain in March, whatever next?' he chuckles. 'Do you remember how hot it was in Morphou the day we were married, Aliki?'

His wife looks up from her papery fish to scan her husband's face. 'Our wedding day?' As usual, she finds it wanting. 'How could I forget? My mamma fainted twice.'

There's an uncomfortable shuffling of wrappers while each of them contemplates the implications of the statement.

Nico sighs. He dips a warm, soggy chip into a splodge of ketchup and shovels it into the back of his mouth. 'So! Where were you going this morning, Miss Melina?'

His daughter nibbles daintily on a piece of cod and he remembers how, when she was eleven or twelve, she decided to become a vegetarian. 'Vege-*what*?' Nico's response was to march down to her favourite chip shop and order her a piece of battered haddock.

She gasped down at her plate in horror. 'Pappa, fish is still meat!'

'Of course it isn't,' he teased affectionately. 'It's a vegetable, like chicken, no?'

Her childish resolve had lasted a whole week after that.

She looks tired this evening, he thinks, finishing the soggy chip and attempting to skewer an uncooperative pickled onion with the complimentary fork. Her light brown eyes are ringed with smudges of grey and her pale skin is almost translucent beneath the kitchen lights. 'Did you not take the bus to Turnpike Lane as usual?'

It's a question meant to satisfy only a nascent curiosity. A mild itch. The truth is, he forgot all about Melina's mysterious detour up Burleigh Street after his morning coffee with Aliki, but the look that now passes between the two women bothers him like indigestion.

There's a sudden onset of coughing. Aliki is choking on a mouthful of food but she raises her hand in the air to signal that she's OK. She can still breathe.

'Bloody fish bones,' she rasps between sips of tap water. 'Melina, go to the English place next time. He's much better than Pappa's and cheaper as well.'

Melina nods. She spies an opportunity to change the subject and snatches it out of the air like a ball player. 'Guess what?' It's an art she's no doubt learned while cutting hair. 'Small talk,' she calls it. An ironic name, Nico thinks, for dreary, never-ending conversation.

'Mrs Karagianni came in for her perm today. You know, the wealthy woman who always leaves a huge tip? Well, her daughter's baby is due the same time as Noni's. The *exact* same day and everything.'

'Noni is pregnant?' Aliki claps her hands together in delight. 'I didn't know! *Marshalla*! Did you know, Nico?'

Nico tries to chime in with his own congratulations but fails to summon any joy for Antigone or her foetus. He feels like he's reaching into a hat and pulling out nothing at all. Not a rabbit, not a sweet. Nothing.

Truth is, any mention of the salon where his daughter works gives him heartache. At twenty-five, she should be a qualified doctor or lawyer by now – a job that she could be proud of and, if he's entirely honest, he could brag about on Green Lanes. There was no glory in massaging Mrs Karagianni's scalp in Noni's salon. Sweeping up discarded hair and gossiping about babies.

'Choices,' Aliki always tells him. They had to let their daughter make her own choices, lead her own life. After all, isn't that what they had done?

Nico's chosen life fits him badly, like a tight nylon tank top.

'We have to let her make her own choices, Nico.'

He wonders, sometimes, if Aliki has any idea what she is talking about, stuck in the house all day washing dishes and sorting out the clothes into piles of darks and lights. Placing them into laundry baskets and stuffing them into the washing machine. Who made her an authority on such important philosophical matters?

There were the little choices, of course. Like what to eat for breakfast. Whether to add milk or sugar to one's coffee or smear butter across a piece of toast. Choices that filled a person's day and made very little difference to it either way. Nico didn't mind choices like these. In fact, he celebrated the flavour and the variety they sprinkled on his routines. Sugar, tea, coffee, marmalade.

Then there were the bigger choices. Deciding which car to buy or where to go on holiday in the summer. These choices left no indelible mark, either. No permanent scar. A person could buy a blue car instead of a red one and enjoy a pleasant life afterwards. Nico wasn't intimidated by these possibilities.

It was the important, life-changing ones he feared the most. The choices that could ruin a life before it had properly started. He'd been faced with a decision of this enormity once, in the old graveyard at the back of their church in Morphou, although he didn't realise it at the time. He didn't recognise its significance and he certainly didn't know that this choice would have tentacles that would reach for him in the years to come. Squeezing the life from his weary body by way of remuneration, in tiny, bead-like drops. Was it so terrible that he wanted to prevent Melina from making the same mistakes?

He sighs as he studies his reflection in the mirror. He licks the tip of his thumb and sweeps it slowly over his eyebrows. First one and then the other, but it's of no use. The grey, unruly arches refuse to be subdued and spring back to life as soon as his saliva has dried. He gives up, pulling a little comb out of his shirt pocket and brushing the grey tufts sprouting at either side of his bald head. The colour and consistency of these tufts is now the same as the stubborn hair emerging from his ears and his nostrils. He wonders if this is how it will end: at sixty-five, with bits of him growing into other bits. Into soft, jellied orifices and cavities. His eyeballs, his lips and eventually his brain, until there is nothing left of Nico Lemoniades to behold except a small mound of grey bristles.

He reaches across for his glasses and pushes them up along the rim of his large nose. He was handsome once. At least, that's what *she* used to say. 'You're not bad for a lemon farmer, Nico' – and if he'd been a little taller, she teased, he may even have been the town's catch.

'Like you, you mean?'

'Exactly like me.'

Her kisses tasted salty, like the Mediterranean Sea.

It's time to venture out. After breakfast with Melina and coffee with Aliki, it's time to zip up his lightweight jacket, lace up his shiny shoes and march down to Green Lanes to buy himself a newspaper. Since retiring from Sonny Smith's cash and carry, his walk has become the best and most important part of his day. It keeps him occupied, allows him to appear useful. How are the shopkeepers of Green Lanes to know that when he returns home and kicks his shoes off, he's not engaged in worthy pursuits but sprawled out on the sofa watching *On the Buses* and devouring chocolate? That sourcing a newspaper is the focal and not the starting point of his day. That since retiring, he's been feeling more morose, more regretful and more introspective than he was in those first, lonely years of marriage on Cyprus.

He calls up the stairs that he's going out to buy a newspaper and Aliki replies that they're out of salami.

'Well, which one should I get, wife?'

'The one you bought last time!' Her voice sounds laboured and muffled, as if it's coming from the inside of yet another bloody basket. A rabbit, forever digging holes through piles of dirty clothes. She looks like one too, he thinks snidely, reaching for his keys. Like an ugly little rabbit with giant crooked teeth.

Nico mumbles an inaudible goodbye that sounds more like an expletive. He stomps up Lancaster

Gardens towards Burleigh Street and Green Lanes and dissolves into the oncoming traffic. The road is long and busy, even on a Wednesday morning. Shopkeepers stand in front of their grocery stores and polish their aubergines and watermelons, and many wave as he walks past. He's a familiar daytime sight and they greet him cheerfully, respectfully. He's 'Kyrie Nico' on Green Lanes – a 'sir', if you will, and not the 'mister' he was in Sonny's cash and carry for so many repetitive years.

'Come on Mister Nico, get a shifty on. You think I have all day to watch you drag a bloody crate across the floor?'

When he first started working for Sonny Smith he assumed, in his naivety, that his boss's rhetorical questions demanded genuine responses. 'I don't know, Mr Smith, since I am no in charge of you.'

Cue howls of laughter. Jokes involving bubbles and banana boats. 'No in charge?' Greece and Cyprus merging into one giant, foreign country. 'What does that mean, Bubble boy?' Nico shrugging his shoulders in confusion.

Yianni's grocery shop is open for business and the proprietor salutes him from behind the till. Nico notices that the man's white apron is smeared with unappealing brown marks, and that his fat stomach bulges out at either side of the gaping material like cream squirting from a cake. A terrible advert for a shop selling food, he tuts. Nico acknowledges the man's enthusiastic greeting with a restrained 'Good morning,' and wanders over to the fridges to choose salami. He smiles knowingly to himself. It wouldn't pay to be too keen, too grateful for the recognition. *On the Buses* was his secret alone.

Yianni follows him. Nico spies him waddling around the counter and across the shop floor and thinks that he's even fatter than he was last time. Cholesterol, Nico thinks, unkindly. Nobody knows when the proverbial axe will fall or what lurks ahead but, for Yianni, the future was definitely saturated with cholesterol.

He peruses the delicatessen display as the shopkeeper wrings his hands on his filthy overalls and hovers excitedly beside him. 'She wants a salami, but easier said than done. Sending a man out to do a woman's work. Honestly, what's next?' he scoffs. 'Asking me to sweep the floors and iron the clothes?'

He turns around and winks conspiratorially at Yianni, who coughs once, then twice, into his large sausage fingers and fiddles nervously with his facial hair.

'You need the toilet?' Nico decides on a branded salami. Lightly spiced and stuffed with garlic and peppers. Bit of everything. That should shut her up. 'I can wait if you need to take a piss.'

'No, no.'

'A cold, then?' He puts a couple of metres' distance between the pair of them, to be on the safe side. 'You sick?'

Yianni shakes his head. 'I'm fine. I'm not sick.'

Nico is feeling extravagant today. Perhaps he'll buy a halloumi to grate over his spaghetti as well. He looks around for the Cypriot cheese and spots it nestled happily between the feta and the anari. Yianni steps out in front of him as if committing suicide by taxi, unable to contain his mounting anxiety any longer.

'Um, Kyrie Nico?' He doesn't mean to disturb Nico's perusal of the meats and cheeses this morning, but there is something he needs to tell him. He chews at the side of his fat cheek. He's been agonising over it since Tuesday, when he saw her at the top of Burleigh Street getting into his car, and if it was *his* daughter he'd want to know. That's what persuaded him in the end, and the wife agreed. That they'd want someone to tell them if the shoe was on the other foot, and it could just as easily be nothing.

'Yes?' Nico's grey arches shoot up in curiosity as Yianni takes a deep breath. The garlic and pepper salami drops to the floor and disappears beneath the fridges.

Nico exhales irritably as he paces around the dusty front room like an animal trapped in a cage. He opens cabinet doors, looking for his bottle of brandy, but it's not where he last stashed it. She's most likely moved it, he thinks. Aliki, the benign tornado. Flinging objects in the air with her useless feather duster so they land in new and random places.

'Aliki! Where's my bottle of Metaxa?' He stops short of demanding that she come and find it for him. He wants to flip the new information around like a pancake first, and to do that he needs peace and quiet. He gives up looking for the bottle when he spies a packet of

Bensons and a lighter hidden behind a paper file marked 'Bills 88'. He groans softly, delightedly. It's been years since he smoked a cigarette. She'll no doubt chastise him when she smells it on his breath, but his lungs are screaming for a drag before he's even straightened up and unwrapped the film.

He'd huffed to Alexi's afterwards and bought his newspaper as usual. Newspapers are more than just rolled-up fly swats to Nico. They offer glimpses into a foreboding world that he can safely scrutinise from his sofa, conveying to him things he needs to know in order to sound knowledgeable, without putting him in harm's way. They allow him to lecture Mr Barnaby next door, for instance. 'Take Maggie Thatcher's poll tax . . .' he once shouted through the small hole in the fence when he noticed the man stooping over his hydrangeas. 'The English elect a woman into power and they're surprised when she squeezes their nuts. It's genius, no?'

Tumbleweed. Nico thinks Mr Barnaby is stupid and uneducated and he enjoys patronising him with the day's news as the man waves back from La La Land. When he doesn't seem interested enough in the point Nico is trying to make, Nico tries to cram the whole paper through the hole. 'Look, Mr Barnaby, look what the woman is doing to the country!'

'Leave him alone,' Aliki yells from the back door when she gets wind of his antics. 'Come inside and have your coffee.'

He sinks into the couch and concentrates on steadying his racing pulse. On the sensation of the grey smoke filling his lungs, on the familiar movement of his hand shifting from his mouth to his side and back again. On the flicking of the ash onto yesterday's discarded paper. The embers, curling up like dead bodies and immediately growing cold.

He loves his daughter the most. Melina. Her name means 'honey' in Greek and she is so named because her lovely brown irises are speckled with yellows and golds. She is the best part of him. A shining star. She is supposed to be going places. She has a bright future waiting for her, a nice career, a doting and – preferably – rich Greek husband and a clutch of kids that will jump into Nico's lap and call him 'Bappou'. If only she felt the same way, he thinks, his face threatening to crumple into a ball. If only she loved him as much as he loves her.

When Yianni finally blurted the thing out, Nico got down on his hands and knees and tried to retrieve the bloody salami. It's funny what seems urgent in the heat of the moment. There was Yianni, wringing his fat sausage hands together and desperately trying to croak out the account that would break his heart, while Nico crawled around on the floor and pulled mouse turds out from beneath his fridges. It had been the same that night in the graveyard. She'd asked him a question, the most important one he would ever be asked in his life, and he'd been intent on finishing that last, fateful cigarette. Blowing smoke into the night sky as if he didn't cherish her with all his heart.

Afterwards, Yianni wanted reassurance that he'd

done right by him. 'You don't look so hot, Kyrie Nico
– you're as white as flour. Leave the salami,' he urged,
'and please sit down.'

Nico replied that he was perfectly fine because he
didn't believe anything that wasn't printed in the newspaper or that he hadn't seen for himself. 'With. My.
Own. Eyes.' He almost poked them out trying to make
the point while the shopkeeper looked like he might
vomit.

'Of course, Kyrie Nico.'

Of course, his arse. Nico opens the back door and
flicks the cigarette butt out into the garden. Its dying
sparks summon the cat. She darts out from beneath
the bushes and advances happily towards him. He
buries his head in her soft grey back and screws his
eyes shut. 'A Turkish boy? Are you joking me?' They've
never bothered to name her, so she's still just 'the cat',
but being anonymous somehow suits her. Of all the
men, he mutters to himself. Of all the men in the
world.

It's time to call Aliki. 'Wife!' Nico clutches the bottom
of the bannister with both hands and he can feel this
morning's breakfast burning a hole through his flesh.
Threatening to spill out of him. Aliki navigates the stairs
carefully, as if they might be booby-trapped, and it
bothers him that she's not rushing to his side like she
usually does.

'Metaxa? Bit early for drinking brandy, isn't it?'

He ignores her perpetually sarcastic tone. 'What time
is Melina finishing work?'

Aliki's brow creases in confusion and her hands fly up to stroke her short grey hair. It's still interspersed with streaks of obsidian black and it suits her, this interesting bob. 'Same time as usual, I expect.' He has to concede that she has weathered the ravages of time far better than he has and it's ironic, really. 'Why?'

Ironic, along with everything else. 'I wish to speak with her, that's why.'

Before Aliki can head back to the safety of her house-work, Nico grabs her firmly by the arm and spits the words into her ear: 'I don't want you there this time, wife.' Her pale flesh is soft and compliant beneath his cold, hard grasp and he wonders how she'd react if he squeezed it tighter. If she would squeal or call out in pain. Search his beady eyes for the reason that she married him and tut at her own desperation.

'This is a father's job, you understand?'

~

The heat felt different that year, the kind of heat that sucked the life right out of your eyes, nose and mouth and left you completely breathless. It was the afternoon of the orange festival of 1954 – he remembers it well because it was the day he first laid eyes on *her*. The Orange Parade, the annual ode to the citrus trees that held the town of Morphou, Cyprus, by the balls. Without them, there was nothing.

He can still recall events in vivid detail. The colours, the smells, the peals of excited laughter. They were out in the streets, maybe as many as a hundred of them from the surrounding neighbourhoods, lining the roads and cheering in unison. Someone was shouting into a crackly megaphone, 'Mind your feet!' as trucks and floats crawled through the tight spaces, each decorated with orange ribbons and brimming with baskets of fruit.

His father was standing next to him, pouring his own excitement into his ear. 'Thank God for the oranges and lemons. What would a couple of dumb peasants like us have done otherwise, hah? We'd have starved, that's what we'd have done!'

'Speak for yourself,' Nico snapped moodily, although they both knew it was true.

Nico's eyes were irritated by sweat and dust, and he thought he imagined the sight of her at first. That she was a magnificent, fruity mirage born solely from his confusion and dehydration.

'Who's that, Pappa?' He jabbed his father in the ribs.
'Who?'

'"Who?" he asks me! How many dark-haired beauties do you see up there on the float? *Her*. The girl on the throne.'

'The Orange Queen?' His father chuckled. 'How the hell should I know?'

She was surely the most beautiful woman at the parade and perhaps on the whole of the island. No, she was *definitely* the most beautiful woman on the island. 'She's wonderful.' The float had stopped briefly to flaunt its cargo and Nico fought his way through the spectators with his elbows to claim a better view, ignoring the ensuing insults.

'Watch it, *garo!*'

'Donkey brains, you're standing in my way!'

'Orange girl? Over here!' He waved frantically and she glanced over, vaguely amused by the commotion in her honour. She tossed him an orange from a basket at her feet and her dark eyes shone with just the faintest hint of impudence. The right amount, he thought later. As if she knew she was very beautiful but was practised enough to pretend. It was a moment between them, really. A passing moment and nothing more, but as he reached up and plucked the fruit as it hurtled through the sky, he knew it was the start of everything.

'Like I said,' his father chuckled, 'thank heavens for the oranges!'

Nico found out where she lived. In a pink, single-storey house on the outskirts of Morphou, they told him. The family was new in town. The girl, her mother and the crazy older brother. The mother was a widow but they were a private family and nobody knew the circumstances of their arrival. 'Be careful,' they warned. 'They're not right.'

He showed up the following evening, rapping eagerly on the door and oblivious to the advice of the town's bigmouths.

The infamous brother answered. 'What do you want, stranger?' His dark shadow blocked the family doorway.

He wanted to see the Orange Queen again, to talk

to her. Perhaps to accompany her on a walk. Desire emboldened his words that night and there was no hesitation. No crack or waver in his voice.

'A walk?' The brother's rancour sprayed from his mouth in a fine mist and infused the air around them. 'You implying my sister is a whore?'

'Of course not.'

'The town's tart?'

'Did I say that?' Nico secretly hoped that she was the town's tart. That she would hear the raised voices and materialise behind open shutters in her thin orange veils. Better still, that she would show up wearing nothing at all, and, as if her brother saw the same filthy fantasy float before his own eyes, he punched him square in the teeth. 'I suggest you go and screw yourself, little man. My sister has her sights set far higher than you.'

Nico collected himself from the dust and staggered off into the night, undeterred by the bleeding and the bruising. The busted, swollen lips and references to his physique. He lusted after his Orange girl for weeks, abandoning the market stall he owned with his father to follow her around like a lovesick dog until, finally, chance threw another citrus fruit up in the air.

'Please, I just want to talk with you. I'm going *insane* here!' He almost licked her face at the delicious sight of her, cornered, at long last, inside a vacant shop doorway.

'Somewhere discreet,' she replied flirtatiously, glancing over his shoulder for reprimanding fishwives.

'I swear to God, if my brother finds out, he'll chop me into pieces with his fruit knife.'

'We can talk wherever you like.'

'Just talk?' The wicked glint in her eyes contradicted her cautious words.

'I promise.'

'The graveyard, then. Tonight.' She pushed past him and fled before anyone could notice the encounter, her long black curly hair trailing tantalisingly behind her.

Tonight? Eight slow and painful hours. Nico's trousers wept in agony.

They met in secret in the old cemetery behind St Angelo's and Nico immediately broke his promise. He couldn't stop himself. He could hear his resolve snapping like chalk as he relieved her tanned body of its flimsy dress and emptied himself into her among the gravestones. He had never felt more alive than in those sweet, delicious moments, completely surrounded by death.

Afterwards, they slumped against the concrete crosses and smoked Craven A cigarettes as the cicadas chirruped admonishingly in their ears. She seemed almost ethereal that first night, sitting among the graves with the moonlight illuminating her face. Nico was almost afraid to speak in case stirring the atmosphere revealed her to be nothing but a ghost.

He withdrew another cigarette and tapped it twice on the red packet, taking his time to shove it under his nose and inhale it before lighting it. As if feeling exultant slowed life right down to a series of magnificent, still images. 'You're really beautiful, you know that?'

'I know.'

'You *know*?' He threw his head backwards and laughed. For the first time since he was a small boy, he really laughed. The sensation of it was so unfamiliar that he almost forced the sound back into his lungs. 'Wonderful!'

She finished her own cigarette and flung the butt into the darkness, sitting up to pull her dress over her small breasts and refasten the knots at the shoulders. 'What's so funny about looking in the mirror and recognising your worth?'

'Vanity?' he teased. 'Nothing, apparently.' It was the relief after weeks of chasing her, more than anything else. Relief that she was finally sitting across from him. That she was his. 'Perhaps your brother's right, after all. You're too good for a sunburned lemon farmer like me.'

They were the very best months of his life. He confided in his Orange girl, told her things that nobody, not even his best friend Giorgio, knew. That he was melancholy living with his parents. An almost thirty-year-old man, sleeping in the back room of his childhood home and listening to them either arguing or praying. He was bored of harvesting the lemons from his father's fruit trees. Waking up at first light to load baskets onto the back of the truck and drive to the market, only to repeat the same interminable morning he'd already endured the day before.

She moaned about missing Limassol, where they'd lived until a mysterious incident forced them to flee. Morphou was too small, it was too far from the sea. 'You should have seen our house, Nico, right by the water's edge. You could walk all the way out along the pier and see the Mediterranean glistening for miles in every direction.' She was afraid of her brother, who'd lost his marbles after their father died. Flinging knives across the room to skewer the mosquitoes.

Nights when they were too tired to talk or share intimacies, they would slump against the crosses, smoking cigarettes and listening to the sound of the cicadas. The stars shone brightly and only for *her*. When there were no stars and no lights, Nico would strike matches so he could read the inscriptions on the worn gravestones. 'This poor, dead bastard has been lying here for more than half a century.' He whistled through his teeth. 'Think of all the things Sergis Katsouris has missed in that time. Two World Wars, the ending of empires, the invention of flight. Doesn't that make you feel, I don't know . . . alive somehow?'

She crinkled her nose in confusion. 'You like all this?'

'I said it makes me feel alive, and it's hardly strange given our desire to exist. Where better to feel that you exist than in a place full of people who don't?'

He could have lived like that forever. Making love to her in the darkness before reading the epitaphs of the skeletons, but, the following summer, something changed. When she came to him, her eyes were no longer full of longing and mischief but brimming with a new and unsettling fear.

'There is something I have to tell you, Nico. But first, I'd like to know what your intentions are towards me.'

He knew what she was about to ask, what she wanted from him.

'Do you ever plan on asking me to marry you, or are we to live like this forever? As secret lovers in a grave-yard?'

His heart sank quickly. He wanted to marry her, of course he did, but part of him agreed with her crazy brother. She was too good for the likes of a sunburned lemon farmer. He had nothing to offer her except the shirt from his back and a basketful of his father's citrus fruit. If she'd been anyone else, *any* other woman in Morphou, he wouldn't have given the thing a second thought. He would have crawled on his hands and knees and proposed to her among the graves and the stars, but this one? This beauty deserved better.

Looking back, he should have shared his thoughts. He should have held her tightly, told her that he was just a farmer and that she belonged with a successful doctor from Greece. He should have given her the opportunity to brush his concerns to the side, but he was too long about the thing and his silence cut her. He could see it in her eyes, in the sudden tensing of her shoulders. He lit another cigarette, blowing a series of flimsy smoke rings into the night sky.

'You're unbelievable, Nico, you know that?' She shook her head slowly in disgust, rising to her feet to brush the loose dirt from her dress and into his upturned face.

If he'd known it would be the last time, he would have run after her. He was sure of it! Chased her through the paths between the neglected stone crosses and out into the dusty streets. Pursued her round the lemon trees and pressed her face to his chest so she could hear what she meant to him. 'What did I do?' Or perhaps he'd have done nothing at all . . .

The next morning, his father loaded the rusty Bedford all by himself. He cursed his son and his rotten luck to have sired him while securing the leather straps around the baskets. '*Garo!*' He swore loudly enough for Nico to hear through the open bedroom shutters before he rearranged himself back into sleep.

Another scorching Saturday in Morphou. The sun had already reached its zenith when Nico arose for the second time and broke his fast with koulouri and cheese. He washed his face to soothe his throbbing head and scurried to Mr Andreas's kafeneon to revitalise his spirits. It was quiet in the café. Most of the regulars were out toiling in the fields or selling their fruit at the markets and Nico sat brooding in the corner until Giorgio showed up to keep him company.

Giorgio, his old school friend, looked like the paintings of the ancient Grecians that decorated his mother's urns. He was a tall, dark-skinned man with large wide-set eyes and arms that could carry a man for miles.

'He's a loyal *shilo*, your Giorgio,' his pappa used to say. 'A loyal dog. A true Greek. They don't make men like that any more.' They certainly didn't make men like Giorgio. He bought a bottle of ouzo for them to share and they drank until oblivion erased his nagging conscience. It was a good day. One of the better ones, in fact, and Nico ended the night on his knees with his braces hanging limply by his side, singing an ode to the moon.

As he prepared to stagger back to his feet and head home, he noticed Aliki standing in the shadows with her father. He wrinkled his nose in drunken contemplation. He'd seen the young woman at the market – it was hard to avoid people in a small town – but that night, as the moonlight caught her brilliant black hair and her impossibly pale skin and turned them both to silver, he convinced himself he knew her well.

'Aliki mou?'

That he liked her, even.

Someone like Aliki, he thought, lurching clumsily towards her, was far better suited to a peasant like him. A plumper, plainer woman with rabbit teeth, who would be flattered by the male attention. 'My sweet Aliki?' A woman who looked like Aliki could not afford to be choosy.

She would later claim, with her father as her witness, that he'd asked for her hand in marriage. Nico would forever protest that he'd blacked out drunk and could barely recall his own name, never mind a proposal. Either way, the seeds of the future were sown.

Still, far better to marry beneath him and feel virile and potent, he commiserated, than to marry someone like his Orange girl and crane his neck like an etiolated sapling.

They moved into the white house Aliki's father had built for whichever one of his daughters should marry first. Nico tried and failed to learn a trade to supplement his income. His father-in-law was a carpenter who ran a small workshop in his yard and, after weeks of invitations, Nico reluctantly agreed to a trial. He managed to stick at the thing for a week, a whole seven days, before his Cypriot temper got the better of him and he almost decapitated the man with a saw.

His mother's brother was a cobbler. The hunched old uncle lent him a wooden desk and some tools – a cobbler's knife, a hammer and a pair of pliers. He taught him how to mix up glue using cardboard and white spirit and they conversed beneath the low arches of Nico's new house as they waited for passing trade.

When Mr Hamboulides hobbled up to Nico's porch with his expired shoe in his hand, the heel flapping hungrily from the under-sole, his uncle stumbled to his feet and smiled encouragingly at the pot of glue. He issued instructions, even standing behind his nephew at one point to bend his arms into the required positions. 'Here, like this.'

Nico's head throbbed from the concentration and the exposure to the midday heat. Beads of sweat pricked his brow and dripped into his eyes as his hands refused to do as he commanded. He soon abandoned the desk and the tools and sent Uncle Artemi back to his rusty tin shack. He was no good, he shouted at the old man, at things that required discipline and application. His stupid mother, claiming to know him best, should have known better. In reality, he was drinking too much and hadn't slept in months. When he held his hands out in front of his face, his fingers shook perceptibly and he could barely see straight, never mind make an acceptable cabinet or fix a hungry shoe.

He went back to harvesting the lemon trees and accompanying his father to the market when he could be bothered to crawl out of bed. It was an unskilled job, but one his limbs at least remembered. More importantly, he was finished by lunchtime so he could slope back home, shower and siesta, and be at the kafeneon before four.

The anticipation of the first drink of the day excited Nico more than anything else. The musty smell of the café; wood mingled with sweat and spirit; the familiar and comforting creak of the chair as he relinquished his weight after a long, laborious morning. Then the arrival of the bottle; its presentation in the owner's large, hairy hands; the twisting and popping of the lid. The glugging of the clear liquid into the glass and the kick of the first sip, like a horse's hoof to the chest. The gradual obscuring and melting away of an increasingly intolerable reality.

Giorgio was always the first to join him. His face was flushed with heat and exertion and his builder's arms were covered in a fine layer of cement dust. Next came Giorgio's friends, Kyriaco and Panayioti. Kyriaco, a short, hirsute man with a mono-brow and an unflattering convict's haircut, made Nico uncomfortable. His volatile outbursts were frequently spliced with fits of troubling laughter, as he shook or stood on the tables to make a point, sending Mr Andreas into a spit-filled frenzy. It would invariably fall to Giorgio to pay for his friend's outbursts but, curiously, he seemed to relish rather than resent this responsibility.

Panayioti was as different to Kyriaco as night was to day, and it was hard to believe that they could complement the same person without tearing his soul in two. Panayioti was a quiet man with floppy black hair and lips better suited to a girl. He played the bouzouki at weddings and had recently stolen his next-door neighbour's bride. It was rumoured that the husband wanted him dead, that he'd offered a reward for his head, and Nico wondered how the pair of them, Panayioti and Helen of Troy, slept at night.

'How could a man with friends like Giorgio and Kyriaco be afraid of anything?' Panayioti giggled when Nico posed the same question. Glancing over at his best friend's biceps, Nico supposed he had a point.

In the summer, Mr Andreas dragged the little tables outside the café so they could take advantage of the evening breeze. As the sun sank below the horizon and the moon rose up to take its place, he lit the foukou to chargrill them a meze of pastirma sausage, halloumi cheese and kalamari rings. Their mouths watering in anticipation, they shouted for another bottle of whichever spirit remained in the decimated stash after an afternoon of heavy drinking, raising their glasses to women with legs that went on forever and to Aphrodite herself.

'To EOKA!' As the day died, Kyriaco ended up on the tables, loudly professing his love for Grivas, and Giorgio would drag him down by his shirt and remind him that Mr Andreas loved his tables and his glasses but he especially loved the British.

Evenings when Nico was still vaguely sober, he would stumble back up the stairs of the white house, kick off his boots and dump himself unceremoniously on the porch like a sack of potatoes. 'Wife, I'm home!' Aliki would prepare a supper of fried rabbit and salad and they would eat outside in near silence, listening to the sounds of an island preparing for sleep. Housewives screaming for their kids to come to bed, doors slamming shut, dogs barking at the moon. The odd car revving laboriously up a hill.

'The jasmine's out.'

Her attempts at polite conversation only infuriated him further and he would shove his empty plate towards her and stumble into the kitchen in search of another drink to wash away the rage.

'A toast!' He filled his glass and saluted the overhanging vines. 'To us, dear wife, and to our *many* happy years together!'

Aliki would have gone to bed by then, exasperated by her husband's drunken moods and, most likely, her own bad luck. Nico would sit outside until the sun rose again, wondering if this heartbreak would always be his life.

The next few years of married life played out like the tentative strumming of a mandolin. Nico waited for the music to intensify and for the notes to burst into a joyful song but, instead, there was only the strumming.

One particular night in Mr Andreas's kafeneon marked a terrible turning point. The evening kicked off with the girlish Panayioti bursting in through the flimsy door of the café to announce he'd become a father. Helen of Troy had given birth to their first child, he declared, as his long hair danced around his silly face.

It was the start of the short-lived winter of 1958, and the three of them were sitting inside the kafeneon to escape the night chill. They were huddled around half-empty glasses of liquor, brimming ashtrays and tavli boards, while Mr Andreas was slumped over the counter with his chin in his hands, listening to a political programme on the radio. Occasionally, he would mutter an expletive or fiddle with his small grey moustache.

Panayioti's jubilation revived the small group. 'I said, I have a *son!*'

A collective chorus of congratulations rang round the café, followed by the drumming of fists on tables and calls for more transparent liquor. Nico wondered how such a small group of men could make such a racket. Giorgio sprang up from his chair to purchase a bottle of spirit, but Panayioti threw his jacket to the floor before he could reach the bar and called for Mr Andreas's finest ouzo at his expense.

It was just as well they weren't toasting Nico's child, Kyriaco sneered, his mono-brow quivering menacingly around his forehead. Their mouths would have dried up waiting for the drink and their tongues would have shrivelled from dehydration.

'I'm skint, file,' Nico growled in response. 'You know I am.'

'So you keep telling us, but I see plenty of lemons and plenty of lemon trees. So go pick them.'

Nico exhaled slowly and in frustration. He slumped backwards in a drunken stupor as his thoughts drifted to her. Always *her*. It was as if she'd disappeared from the face of the earth after that last night in the cemetery. He wondered if she'd gone back to Limassol where she was happiest, or perhaps – he swallowed the bitter lump threatening to shoot out of his throat – to marry a worthier man. He often considered going over to the house and asking after her, but these theoretical visits usually culminated with the brother's fist in his mouth.

'Did you hear what Panayioti just said?' Kyriaco's voice pierced his thoughts like a pointed skewer. The cuckolded husband had called off the hit, so Panayioti could sleep safely in his bed. 'Turns out, nobody wants to raise another man's child, and who can blame them, hah?'

Kyriaco reached over and poured himself a third glass of ouzo and surmised that it could all have been much worse. 'It can *always* be worse, file. Trust me.' Helen of Troy could have run off with a big, hairy Turk. What would the ex-husband have said then? He would have been laughed out of Morphou with horns sticking out of his head and his tail between his legs. Giorgio rolled his eyes to the ceiling good-humouredly and Nico braced himself for the evening's inevitable descent into anti-Turkish rants and pro-EOKA chants, culminating, most likely, in their eviction into the night.

'A song!' The man of the hour was not ready to relinquish his moment of glory to Kyriako, or to Grivas for that matter, and began a hoarse lament of his own. A peasant's heart was torn in two by a beautiful woman with eyes the colour of midnight and lips as red as blood. The poor devastated bastard followed her to the ends of the earth in search of an explanation. 'Why, why, why?' The clicking of fingers and the imaginary thumbing of a bouzouki accompanied the absurd refrain. The beautiful woman refused to see him, so the man sank to his knees to kiss her feet, begging her to release him from her spell.

The song changed tempo, suddenly, and the rest of the men joined in. Panayioti's voice grew louder and more insistent and he stood up and waltzed around the room with his invisible bouzouki in his embrace. 'Please, please, please!' Nico's ears began to ring and his own hands were no longer drumming or clicking but trembling in front of him. By the time the woman's son emerged from the shadows to plunge a dagger into the wretched man's heart, Nico had vomited all over the kafeneon floor.

He was banned from the kafeneon for a period of three months, or until his liver regrew. Those were Mr Andreas's orders. As it turned out, Nico could barely leave his bedroom, never mind open the front door and walk the hundred yards to the café for a drink. He lay in his bed for weeks, sweating and shaking and vomiting into the bowl Aliki left beneath the bed. He wondered, in his more lucid moments, if he might die. He could imagine the confused looks at his funeral. The sympathetic tuts.

'What did the poor bugger die of?'

'Nobody knows! His wife told mine that there was absolutely nothing the matter with him. What a thing, hah?'

She wanted to send for the doctor, although Mandrides was the last person Nico wanted to see hovering by his sick bed. Prescribing pills and slipping Aliki the bills, and waiting for him to croak so he could make more profit from recommending the undertaker, no doubt.

'No thank you, wife, I would rather croak than line Mandrides' pockets.'

'Why don't you close your eyes for a bit, then?' Her soothing voice cut through the intense ringing in his ears.

When he did manage to sleep, his head was thick

with dark, twisted visions. Mr Andreas listening to the radio and fiddling with his moustache while the characters from Panayioti's songs came alive to bury his stinking corpse. Sometimes *she* was there, watching from the shadows, and other times he had a sick sense that he had eaten rat poison and that it was killing him slowly, from the inside.

They spent Christmas by themselves, just the two of them, and it was a relief not to have a house full of relatives banging pots in his kitchen. He'd always hated Christmas and he wouldn't have been able to force the merriment this year. Instead, Aliki pushed back the shutters and propped him up against his pillow. They sat together, in grateful silence, eating roasted chestnuts and listening to the chants of '*Kala Christouyena*' that echoed around the cold, dusty streets on Christmas Eve.

Gradually, he could smell things again. The familiar scents of coal, pine resin and smoke infused the winter air and he could feel that he was starting to get better. By the new year, he was well enough to shuffle outside and sit beneath the arches. He watched Aliki patiently mending the neighbours' clothes to throw a few extra coins into their tin as he slurped egg and lemon soup the way his grandfather used to. A toothless old man hunched over his pot. Careful not to spill any down his shirt and humiliate himself in front of his grandson.

He'd aged half a century or more in the space of a few short months. He looked down at his loose-fitting jumper, his worn pyjamas and leather *pantofles* and he wondered who he had become. Who was this eighty-year-old man who had snatched the body of his thirty-three-year-old self?

He finished his soup and pushed his bowl towards Aliki. He stared at her long pointed needle as it weaved skilfully in and out of the thin fabric on its way towards the sky. As she stitched, her brow was knitted in concentration, and something else: satisfaction. He envied her ability to feel this joy, however fleeting.

The cool breeze that whipped around their porch sounded like curses and ominous whisperings. It carried with it a fine yellow dust that reminded him of his mortality. Of the crumbling bones in the graveyard behind the church, of time running out. Nico lit his first cigarette of the year and decided it was time to get dressed.

~

Nico Lemoniades is a hungry man. He pads into the kitchen in his Marks & Spencer's slippers and throws a can of cold baked beans over a slice of stale bread. He imagines Aliki poking fun as he scoffs. Tomato sauce dribbling down his chin. 'Oh! A man of the herbs and the spices, are we?'

Baked beans remind him of Ricky Smith's acne-covered face. Ricky was Sonny Smith's son and he used to show up at the cash and carry under the pretext of helping. A spiteful, lazy little weasel who would call him 'boss' and 'guv' and then grass him up if he spent too long on his smoke. For years, it was his worst nightmare: his beautiful Melina ending up with the likes of Ricky Smith. Spending the rest of her life on benefits with a wailing brat beneath each arm.

Mind you, he thinks, shovelling more beans into his face, this new scenario is worse. *Infinitely* so.

He sits in front of the television with his plate of lumpy, cold beans and waits for her to return from work. He sighs as he remembers how she used to poke sticks through the holes in the triangular borders of their lawn when she was a little girl. Collecting the snails that hid inside them and arranging them in order of size and colour. 'Look what I found, Pappa!' He can still see her in her dark green school uniform and black and white checked skirt. Her white socks pulled up to just beneath her knees and her long hair fastened with ribbons from Aliki's sewing box. He used to knock on the window and wave to her, sticking his thumb in the air to signal his approval. 'Very good, Melina!' Her hands, when she waved back, would be sticky with snail slime.

He's still thinking of the childish simplicity of these memories when he hears her key clicking in the lock. Her wavy hair catches the evening light as she spins around to close the door behind her. She hangs her jacket on the coat hooks and slips off her shoes. It seems to him that she is biding her time. First one foot, then the other. She runs her fingers through her hair and massages sticky goo from a pot in her pocket into her lovely lips. When she finally walks towards him, her face is clouded with doubt. The cynic in Nico wonders if her mother has called the salon to warn her of his mood. His insistence that he speak with her alone. What would *she* know? he thinks, as he dismisses the thought as too paranoid even for him. Stupid woman that she is.

'Hello, Pappa.'

'How was your day, miss?' He gets up with a groan to silence the television and gestures to the saggy brown sofas.

'It was fine, Pappa. How was yours?' She sits on the couch opposite him and he's struck, in moments like these, by the stark differences between mother and daughter. Melina's honey eyes and wide, expressive features, contrasting with Aliki's scrunched-up rabbit face. It was almost as if they were two strangers at the breakfast table some mornings, two strangers thrown together by chance.

'Funny you should ask. I popped into Yianni's to buy your mother a salami.'

'How is he?' Is it his imagination, or do her eyes grow wider and more fearful?

'Oh, you know. A walking warning for heart disease and bowel cancer. Maybe diabetes too.'

She has the good grace to smile. Her face relaxes around her lips as if her mouth is the centre of the universe.

'He said he saw you on Tuesday.' He clears his throat nervously. 'Getting into a car with Ozil's son. He says you looked like lovers, the pair of you, and that I would want to know. Is it true?' The words almost stick in his throat as her lips part in surprise. 'Are you and Ozil's son lovers?'

He looks around the room as if he's searching for the answers in the walls and the ceilings. He notices that everything in his little world is brown. The sofas, Aliki's sewing chair, the carpets and the curtains. How could anything good happen in a room as brown as this?

'Well, Melina?'

'What are you asking me, Pappa?'

He can hear his heart thumping in his ears. He remembers how, when he made love to his Orange girl among the stone crosses and the lemon trees, he'd never felt more alive.

'I'm asking you if Ozil's son is your lover.' The words stick to the roof of his mouth and he can barely get them out. He knows what the answer will be before her lips have even parted. It's written all over her lovely face, along with something else. A glimmer of relief.

He steps out into the chilly night. The wind is damp and has a bite to it and Nico pulls the collars of his jacket up around his ears to shield them from a whipping. It feels far too cold for the end of March. It's *always* too bloody cold.

He marches up Lancaster Gardens in his shiny black shoes but he's deflated. There is no longer pride in his step. He notices that the cat is following furtively behind. He turns around to shoo her away as she darts in and out of the parked cars, defying him. 'Piss off home, you hear me? You'll get yourself run over!'

He lingers briefly at the corner house in the middle of their street. It's twice the size of theirs, maybe even bigger, and he wants to ring Mr Robinson's doorbell and shake the man's hand. 'Congratulations to you,' he wants to sneer in his neighbour's face. 'On your admirable house with the sweeping driveway and your beautiful wife with the nice big breasts. Congratulations, Mr Robinson, for having the guts to grab your own life by the balls. I hope you're very happy!'

It's a lie, of course. Mr Robinson's happiness is the last thing on Nico's mind. In fact, he hopes that his own stuck-up daughter will come to him one day with the news that will break his heart into tiny pieces. That would serve the smug bastard right.

The cat jumps up on the garden wall while he's glaring menacingly through Mr Robinson's front windows and startles him. He scoops her up and whispers into the back of her soft, pulsing fur, 'Don't look at me like that.' He gestures at the glistening pavements and the rows of parked cars surrounding him. 'All of this is because of *you*. Because of what I did to you. Because I'm trying to fix things so that she doesn't end up as miserable as me. Can't you see?'

He lowers the cat to the ground with another grunt of effort. He turns right onto Burleigh Street and then left onto Green Lanes. His glasses have misted over and the lights seem broken and distorted, as if he's viewing them through a dirty car windscreen. He pauses while he takes them off and cleans the lenses with the edges of his sleeve.

It all made sense, suddenly. The pointed comments over fish and chips and the looks that passed between mother and daughter while he was regaling them with his tales. Melina's late hours in a salon that supposedly never closed. Geriatric haircuts at ten o'clock at night? He was a stupid fool. He should have guessed!

'Were you in on this too?' he spat at Aliki, resisting the familiar urge to dig his nails into the soft, fleshy part of her arm. 'This deception?' To make her yelp in pain.

'Of course not, Nico.' She was a terrible actress. The very worst. 'What do you take me for?'

It's late, but the twenty-four-hour grocery shops that line the main road on both sides are open for opportunistic business. He stops outside Ozil Groceries and watches Mr Ozil stocking his shelves with tins of beans. Rumour has it that the man sells marijuana on the side but if he does, he can't be very good at it. His shop is old-fashioned and his overalls are scruffy. He's not a young man either, maybe even older than Nico, and Nico doubts he'll be able to stand up again once he's finished tending to his tins. He wonders if Mr Ozil knows what his son has been up to in his red car on Burleigh Street? The damage he's caused his family?

'They're just the same as us,' she cried naively as he hunted for his jacket. 'They have the same blood running through their veins.'

He laughed out loud, then, at her ridiculous arguments. Her simplistic way of looking at a complicated world. 'Tell that to the Greek-Cypriots they kicked out of their homes in '74,' he snapped, as his lungs itched for a secret cigarette. 'Go and tell them it's perfectly fine that you lost everything during the civil war because my Turkish boyfriend has the same blood!'

To think, he tuts, as he watches Mr Ozil labouring away in his shop, that she was apparently a shining star. That he once dreamed of her becoming a successful doctor and owning a huge house in Hampstead with a successful husband. Filling their six bedrooms with kids that he and Aliki could dote on. Hell, some grandchildren may have even given them something to talk about besides salamis and laundry.

The shopkeeper stumbles to his feet and notices Nico standing in the drizzling rain. He beckons to him warmly through the half-steamed window but Nico shakes his head and sinks back into the collars of his jacket. He bids him goodnight. Better to stay away, he thinks, shamefully. In fact, the world would be a much better place if people just stuck to their own kind. Mr Ozil can sit in his shop and play with his fava beans, and he can lie on the sofa and read the Greek-Cypriot announcements in his newspaper. Like with like.

Anger suddenly displaces his grief and, abandoning his walk, he turns around to head home.

'You're killing me.' He stomps up the stairs full of renewed rage and barges into her bedroom without knocking. He startles her, he can tell from the expression on her face. The way she leaps up from her bed

as if someone has set fire to her feet. 'You hear me?'
He's pleased that he's shattered her peace.

It's been years since he's set foot inside her bedroom.
A woman's room is sacred. Forbidden, even. Like the
mysterious interior of her handbag, its inner pockets
stuffed with strange and exotic things. Lipsticks,
perfumes, little feminine pads. He feels like he's violating
her by being in here.

He looks around. Her walls, once pink and plastered
with posters from the magazines he used to buy her
from Mr Patel's, are now white. Photos of strange men
at parties are arranged, rainbow-like, over her bed.
Were these friends from her college days, he wonders,
examining the faces. Friends from work or yet more
lovers? Their pierced tongues goad him from beyond
their papery stillness. Their faces, shiny with sweat and
God knows what else. Beer? Drugs? Ecstasy? Is that
what they called it? He can almost hear the walls jeering
at him.

A string of fairy lights twinkles around her mirror
and the place feels more like an apartment than a
bedroom. A home inside a home, and he's hurt by
another betrayal. By his daughter's desire to distance
herself from the brown life that he's carved out for her
downstairs.

'How could you do this to me?' He's huffed all the
way up here to tell her that she's wrong, and here she
is wearing pink pyjamas and getting ready for bed as
if it's nothing! As if she isn't about to destroy her bright
future with her silly choices! He stood outside Mr Ozil's

shop in the rain and watched him stocking his shelves with his tins and they weren't the same, the Greeks and the Turks. They *were* different. They didn't share the same blood no matter how much she wanted to believe it, how pink her pyjamas were.

Did she know that among his friends back home, he had been the least concerned about the politics of the island? Giorgio always had his finger on these things, but Nico couldn't have cared less about their civil conflicts, the Greeks, the Turks and the British. As long as he had money in his pockets and a seat in the kafeneon at the end of a long, hot day, he was happy to let them all kill each other.

Then they invaded the north of the island, taking his parents' home. His fruit trees. His own daughter's legacy. Morphou is no longer called Morphou, he tells her, but something else. Something unpronounceable. Something *Turkish*. Did she even know that? 'Thank God for the oranges and lemons,' his father used to exclaim as the floats paraded up and down the dusty streets. 'What would we have done otherwise?' He was proud to hail from a town where the citrus trees grew big and strong and the blossoms smelled like honey for so many months of the year. They all were, once. Now generations of hard work had been lost. Swallowed up by the war. People literally disappearing through the cracks in the earth, never to emerge again. The Turks were no longer a political discussion after a drinking session at the kafeneon, but a real and tangible enemy. Did she know *that*?

'I understand, Pappa, but they're your enemies,' she replies, 'not mine. Your memories. These trees, the lemons, these lands you're talking about, they're your legacy.'

'It's not just about the war, Melina.'

'Then what else?' She stares at him, mouth agape, and he shakes his head incredulously. He wants to pounce on her. To grab her by the shoulders and squeeze her until the apathy drips out of her like a juice. He sees *her*, then. As clear as that last night in the moonlit cemetery. He sees her gathering up her skirts, her eyes round with hurt and disbelief, turning away from him for the last time.

'Everything else! By choosing this boy, you are ruining your own life too. Don't you see? It might be all chocolates, hearts and flowers now, but he will eventually want different things to you and these arguments will tear you apart. He'll want to marry you in a mosque, to circumcise his sons, to give them Turkish names. These are big differences, Melina. You can't sweep them aside with a make-up brush.'

'So what if our children have Turkish names?' she asks. 'Is it really such a big deal, Pappa? We live in London, not Morphou. Everything's cosmopolitan.'

'Cosmopolitan? So what? Big deal! This is the respect your poor pappa deserves after everything I've done for you? The sacrifices I've made by emigrating to this cold, miserable country to haul boxes for Sonny Smith? For my grandson to be named after Ozil from the grocery shop on Green Lanes?'

'What's so wrong with Mr Ozil?' She makes her disappointment in him obvious by clicking her tongue against her teeth and he can see it in her eyes. The consequence of the passage of time and her lazy, second-generation perspective. He's given her too much, that's the problem, and he wants to piss his own pants at the irony of the thing. The mess he's created for himself by coming to England in the first place.

'Nothing if you run out of tomatoes in the middle of the night, but to invite him into the family? It's a kick in your pappa's teeth, no?'

'So, this is about you and your ego?' she mocks. 'Your silly pride? You're not worried about cultural differences and unhappy marriages at all, but about what your shopkeeper friends might say behind your back?'

'This is about what is right and what is wrong, and marrying a Turkish boy is *wrong*.'

'Right. So he has to be Greek, that's what you're saying? I can marry anyone I like as long as he's Greek?'

'Yes!' Nico quickly corrects himself as images of his lovely Melina and her Greek husband dissipate like her vanilla perfume. 'I mean, you have to be the same as the person you marry. Share common interests, similar ideas and goals for the future. Relationships don't work otherwise. If he's Greek like you, then it works better, see?'

'Similar?' she scoffs. 'Like you and Mamma, you mean?' She's making fun of him, and his stomach threatens to reach up his gullet and grab him by the throat. To shake him from side to side as if he were a chicken being strangled.

'Maybe if you actually *met* Hassan you'd realise that you're worrying about nothing. That we do have things in common. We like to eat the same things, we go to the same places to chill, and he even likes my soul music.'

'Chill? What is this "chill"? This is not what I'm talking about, Melina!'

'*Please*, Pappa?'

Nico shakes his head. 'You want me to welcome him into my home for a barbecue, like I am approving of this bloody thing? Are you so very stupid, Melina?'

'She's going to leave home.' Another doorway lecture from Aliki. If he didn't accept Melina's relationship, she was going to move out and start her own life, away from his expectations. 'She can't live your way, Nico.'

'Move where?' he scoffed, shoving her roughly out of his way so he could go and spy on Mr Ozil. 'Melina doesn't know the first thing about life, the way you've wrapped her up in cotton wool since she was two years old!'

'The way *I've* wrapped her up?' she called after him. 'Me, Nico?'

His daughter is finally crying and if nothing else, her tears are a welcome sight. At least she feels sorry for him.

'Do you understand? Do you know how hard you make it for us to love you?' Melina cries.

'What are you talking about now?'

'Me and Mamma. Sorry to say, Pappa, but you make it really hard for us to love you sometimes.'

Defeated, Nico turns and walks out of her bedroom. He's afraid, more than anything, of what she might say to him next. As his own mother used to say, words flung in the heat of the moment had the sharpest points of all.

~

He could tell Aliki was flustered by Giorgio's appearance on their porch. It was late and she was dressed in her flimsy nightgown, her face washed bare of the pinkish powders she liked to dust on her cheeks. She looked younger without these things. Without her clothes, her sandals and her face paints. Younger and more vulnerable, and an unfamiliar pang of jealousy almost thrust him into the doorframe.

She changed hurriedly back into her day dress and prepared them a supper of bread, halloumi and salted turnip. They ate beneath the arches and swapped stories between gulps and slurps. The local *manavi* was getting on Aliki's nerves. While his vegetables were shrinking, his prices were creeping up like weeds. Giorgio offered to wrap the man's bicycle tyres around his neck in retribution for his greed, and Aliki's cheeks flamed the colour of ripe tomatoes. Between the short gaps in their conversation, they could hear Mrs Kamilari across the street bellowing at her unruly brood of children. Calling them lazy bitches and bastards and threatening to hang herself from the branches of the trees if they didn't come home at once.

'She has twelve,' Aliki chuckled good-naturedly, passing a basket of koulouri to Giorgio and imploring him to eat. 'No wonder the woman's gone completely crazy.' Nico noticed that she didn't offer any of the bread to him.

Giorgio's large dark eyes danced in the faint glow of the candlelight. 'She sounds like my own dear yiayia.'

Giorgio's parents had died when he was still in nappies and he'd been raised by his grandmother, a cantankerous cow who, fittingly, sold milk curd for a living. She'd been more upset by the child-shaped hole in her freedom than by the death of her only daughter and her husband. At least, that's what Nico had heard. Giorgio appeared blind to the woman's imperfections. His loyalty to her, as to everyone else who surrounded him, as unwavering as a Cypriot summer.

'It's just as well he's not married,' Aliki had once remarked sarcastically and referring, no doubt, to his own friendship with the man. There was no room for three of them in Giorgio's bed.

After supper, she gathered the empty plates towards her bosom with a clink and bid them both a *kalinihta*. Nico could tell she was grateful for the imminent privacy of her bedroom and he was similarly relieved by her departure. He wanted to reclaim his guest. He pulled out the packet of cigarettes from the pocket of his shirt. Besides, after ten at night, the porch was a male arena. A place to drink liquor, enjoy a smoke and contemplate lost loves while the moon shone through the gaps in the grapevines. It was no place for a nagging wife.

He offered a cigarette to Giorgio, who wedged it behind his left ear. Nico shrugged. 'Please yourself.' He paused to light his own with a burning match. 'How are our friends at the kafeneon, by the way?' He shook his wrist in the air until the flame eventually died. 'Is Mr Andreas missing my *lires*, or am I still banned from the premises?'

'Missing you? I think Mr Andreas is too busy spying for the British to miss anyone except the Governor General.'

Nico sniggered. It was a running joke between the pair of them that Mr Andreas's anglophilia was more than just a passing admiration for his superiors; that he was on the British army's payroll, spying on the clientele he suspected of being EOKA sympathisers and pointing them out to the administration.

'You think he does it for a fee? This espionage?'

'I think he does it for the good of the British, *file*,' Giorgio surmised. 'He's better than us and he wants to prove it.'

Nico smirked. 'I see. Who'd want to be a Cypriot peasant selling fruit on the back of a donkey when you could sip tea with the ruling classes in nice china cups?'

'Exactly, my friend. Exactly.'

The lemon-scented breeze was damp and stifling and Nico's shirt felt like it was squeezing him to death. He leaned over the porch to fling his still-lit cigarette into the dust as Mrs Kamilari slammed her shutters closed and the sounds of her numerous children were smothered by the darkness. 'Kyriaco had better watch out, then – all those odes to Grivas after one too many ouzos. Mr Andreas will have scribbled down the dates and times of the offending refrains and passed the intelligence on to Sir whatshisface by now. The one in charge.'

'I think our friend Kyriaco is too stupid to be suspected of anything other than being stupid. In the nicest possible way.'

A few years ago, a young man from their neighbourhood had supposedly been caught snooping for EOKA and arrested by the local British army in the middle of the night. He'd been thrown into the back of a truck under armed guard and driven to a detention centre on the outskirts of the town, a foreboding place, bordered by fences and barbed wire. Rumour had it that he was interrogated for three days straight before being sent home to his mother with a pair of black eyes and a handful of broken ribs. Nobody knew if this strange story was true but, if it was, Nico wondered if Kyriaco might succumb to the same fate. That he, too, might vanish one night on his way home from the kafeneon and re-emerge a week later with no teeth and no fingernails.

'Stupid?' Nico wondered aloud. 'Perhaps.'

'Besides, they're leaving next year. The British army. Then Mr Andreas can go spy for the Turks if he hates us so much. Kiss their hairy arses instead.'

Giorgio retrieved the cigarette he was saving from behind his ear and slid it gratefully beneath his nose. 'Time to savour this, *agabi*.' He struck a fizzy match, his face glowing orange in the darkness. 'You look like shit, my friend. You sick or something?'

It had been eight months since Nico's strange breakdown in the kafeneon and they were all wondering the same thing. 'What's wrong with the lemon farmer?' But they were afraid to *actually* pose the question in case his affliction was mental and not physical.

Nico sighed sadly. 'To tell the truth, friend, I'm not quite sure myself.'

It was a lie, really, but how could he confess that he was more lovesick than a schoolgirl to a man as impressive as Giorgio? That he was lonely and heartbroken and that he longed, not for his wife, but for a woman he'd once wronged in a graveyard? That he would do anything to relive those months. To go back to the old cemetery at the back of the church and give her the answer she had deserved. That in between his sickness and his yearning for her, he felt a guilt so powerful, so corrosive, that he still vomited into bowls hidden beneath the bed. 'You've nothing to be guilty for!' he would console himself after he had finished spitting and retching. 'We weren't even together. Not in the *official* sense.' But he hardly believed the voices in his head.

What would Giorgio do, Nico finally asked, if he was living a life so miserable, a life he felt so trapped in that some days, he found it difficult to breathe? That when he opened his mouth, the fine yellow dust that floated in the Cypriot breeze invaded his orifices and smothered him? What would Giorgio do?

Giorgio turned around to face him and his strong back flexed against the circular porch wall.

'Assuming this is all hypothetical?' His dark eyes searched Nico's for several quiet moments.

'Of course, what else?'

'Then hypothetically speaking, I would discard the life that was making me so depressed and find a more tolerable existence.'

Nico waited patiently for the headlights of his father's Bedford truck to pierce the purple gloom so they could drive the short distance to the market. Most mornings, Nico dozed in the passenger seat while the stench of pig farms wafted in through the open windows. Mosquitoes sneered in his ears. 'This is your life,' they would whine while he smacked irritably at his face. 'This is your miserable life.'

Once beneath the shade of the market canopies, they unloaded their crates of lemons into showcase baskets and waited for the first eager trickle of customers to furnish their rusty tins. The work was short-lived but monotonous, and Nico's father was at just the right height to pour incessant misery into his ears. He was worried about the dwindling numbers at the pantopoleio, the success of other stalls that sold produce all year round. 'Sustainability, son. You know what it means to be sustainable?' Which reminded

him that he was the opposite of viable. Everything
hurt. Parts of him hurt today that hadn't hurt yesterday.
Soon, he would exclaim proudly, there would be more
of him hurting than not hurting, and his son would
have to manage the stall by himself. A scenario that
grew more and more appealing with every passing
minute.

Lacking any discernible attributes of his own, Nico
learned to mimic the qualities he admired in those
closest to him. Aliki's willingness to swallow her pride
and sew the neighbours' clothes. His father's unwavering dedication to the market. Giorgio's ability to
win people over, to charm complete strangers. His disciplined work ethic and his even more disciplined
drinking. 'The secret, *file*, is to know when to stop.' Until
finally, Nico found that he was devising the very plan
his friend had spoken of beneath the moon-drenched
grapevines. He was on a path.

They usually packed up the stall at midday and his
father would drive them back to his place for a lunch
of barbecued fish, fried potatoes and salad. It was an
expedient way for Nico to fill his stomach, save his *lires*
and fulfil his filial obligations all at once.

During these visits, his mother sat in her wooden
chair in the back yard with her dark skirts sagging
between her knees, mumbling about life's interminable
hardships and stroking her long grey hair, Nico thought
she looked twenty birthdays older than her supposed
sixty-four years. The sun had cracked and blackened
her skin prematurely and he could tell, when he looked

deep into her droopy eyes, that she was disappointed he was their only child. That *he* was a disappointment.

Most afternoons, he would rather have been at home with Aliki than waiting for his father to sear the fish while he listened to his mother muttering, engaging in idle gossip on their porch while she sewed in the sunlight, and Nico was surprised by these new feelings; by the nascent changes in himself.

They would move to England, he decided. Australia was too far away and America, or at least what he knew of it, intimidated him. There were too many opportunities in America and no room to fail. England felt like a compromise and more conveniently, Aliki's uncle lived in London and could officially invite them into the country. It was a start, and everything, good or bad, had to start somewhere. All he had to do was lower his head and endure his father's complaints for a little longer.

The darkness seemed to wrap itself around him. There was still a nip in the air but he could smell the arrival of summer: the scent of jasmine blossom and hard-baked dust; the promise of unrelenting heat for months to come; the hazy smell of sea salt blowing in from the northern coast.

He found Giorgio sitting beneath the lime trees, drinking zivania straight from the bottle. He beckoned Nico in through the small iron gate that separated his neglected garden from the equally neglected street, and he could tell from his slurred voice that he was well on the road to inebriation. It didn't take long with the hard stuff. There was no arguing with zivania as Nico, who'd valiantly fought with most spirits, should know.

The small wooden chair gave a creak as he sat down and prised the bottle eagerly from Giorgio's sweaty palms. Nico envied his friend's ability to relish his own company in a way he himself never could. To drink contentedly instead of crying into his glass and bemoaning his lot in life. There was a skill to it. An art. They swilled in silence, their shirts unbuttoned to their navels, until the trees began to sway of their own accord and the lights in the houses opposite blinked at him in code.

It was a moonless sky and after a few more shots, Nico felt like cowering behind his chair, paranoid about what might be slithering around in the thistles in search of an ankle to vampirise. 'I think I've drunk too much.'

'No such thing for Nico.' Giorgio chuckled, savouring another long glug. 'Although you're still here, I see? On this beautiful island of ours?'

He still was. Only now, his father was half blinded by cataracts, so Nico was hauling him to the market as well. 'Not for much longer, my friend. Not for much longer. Pass the bottle back then.'

'Oh yes?'

The news that called for a drink caught him unawares, and the plan he'd been keeping to himself for so long poured from him like piss. It was the last thing he'd expected her to announce yesterday, the very last. Having long ago reconciled himself to the fact that there would be no children for them to raise, no little Nicos to grace the future, that he and Aliki would spend their lives together on the porch, gossiping about the neighbours' affairs and eating salted turnips until one of them, most likely him, dribbled their last.

She told him that the doctor was sure and he could think only of *her* in those moments. Where she might be living, what she might be doing. If she was still as beautiful as the last time they'd made love or if she'd been altered by time and commitments.

'Aliki is pregnant, *file.*'

Whose lucky lips were tasting her salty kisses and, worst of all, he was unashamed by the thoughts floating before his very own wife. Exhausted, but quite unashamed.

'Pregnant?' Giorgio fell from his chair and onto his hands and knees and slapped the ground in drunken jubilation until his grandmother shrieked, 'Shut it, donkey!' from the open bedroom window.

'Bravo, bravo. You're a real balikari, you know that?'

Nico was a hero. The man of the moment, like their friend Panayioti had been in the kafeneon that fateful night. They'd had three in the ensuing years, Panayioti and Helen of Troy. Nico had barely seen him since his strange collapse or even cared to ask how he was.

'Are you pleased?' She'd returned from her visit to Dr Mandrides and had been happily brewing a pot of tea while he stood behind her in a daze. His mouth hung open like a carp fish. 'Well, *are* you?' He'd stared at the back of her head as she threw cinnamon and cloves into the teapot and swirled it around hypnotically, her skirt sashaying this way and that as she danced around the kitchen, and it was as if an unfamiliar sun streamed in through the kitchen windows to vaporise his disbelief. A sun that blazed across the sky in otherworldly colours.

'It will take me a little time to get used to the idea of a baby but, yes, Aliki, I am.'

Nico expected to find the English streets filled with pale-skinned men strutting around in khaki army uniforms, but instead they were full of sons. Williamsons, Robsons, Hendersons, Richardsons. Sons, everywhere he looked, and then, of course, there was Sonny Smith. A man more like a rain cloud than a slice of sunshine; his mother must have been having a nice laugh when she named him Sonny, no doubt about that.

Aliki's ancient uncle received them with courtesy, letting them share his small Victorian terrace on Warwick Street until they stumbled back to their immigrant feet. 'Please. Stay as long as you need.' Recently widowed and deaf in one ear, although not in that order, he claimed to welcome the company of his beloved niece, her grumpy husband and their small baby.

The house was tired. The rooms were carpeted in greenish rugs that tickled like grass beneath bare feet, and the walls were painted the colour of parsnips. The taste of the dead wife for sure, Nico thought, wrinkling his big nose. 'It's like living in a wheelbarrow full of rotting vegetables,' he grumbled to Aliki as they undressed for bed at night. 'Stinks like one too,' and she would silence him with an embarrassed, 'Hush, Nico,' or sometimes a conspiratorial, 'Well open a window, then.'

As well as smelling like a compost heap, the place was also a shrine to the ancient uncle's former life. There were pictures of the couple everywhere. Photographs of past holidays, dusty cups and medals their only child, Sophie, had won as a curly-haired teen at some club or other. Trophies in the downstairs toilet. Certificates proclaiming her magnificence in the spare room and her excellence on the fridge in the kitchen.

She'd moved out shortly after her mother's funeral, evidently glimpsing the future for what it was. Bleak and miserable. A life filled with hospital appointments, blood tests and long-term geriatric care. 'She couldn't have been that great, your cousin, like her certificates say,' Nico would point out snidely, while fumbling with the buttons on his stripy pyjamas. 'Abandoning her father in his hour of need and leaving him with her stupid cups for company. The medals aren't going to take him to the toilet and wipe his arse for him, are they?'

'You're one to talk,' Aliki would mumble back from the inside of her cotton nightgown. 'We abandoned our parents.'

'This is different, wife.'

'Different how?'

Still, Nico quite envied the ancient uncle his daughterless home and wax-clogged ears. His ability to check out of a conversation when he lost interest in the thing without offending the other party. Snuggling comfortably back into his own thoughts as if they were warm blankets while he and Aliki flailed about on their own.

Nico spent a lot of time slumped inside his own thoughts, too. Especially in those early months. Thoughts about how much he still missed *her*. About the miles and the years that now separated them and their secret cemetery in Morphou. Two thousand, according to the pilot as they took off from Paphos airport, and he'd wondered, looking down at the rapidly retreating landscape, what had become of her since.

He needed to find gainful employment. He was better when he was useful, engrossed in the pursuit of things and not staring at the parsnip-coloured walls, and through ancient Uncle Spyro he secured labour in a local cash and carry in nearby Manor House. So close, in fact, that he could walk there by himself with his carrier bag full of lunch dangling from his wrist.

Disappointingly, there was no actual manor in Manor House and the boss was a bastard named Sonny Smith. A middle-aged middle manager with coarse yellow hair and the complexion of an experienced alcoholic. He spent most of the working day firing sarcastic remarks over his clipboard, gems such as, 'You having a laugh, my Bubble friend?' and 'Do they walk backwards instead of forwards where you're from?' But the racist banter, like most things about England, was lost on the newly emigrated Nico.

His job was easy. To wait for the large delivery trucks to pull into the unloading bays, unburden them of their goods and restock Sonny's shelves. A perpetual cycle in an unskilled role, but a role with which he was familiar. Though in England, instead of citrus fruits and sunny markets there was corned beef and fingerless gloves.

He worked the floor with Frankie Goodwin. A small, rat-faced cockney who stank of piss and bragged about knowing the Kray Twins.

'Well, is a shame as they are in prison, no? Maybe you can call whatshisname? Ronnie Biggs?' said Nico, barely suppressing a chortle. 'Go ride the trains together?'

'Oh yeah? What would you know about it, my little immigrant friend? You just washed up from Greece in your banana boat and you're already bad-mouthing my mates in your terrible accent.'

'Cyprus, actually. Greece is a whole other country, my friend.'

'Same ole shit.'

Nico quite liked Frankie. They were a team, at least on the floor. It was Nico and Frankie against the boss and he liked him a whole lot more than he liked Ricky Smith. Sonny's sneaky son would skulk into the warehouse just to scratch his balls, squeeze his spots and eavesdrop on their conversations, make sure they weren't insulting his father. Nico would walk home in the evenings, his empty carrier bag still dangling from his wrist, and thank his stars that Ricky Smith was not his son or his son-in-law.

'What is his problem you think, the boy?' Nico's English was not yet good enough to convey his true contempt.

'He's a weasel, that's his main problem. His other problem is that he's a bastard.'

Sonny paid Nico sixteen pounds a week. Sixteen pounds to replenish the shelves with cans of tuna and baked beans while the Beatles played cheerfully in the background. He offered five of it to the ancient uncle, who politely shook his head. 'Save it for a house of your own, God willing, and therapy for your poor knees. I don't know how you stand it all day, I really don't.'

'Technically, I'm kneeling. Besides,' Nico would point out, 'my knees are numb from the English cold.'

Other bits of him were numb, too. The end of his nose. The tips of his fingers and the ends of his toes. The tops of his ears. He melted when he saw the baby, though. When he peeled off his frozen boots and unbuttoned his icy, wet coat and Aliki shoved a gurgling Melina into his arms. He glowed like the advertisements on Sonny's boxes of porridge.

They called her 'Melina' because her lovely eyes were the colour of honey. A syrupy brown flecked with spots of yellows and golds and, if you looked close enough, a few black ones, too. The name belonged to her. As if there had always been a Melina hole in the world and she was born to fill it.

She was a slow developer; late to walk and talk, late to grasp things, and Aliki's brow creased in concern when she compared her milestones to the achievements of other babies.

'Look at her, Nico, she's just sitting there and staring at the wall. Something must be wrong with her . . .' but by the age of two and a half, and without any fuss or explanation as to why it had taken her so long, she was suddenly up and away. Whizzing around the uncle's house like a stray firework and there was no telling her otherwise. 'See?' Nico chuckled as he darted out of the way of a flying toy. 'She just likes to watch and learn and bide her time. To do things at her own pace like her pappa.'

Something else happened that year. An accountant named Rajiv joined the team at the cash and carry, a reflective, nicely dressed man from India who'd recently emigrated to London to offer his family a better life. He spoke English fluently and addressed Sonny Smith with more respect than he deserved.

He began to notice it, then, the so-called 'warehouse banter', although it was nastier with Rajiv. They soon forgot about Nico. It was much more enjoyable to spew offensive remarks about the colour of the new boy's skin than it was to laugh at Nico's accent or the contents of his lunch. Rajiv was more exotic, his differences much more obvious.

Nico learned something else that year. In 1965, he learned how to retaliate with a 'piss off' when Frankie called him a 'Bubble'.

~

'Mrs Vlahos tells me they're announcing the winner of the Local Businessman of the Year competition tomorrow. She says it's going to be in the Greek-Cypriot paper.'

'Why should I give a damn?' They've been sitting in near silence for days, with only insults hurtling between them.

'I'm just making conversation, that's all.' Aliki continues sewing her infernal clothes while Nico pretends to watch an episode of *On the Buses* that he's already seen a million times.

'It's being sponsored by that estate agent you hate.'

'So what?' He knows the lines coming from the TV by heart: *'You're a really pretty girl' 'You think so?' 'Oh yeah I know so.'*

'Don't get your knickers in a twist, Nico. I'm just making conversation.'

'Do me a favour, wife, and don't bother.'

Melina moved out in a flurry of tears and goodbyes when he refused to accept Ozil's son. Nico couldn't bring himself to call the boy by his name for fear of making him a reality. Aliki was distraught – blamed him, even. What a thing, when the pair of them had been conspiring behind his back for months and probably even years. He crept up the stairs afterwards and pulled back the curtains. Watched her drifting away from him like a lost balloon, its string just out of his reach.

'Demetri, I think he's called, anyway. The estate agent you hate.'

He was undoubtedly waiting for her round the corner in his ridiculous Ford Escort. It was the stupid car that had first caught Yianni's eye and, if it hadn't been so bright or so red, he admitted, he might not have noticed it and they'd all be none the wiser. He wanted Nico to absolve him afterwards. Begged pathetically. If it was *him* he'd want to know, he reasoned with himself. Wasn't it better to know things than not, to live in light than without it?

Aliki scurried into the kitchen to check on him a few hours later. To tell him that Melina was safe. That she was renting a room in Irini Iacovou's house a couple of streets away.

'Who?'

'The woman with the boarding house on Liberty Street. You've met her before, at Eleni's wedding?'

'Never heard of her.' If she existed at all, he thought. Another lie. 'She with him, then, Ozil's son, in this strange woman's home?'

He wanted her to confirm his betrayal so that he would be right, but the nodding of her head only re-ignited his guts in the most unpleasant and unexpected way. He shoved past her to grab a pint of milk from the fridge and pour it down his throat. Then he told her what he'd been telling himself all morning: 'Good riddance.' She didn't reply, but he could tell from her eyes that she pitied him.

'Demetri Lettings, that's it. That's who is sponsoring the competition.'

'Damn it, Aliki. Will you stop wittering on? I don't care about the bloody competition!'

Suitably chastised, she returns to her pathetic pile of sewing and he wanders out into the garden to look for the cat. His last loyal friend. 'Psst!' His eyes survey the small back yard and widen in panic when she doesn't immediately approach him, wrap herself round his legs and arch her back into his palms. Last year, someone shot Mr Barnaby's cat with an air rifle and flung it into the thorny rose bushes for the poor man to discover. What a terrible thing to do to an animal and you just knew, he said to his distraught neighbour, you just *knew* that whoever had done it was on his way to becoming a serial killer. He didn't berate him over the fence about Maggie Thatcher for a long while after that.

'Psst!' He finds her hiding in his damp tool shed and is relieved she hasn't met the same fate at the hands of the Harringay Cat Killer. She has a present for him. A bloodied bird with its head half chewed off. It takes him a few moments to catch his breath, before he regains his composure and chuckles. She liked to startle him, this one. Always with the little surprises.

He reaches in and tickles her behind the ears. It's hard to feel stressed when you're stroking a cat. Damn near impossible, in fact. She's not in the mood for him, though; intent, instead, on toying with her prey. 'It's OK,' he whispers in collusion. 'I'll leave you alone with your secret.' He turns around begrudgingly and walks back to his television.

On a misty Monday at the start of April, Nico guzzles a hurried breakfast with Aliki before trudging up the stairs to indulge in one of his favourite pastimes: staring at the good people of Lancaster Gardens as they're flung from their houses like slices of toast. Mrs Richardson, he thinks, is getting fatter and angrier, while Mr Williamson hasn't kissed his lovely wife on the mouth for days. A curious thing. If only the little blonde beauty was *his* wife. Now there was a stirring thought.

'Nico! Kettle's boiled. You want more coffee?'

He slurps a few hot sips from a cup with 'Have a great day!' printed on the side before lacing up his shiny shoes and heading out to buy a newspaper.

Green Lanes is littered with bunting and burst balloons. A green and white 'sponsored by Demetri Lettings' sign has been tossed on top of a pile of stinking black bin bags and Nico sneers at the symbolism of the scene. It's where Demetri belongs, in the rubbish along with his morals. He's probably made the entire competition about free publicity, he thinks, kicking a rotting banana skin out of his way. Meanwhile, the real winner of the thing got a bag of fish and chips and a catalogue of Demetri's available properties.

He marches straight past Yianni's shop. He's not going to buy newspapers from his establishment any more. While Nico doesn't entirely blame the man for the way things have turned out, he still considers him a key player in his misfortune, along with the infernal Ozil. He turns left and heads up towards Alexi's instead. His supermarket is further along the Lanes but the man is a renowned purveyor of news and confectionery, as well as a very good laugh, and God knows Nico could use both this morning.

Alexi's bell tings a cheerful salutation and Nico reciprocates with a wave but his head refuses to surface from the collars of his jacket. He makes his way over to the newspaper stands. Poll tax stories dominate the back wall. He's sick and tired of hearing about them. Margaret Thatcher's face sneering at him from the cover of every newspaper in the country, along with a montage of black and white fiery photos.

'Why don't you put the Greek-Cypriot papers at the top?' he challenges the shopkeeper. 'Instead of the tabloids? How many English people come in here?'

'You'd be surprised,' Alexi replies from his crossword, his chin resting lazily in his hand.

'Really?'

'Yes, they come to gawp at Stalin. Or Saddam Hussein, depending on which way the wind is blowing my moustache.'

Nico guffaws. 'You're a real joker. You know that?' He wishes his breakfast anecdotes were as entertaining as Alexi's. Then Melina might never have fallen in love with a Turkish boy and moved out of his house.

'I have to be, this far down the street. I have to

incentivise people to walk the extra hundred metres past all the other sweet shops.'

Nico crouches down and picks up the *Foni*. Let the English tear themselves apart in the streets, he thinks. And Frankie used to say that the Cypriots were peasants! He'd rather read about his compatriots and their exploits and this way he can find out who won the ridiculous competition Aliki cares so much about. Ambush her with the information when she returns from this Irini's place and spoil her nice surprise.

He hauls himself back up with an 'Eiy!' remembering how Mr Ozil had rubbed his back while stocking his shelves with his tins.

'See, Pappa, we're all the same,' he imagines Melina taunting. 'Look, you're both old men with arthritic backs.'

He grabs a bar of chocolate on his way to the counter. 'Same, my arse.'

'Sweets?' Alexi tuts in feigned disapproval. 'Give you a heart attack, this stuff.' He waves the bar in his face and Nico snatches it from his hand and drops it into his partially unzipped jacket. 'Man of your years should be more careful with his diet, no?'

'It's my only vice, file,' Nico grumbles. 'This and the cat.' He grabs the paper and tells Alexi to keep the change. It's the least he can do for all the laughs.

'Well, Kyrie Nico, I suppose I'll be seeing you?'

'I suppose I'll be seeing you, too.'

There is nobody home and the rare freedom this affords both excites and agitates him. He discards his jacket by the front door and throws his bar of chocolate and newspaper on the coffee table. He sags gratefully into the squeaky brown sofa and kicks off his shoes. They fall to the carpet with a muffled 'thud, thud' and he closes his eyes for a moment, enjoying the stillness. He's breathless. He must have been walking faster than he thought, eager to get away from the noise of the Lanes.

Yesterday, he crept back into her empty room to stare at the montage of men on her wall, searching for the clues he missed the last time. Wondering which of the many boys on display was *him*, this Ozil's son. If his tongue was protruding from his face like the others, a celebratory gesture for having stolen Nico's daughter. He picked up the hairbrushes and make-up powders she'd left behind and brought them up to his nose, inhaling the lingering scent of her. He ran a palm along her dressing table in an effort to uncover who she really was, who she'd been all along, because the Melina who'd collected snails in the back garden as a child and screamed with delight when he pushed her high on the swings, was not the stranger who inhabited this bedroom.

'Please stay,' he murmured into her pillow, her duvet, the dressing gown behind her door. 'Don't marry this Turkish boy and spend the rest of your life regretting your decision. Not when you have a chance at a proper future.'

He sighs. He reaches over to the coffee table, picks up the *Foni* and thumbs through it. There's an article on page eight about rising rent prices on Green Lanes. A fat man named Lefteris Diamandis, the so-called president of the Shopkeepers' Association of North London, is bemoaning their lot. Does the landlord know, he whines, how many tomatoes these poor shopkeepers would have to sell just to afford a month's increase? 'Ten thousand?' Nico mutters to himself. 'Twenty thousand?' The papery portrait is unflattering. 'Perhaps they should be selling drugs instead of tomatoes!' he shouts to Mr Diamandis. The Shopkeepers' Association should talk to Ozil. He knows all about that nefarious sideline.

Nico tuts and licks his fingers, flicks through to the Local Businessman of the Year Competition. The newspaper has dedicated its entire centre spread to the event. 'Come on then, who bloody won it?' he mutters sarcastically. 'The suspense is surely killing me.' He pushes his glasses up over his head and brings the paper to within an inch of his eyeballs. He squints at the caption beneath the main photograph. 'Mr Angelides, a funeral director from Holloway, north London.'

'You're bloody kidding me!' He laughs aloud and slaps the sofa cushions wedged on either side of him. No shit the undertaker is going to boast the best profits – the man has a guaranteed supply of clients. It really is ridiculously funny.

The local Greek-Cypriots flocked to him, no doubt, because he promised to do the right things in the right order. This Mr Angelides probably knew the holiest of priests who would mumble the Trisagio prayers over the corpses. Promise a safe passage to the next life. Passage to nowhere, more like it. Where did these people think they were going? He taps the page with his forefinger. 'Maggot land, that's where you're heading, my friend!'

Not that Nico really blames them, the dying and the families of the deceased. He doesn't believe in God himself but he can understand people wanting to hold on to their rituals and superstitions because they're afraid. 'Well done, Mr Angelides.'

If he had a hat, he'd take it off to him. He's accepting an award from Demetri the Crook. He's not a tall man, this Angelides, and his large bent nose and jutting Adam's apple give him the unfortunate appearance of a bird – and not just any bird; a vulture, of all things! Nico sniggers at the image of the scavenging undertaker picking over the carrion. His hair is thinning as well and although he's attempting to hide it with a sweeping hairstyle, Nico can tell that Mr Angelides is well on his way to baldness.

He readjusts his glasses and peers more closely at the picture. The odd sensation of walking into a stranger's house and recognising the objects within it suddenly washes over him. What did they call it, he wonders, this perturbing feeling? Reincarnation? No. Intuition? Déjà vu? His mind is thick with fog and things no longer appear as clear to him as they did a few short moments ago.

A photograph in a silver frame. He knows that the answer is lurking in the photograph he keeps on his bedside cabinet. An old black and white picture of him and Aliki standing in front of a row of palm trees sometime in the early sixties. She hated it. Claimed her teeth stuck out, that she looked like a rabbit, but he refused to let her pack it away and he perched it proudly beneath his reading lamp. It was one of the few pictures that survived their move to England. Visual evidence that he wasn't always sixty-five, bald and bad-tempered. That he was once a young man in his thirties and that *she* thought him attractive.

'Where is it?' He sits up, suddenly, determined to find it so he can compare their faces. Show it to Aliki and make her laugh. 'Oh he does!' she'd exclaim. 'He does look like you! What a thing!' He rolls up the newspaper and tucks it beneath his arm as he trudges towards the stairs.

He's sweating and there's a tension brewing inside him along with the sensation that insects are crawling all over his skin. He counts six steps and stops, leaning over the bannister to catch his breath, trying not to regurgitate his coffee. It was the trot up the Lanes, he thinks. That's what's induced this funny turn. He marched up there too fast in his shiny black shoes. Or maybe the years of guilt and regret over what could have been his life have finally caught up with him. The suppressed memories, trickling out of him like urine. The piss making its way down his trouser legs to pool embarrassingly on the carpet.

'The smell will never come out, Nico!' He can hear her rebuke in his ears. 'Couldn't you have waited until you were on the toilet?'

He looks up at the ceiling instead. 'Do you know,' he says to the air, 'that I named the damned cat after you?' It's a secret, of course. 'Don't tell Aliki. She'd go crazy and who could blame her? All these years of being overshadowed by your memory and never even knowing. Do you promise?' he whispers to her with his very last breath. 'Do you promise not to tell?'

Evgenia

October 1988

SHE LIKES TO wear bold, statement colours. Her wardrobe is a soft smorgasbord of fuchsia pinks, brilliant vermilions and bright apricots, colours that complement her voluminous blonde hair and her red-stained lips, but, today, on a fine, crisp morning in October, she decides to wear a black satin blouse with a matching cardigan. Later, she will look back and wonder if she jinxed herself. If she could have altered the course of the day's events by wearing, say, emerald green or cornflower blue.

'It can't be good news if they've called you in, Ev.' Jimmy scratches his forehead uncertainly, offering to go with her to the appointment. 'Don't they usually send the results by post?' Evgenia shakes her head as she sprays deodorant under her wobbly arms and pretends that she doesn't know what he's talking about. That it's all going to be OK. 'I'll be just fine, love, you'll see.'

In reality, she doesn't want him to accompany her to the hospital because she suspects the results of her tests will be bad, or at best not good, and he won't be able to cope. She loves her Jimmy, she really does, but she knows too well that he's a chocolate teapot in a crisis. There will be two of them, then, snivelling in front of the nice young consultant with the lovely teeth and the million other places to be. Two of them instead of just her.

Mr White Teeth, they nicknamed him behind his back, because his expensive suntan illuminated his smile. 'I'm off to see Mr White Teeth and I'll be back early afternoon,' she yells up the stairs as she pulls the door closed.

Mr White Teeth never ages and, if anything, he seems younger this morning than he did when he delivered the first hammer blow three years ago. The unforgettable initial diagnosis. She wonders if he's the same age as her James-Dean and if he's even completed the qualifications an important oncologist whatsit needs in order to *be* important, but he appears to know what he's doing. He certainly holds her images up to the light in a very reassuring manner. Between his thumb and his forefinger, like they do in *Casualty*.

'I'm sorry, Mrs Theocaris, but the latest scans show that your cancer has returned.' Time grinds to a halt and, in the stillness that follows, she can hear Mr White Teeth's breath.

'Are you OK, Mrs Theocaris? Is there someone I can call for you?'

'I'm fine, thank you, doctor,' and as she bends over to scoop up her handbag, she really believes she is.

Standing patiently in the queue at the appointments desk to book herself in for a new course of chemotherapy a few moments later, she decides that she's not fine at all. She's quite upset at the way Mr White Teeth labelled it *her* illness. '*Your* cancer has returned,' he explained. Not '*the* cancer'. As though it was her problem and hers alone – or worse, as if she deserved the diagnosis.

Not that she supposes he meant for it to come out like that, and maybe she's feeling overly sensitive but, under the circumstances, she's allowed to be sore. Besides, it's like she's always said to her Jimmy: these doctors need to be mindful of how they come across.

'All doctors?' he used to wink, playfully. 'Or just Dr Theo Angelides?'

It's all over by midday. She knows he'll be waiting anxiously for her to call him from the sticky payphone outside the hospital entrance, but she can't face speaking to him and especially not from a cubicle soaked in urine and decorated in sex cards. It wouldn't feel right. Instead, she gets off the tube at Finsbury Park station and walks the fifteen minutes to her best friend's place because she'll know just how to cheer her up.

Her Best Friend of Almost Thirty Years, to give Emiliana her full and proper title, lives in a ground-floor maisonette on Missouri Close. Such a pretty word, Ev thinks to herself, as she clip-clops towards it. *Maisonette.* It sounds like a French girl's name. A girl who is as posh as she is frilly. When she arrives, Emiliana is in the middle of making herself a tuna fish sandwich for lunch and the smell of it, like dirty cats on a hot summer's day, sends Ev retching to the loo to bring up her cornflakes.

'Ev?' Emiliana's concerned voice sounds almost

distorted as it carries through the locked bathroom door. 'You all right in there?'

'I'll be with you in just a minute, my darling.'

She's in tears when she staggers into her best friend's front room, although she doesn't particularly want to be, and now there's a faint stench of sick to add to her long list of problems. Emiliana puts down her half-eaten sandwich, wipes her mouth with a napkin and rushes over to comfort her.

'It's back, he said. Mr White Teeth. I haven't told Jimmy.'

'Oh, my darling!' For just an instant, more like a nanosecond really, Emiliana's big dark eyes tell her what she already knows. That this time, she's a goner.

'There's always a light at the end of the tunnel, though, you'll see.'

'Yes, my darling, but sometimes it's a bloody big train.'

They sit on the sofa and Ev weeps silently on her best friend's shoulder for all the things she'll miss – making sure to brush her lovely grey curls aside first. Mr White Teeth told her that they'd found it in three different places this time. In her bowel, which is where it had started its malignant journey; in her pancreas; and, unbelievably, there's also a spot on her left fibula. She almost made a joke about being grateful she didn't have one of those to hand, but something in his expression stopped her from doing so.

'Your lower leg bone, Mrs Theocaris.'

He used words like 'persistent' and 'aggressive' and

delivered them impassively and as if he was running late for lunch. Although he didn't quite say it was terminal, she could tell from his eyes that it was. She was getting good at reading the eyes.

'I'm scared, Em. This time round, I'm *really* scared.'

Emiliana pats her arm and strokes her blonde halo-hair, hardened by this morning's over-enthusiastic use of hairspray. She tells her that if the worst did happen, Angelo would take good care of her. 'He treats them like gold, Ev. I don't know the correct word for them, but you know what I mean.'

Evgenia shudders slightly because for the first time since this thing started, she can see herself dressed for her eternal rest. 'I know he does, my love. He's a good boy is our Angelo.'

Emiliana offers her the phone so she can call Jimmy but Evgenia pushes it back towards her. 'Let me gather my thoughts and my strength first, because you know my Jimmy. He's going to need me more than I need him.'

She could certainly use a drink though.

Emiliana springs up with renewed zeal and purpose and heads into the kitchen to mix up Something Soothing. Evgenia can tell that she's glad to be assigned this practical task. Something to ameliorate the situation besides offering tissues and patting her wobbly bits in sympathy. While Em crashes around in her little kitchen, Evgenia looks around the untidy living room and chuckles in disbelief. 'You should clean up in here, my darling, it really is a pigsty.'

Piles of magazines obscure the sticky coffee table. Half-drunk cups of coffee line the windowsill, the greenish swamps inside, she imagines, in various states of decomposition. Dust hangs happily in the air, clarified by shafts of sunlight streaming in through the curtains. 'It's turning into my late mother's place. You remember how she loved to hoard after my father died?'

'Don't start! Angelo's always going on at me. I think he has that obsessive cleaning disorder thingy.'

Emiliana emerges from the kitchen with two cocktail glasses filled to the brim with gin and lemonade, and thrusts one in her face with a 'ta-dah!' Evgenia suspects there is more gin than lemonade in the concoction, but still, the welcoming sight of the cloudy liquid in her friend's posh glasses lifts her spirits no end.

'He says it makes him physically sick coming here. I mean, *sick*?' Emiliana gasps between satisfying mouthfuls. 'He's so melodramatic, honestly. Not to mention a complete arse to his mother.'

Her hands and mouth occupied, Evgenia nods her head in agreement. 'And how is the lovely Angelo?'

Emiliana purses her lips. 'Not sure "lovely" is the word you're looking for, Ev.'

They slurp determinedly and until they reach the bottom. Creases of concentration dent their already wrinkled brows. 'He's bought a dump in Seven Sisters and he's supposedly busy doing the place up. Just another excuse not to visit, if you ask me.'

Evgenia drips the last drop of gin down her throat while Emiliana fumbles for a cigarette in the pockets of her blue cardigan, the very thought of her son provoking her need for nicotine. They both know what's bothering Angelo, but it's not the right time. For once, it's Ev's moment in the spotlight.

'Let's save Angelo for the cards.' Emiliana appears to agree. 'Next Tuesday as usual?'

'I wouldn't miss it for the world, my darling.'

Evgenia sways like a branch on the way to her best friend's front door and she misses the handle twice. 'Oops. What am I like!' She kisses Emiliana on both cheeks. 'Mwah. Mwah!' She tastes of tuna, fags and perfume. 'Thank you, my darling. That was a real tonic,' she tells her, before tottering the mile and a half along Seven Sisters Road towards her house on Addison Avenue.

Fonthill Road is bustling with afternoon shoppers. Customers dart in and out of shops with pushchairs, shawls and carrier bags, and she wonders, surveying the busy and somewhat blurry scenes now pulsing before her, how she's going to break the news to her Jimmy? To the kids? How much longer she's going to be around to enjoy all of this? The colour-filled streets, colourful people looking for cheap, colourful dresses against the backdrop of a pink autumn sky?

She wobbles up to their front door with flushed cheeks and searches for her house keys. 'Oh dear!' She's left her handbag on the floor by Emiliana's sofa. No wonder her armpits felt light and airy on the walk home; she can even visualise the thing sitting in the space where her legs would have been. She drank more than she intended and she suddenly feels like a foolish sixty-three-year-old woman, because only foolish women do things like this. Drink gin in the middle of the day and lose their blooming belongings.

'Scatty' is what her Jimmy will call her. 'You're so bloody scatty, Ev. Always losing things.'

She crumples into a heap on the front step, thrusts her forehead between her knees and allows herself the second cry of the day, because it's been a crying sort of a day. 'Ev?' It's Jimmy, and the sight of her husband walking through the front gate, which gives a faint squeak when you open it, makes her heart ache for their former life. This morning's life. A life when walking through the squeaky front gate was just that. Nothing more and nothing less. 'Why didn't you call me, love? I've been worried sick.'

He's been standing on the Victoria Line platform at Finsbury Park station waiting for her since lunchtime and she feels so bad for him and for everything she's about to put him through, that the words gush out like Niagara Falls. Mr White Teeth, sitting in his white room with his white coat and his bad news. Her drink at Emiliana's that was more gin than it was lemon. Her forgotten handbag with their house keys inside.

'I'm so sorry, Jim.'

'Oh, Ev!' He half picks her up from the step and squeezes her in an awkward embrace and after all these years married, they still don't quite fit together, the pair of them. He's all bones while she's mainly fleshy folds.

His muffled cries rattle in her eardrums and she knows from experience that his skinny legs will buckle at any moment and then they'll both collapse in a human heap on the doorstep. She decides enough is enough. She's spent all morning and most of the afternoon feeling sorry for herself. For all she knows, she has years left to walk the earth and it won't do to melt beside her husband in a puddle of whatsit and wait for the children to mop them up. Besides, she might be hit by a bus tomorrow and then it won't matter about her fibula.

'What we gonna do now?' Jimmy's brown eyes desperately search hers for the answers to life's ongoing hardships.

'We're going to pretend we're a pair of curtains and we're going to pull ourselves together, that's what!' Her voice, when she finally summons it from her depths, is unwavering. 'Then I'm going to batch cook for the freezer.'

She calls the kids in the order in which they were born. They insist on coming to see her and the thought of it, of her Despina and James-Dean descending on her from various angles and assailing her in their unique and personal styles, exhausts her. 'No thank you, my darlings. Not tonight.' She would much rather pour herself a large glass of pinot noir, curl up on their sofa and watch *Dynasty* with Jimmy, and she tells them as much on the phone. 'Another time, my lovelies.'

Her Dezzy, at forty-three, is a big enough girl, but she feels a stab of guilt for her youngest. Twenty-five-year-old James-Dean, stuck all the way down in Brighton by himself with only the squawking seagulls for company.

He was a complete surprise. She had no inkling she was pregnant until the poor thing was dangling upside down in the toilet bowl and Emiliana laughed hysterically when she popped round to meet him. How could she lug that lump of a child around for the best part of a year and not notice? That massive head! 'Mind you,' she conceded, 'every baby is a bloody bombshell. Just look at me with Angelo.'

The truth was, she didn't suspect him at all, not one bit. She was a martyr to her guts at the best of times and she attributed the tummy aches to the all too frequent takeaway curries from Taj's round the corner. When her periods stopped at thirty-eight, she chalked it down to pot luck. It did seem a *little* early for the menopause but there were so many other things going on that year, her poor father's passing for one, that she didn't give it a second thought.

The day he came into the world, she thought it was food poisoning courtesy of the Taste of Taj. She'd popped in the night before to order their tikka masala with a side of sag aloo and the gangly teenager who took her order was picking his nose as she strolled through the door and walked hesitantly up to the counter. Bold as brass, he was, without the faintest tinge of humiliation at being caught with his fingernail up his hole, and she moaned about it to Jimmy when she plonked their bag of steaming food on the kitchen table. 'Place has gone downhill since Taj sold up to Mr Whatsit, so eat dinner at your own risk!'

She thought she was right, too, because the chicken tasted fine but she spent the next morning hunched over on the toilet, and, in between the delirious moaning and shouting at Jimmy to bring up more toilet roll, she had a bloody good mind to lurch over there and give Germ Boy a piece of her mind.

After hours of interminable retching and cramping, something seemed to 'plop' inside her, and she wondered if her appendix had burst with all the exertions. 'Jimmy!' she screamed down the stairs, 'Come up, something's sticking out of me!' It was only when she touched herself 'down there' and felt a wet, hairy ball where her whatsit should have been that it finally dawned on her that she wasn't giving birth to her internal organs but to their second child.

Everything happened in slow motion after that. Jimmy, holding on to the doorframe with both hands and screaming, 'A baby? Bloody Nora, Ev, you don't do things by halves!' The sound of her own voice crying out for an ambulance before he passed out and slid to the floor, cartoon-style.

Later, as she lay in St Mark's Hospital by herself and stroked the baby's smooth pink cheeks and tiny button nose, the little mite had looked up at her with such astonishment that she couldn't help but giggle at him. 'Oh *you're* surprised, are you, sir? And how do you think I bloody feel? I thought you were a dodgy curry!'

Jimmy wanted to call the new baby Gonzales as a tribute to his swift entry into the world, but she'd long ago fallen in love with 'James-Dean' because, well, she'd long ago fallen in love with James Dean. Despina was a tribute to Jimmy's ungrateful grandmother, Despo, and it would have been infinitely worse if she'd been a boy because Jim's grandfather's name was Sody. James-Dean it was. She announced her decision in the car as they drove home with their bundle of joy and work-horses couldn't have changed her mind.

Jimmy chuckled cheerfully into the rear-view mirror. 'Workhorses, eh?' he winked, fiddling with the indicators. 'You sure? So be it, Ev!'

Her surprise baby and his unexpected arrival into their toilet seemed to set the scene for a whole lifetime of revelations. James-Dean deciding to move away to Brighton University to study English Literature when he had a perfectly comfortable bed at home. Despina's unforeseen inclinations and then, of course, the thing she learned about Em and Angelo. 'My son off to read English!' Jimmy was angrier than a tornado the day their son packed his bags for halls. 'English is not a *real* qualification,' he blustered, as James-Dean hastily relieved his wardrobe of baseball tops before Jimmy combusted in front of him. What sort of a job was he going to get with a piece of paper that said he could read nice poems?

Jimmy sulked for England and James-Dean brooded

for Brighton, and the farewell dinner she'd been planning for weeks was thoroughly ruined by their childish antics. Not just for James-Dean, but for all of them because, despite Jimmy's reservations, the family were all excited for their son's next chapter. Jimmy regretted it afterwards, she could tell. He drove his son to Finsbury Park station to catch his train with his head stooped like a grazing giraffe's, and Evgenia was a *teeny tiny* bit sorry for him because the truth was, Jimmy had grown into his Greek-Cypriot skin over the years and he just couldn't help how he felt.

He was certainly more Greek than when they'd first met. A handsome east London chappie, dressed to impress in his posh suits and cream scarves, with his apprenticeship in a jeweller's workshop in Hatton Garden. They were the newly established 'Ev and Jimmy' back then. Their whole lives ahead of them. 'Get us,' she used to squeal into his ear as they swanned around Leicester Square, arm in arm, 'we're a proper *English* couple,' and Jimmy would reply, 'It's just you and me, Ev. Without you, there's no me, see?'

Her James-Dean never did return from Brighton. There would be no welcome home dinner from Zeus Doner Kebab on Drayton Park Road because after his degree, he decided to stay by the sea and look for a job. At least, that's what he claimed, and she hauled her shattered heart around like a bag of broken glass for weeks afterwards. She was secretly counting down the days until her Best Boy moved back home, even buying a new quilt cover for his bed so that his room wouldn't look too babyish when his friends visited. While she didn't *entirely* blame Jimmy for her son's absence, she did wonder whether his disapproval prevented the boy from returning to London without a career to prove everyone wrong.

Jimmy, of course, stuck his giant Greek nose in the air and huffed aloud, 'He'll be back all right. He'll be back when the girlfriend dumps him, the beach is too soggy and the grant runs out.' He tried to make a joke out of the whole thing and she was hurt by the dismissive tone in his voice. 'Ev?' Stomping around their house like a right one for weeks. 'What did I say, Ev?' She dealt with it by fixing herself decadent, alcoholic cocktails in the middle of the day and burping all the way through *Sons and Daughters*.

She quickly dropped the act when she heard him sobbing into his pillow one night, though. Leaning across the bed to plant a kiss on his clammy forehead, she said, 'Hush, now, my love.'

'I'm so sorry, Ev. It's my fault he's staying down there.' Wiping away tears on the edge of the bedsheets. It appeared Jimmy did miss their son after all.

'It's not your fault, love. Boy's grown up, that's all. Would have happened sooner or later.' She was never very good at nursing grudges.

She awakes at the crack of dawn and before the reddish rays of the sun have penetrated the chinks in the curtains. Jimmy is snoring softly next to her and these rhythmic sounds of his life offer Evgenia a few crumbs of comfort. She sips a mouthful of tepid water from the mug next to the bed. Flips the pillow over for a fresh start but her attempts at readjusting herself are futile. Sleep, it seems, has turned its back. She swallows a couple of the stronger painkillers Mr White Teeth prescribed and grabs her fluffy pink dressing gown from the hook behind the door. The feel of it around her bare shoulders is like a comforting embrace and by the time she pads down the stairs to watch the sun emerging over Addison Avenue, Ev has a renewed spring in her step.

Before the maisonette filled with coffee cups, Emiliana lived two doors up from them, which was just as well because Jimmy's nemesis, Aunty Maro, lived two doors down and Jimmy was apparently allergic to her. 'She's a yenta, Ev. I get the same rash when I think about her as I do when I wear fake gold. What does that tell you, eh?' Yenta or not, they *both* pressed their noses up against the window in excitement when a removal van pulled up outside their house with the prospect of a new friendship inside it.

'They sound Cypriot.'

'That's because they are.'

'She's gorgeous . . .'

'Ev, they're looking over here, duck!'

They peeked out from behind the living-room curtains until Theo Angelides dragged the last of the boxes inside, then they rang their new neighbours' doorbell with an excuse. 'Surprise! We've bought you a . . . er, teabag?'

Introductions followed. The couple had just emigrated from Limassol so that Theo could accept a prominent position at Queen Charlotte's Hospital.

'My husband's just qualified as a consultant, you see.' Emiliana flicked her dark curly hair from side to side. 'Women's whatsits.'

'Oh my!' Ev rubbed at her chest nervously while Theo strutted about the place like a peacock in case his neighbours missed the part about him being a consultant. 'You've brought us a teabag?' She remembers his eyebrows shooting up in derision. 'Should we all share it?'

They had a young son. Evgenia was quite startled when the poor little creature appeared at the top of the stairs in his pyjamas and she wondered how she'd missed him earlier. The boy's small dark eyes nervously surveyed the scene beneath him as if he was stranded in a very tall lighthouse with no hope of escape. 'Help me,' the eyes seemed to say. 'I'm stuck.'

'This is my son, Angelo. Say *yia sas* to our new neighbours, Angelo.'

Evgenia waved back at him reassuringly but the little mite shook his head from side to side and ran away to crouch in a corner somewhere. He was no doubt missing his warm, sunny home and lamenting his exile to an unfamiliar street full of strangers who spoke a funny language.

'Shame *she's* not bloody shy.' Jimmy had decided he didn't like Emiliana after less than a fortnight's worth of visits. Not that it took much for Jimmy to find fault.

'She's completely self-absorbed. Never asked us a single thing about ourselves; we may as well not have been there tonight.'

'She's not self-interested, she's *interesting*. There's a difference, love.' Ev sighed in disappointment as she relieved her show-plates of the remnants of their third, and possibly last, social gathering. Discarded pistachios and spicy crisps along with any future hopes of double dating.

'Interesting?' Jimmy scoffed. 'Where was she hiding that, then? Up her skirt?'

Then, of course, there was the great Dr Theo.

'He's a snob. Or at best, a patronising git.' Evgenia couldn't work out which was the better insult so used them both together. She did her best impression of him as she bashed the dirty ashtrays on the inside of the dustbin. 'I'm a *doctor*, you know. I mean, heaven forbid we forget for a minute and talk about something else!'

Jimmy guffawed from the sofa in the living room. 'Told you! Didn't I tell you they deserved each other?'

The great Theo thought them too common, she could tell, their rusty Greek and Jimmy's struggling jewellery shop on Old Street no match for his good looks, expensive accent and even more expensive education. 'I'm surprised there was room for snacks when he was clearly so full of himself, that's all I'll say.'

'Oh, I'm sure you can say plenty more than that if you put your mind to it, love,' Jimmy chuckled.

She was ready to consign their fabulous foursome to wishful thinking – and would have done so, too,

were it not for her growing fascination with Emiliana.
There was something lovely about her, despite what
Jimmy thought. She was honest, refreshingly so –
unlike the two-faced Aunty Maro two doors down
– and she was beautiful. Not just conventionally but
elementally so. 'Don't you think she could be Mother
Nature, with all that lovely curly hair and those big
eyes?'

'Mother Nature?' Jimmy, mumbling from the inside
of his newspaper. 'How should I blooming know?'

'Suit yourself then, love,' and she wondered, as she
turned on the taps and submerged their poshest glasses
into the soapy sink, if despite his contempt, her husband
secretly fancied her.

Ev and Emiliana played cards together every Tuesday
after that. Drinking copious gin cocktails, smoking too
many cigarettes and sharing far too many confidences
in their newly forged 'Greeklish' language. Emiliana
admitted she fought with the great Theo. 'So many
arguments, Ev. That hole beneath the light switch over
there? That's where I threw a vase at the wall . . .'

She had been furious with him, that first night in
their new house, for moving them so many miles from
home to a place where she had nothing and nobody,
and all so he could chase *his* dreams. 'I see, my darling.'
It was hard for Ev not to think of her melancholy
mother in those moments – Sotira, whose own trans-
planting into foreign soil almost finished her off.

Emiliana loved him, though, at least on the good
days. 'Isn't he handsome?' she would croon. 'I suppose

he saved me.' Ev had to concede that Theo looked *a bit* like Paul Newman, but only after a couple of stiff ones and if she squinted hard.

'Saved you from what, my darling?'

'All in good time, Ev.'

Was there ever a good time to blurt the thing out? Evgenia wonders, satisfied that the sun is peeking properly over the rooftops and that the hazy light will shortly rouse her Jimmy from his bed. Would their friendship have been simpler if she didn't know, if Em hadn't made her complicit in the lie? She sighs as she switches on the television, skipping past a programme about the Pope in favour of a Bollywood film on BBC2. She's mesmerised by the lovely Indian dancing, the brilliant colours and the songs that sound like whiny, tormented tears.

She's always wanted to go to India, but Jimmy isn't keen on the idea. 'Why would we want to go there?' They would get 'Delhi Belly', he declared proudly, his conviction contradicted by his limited life experiences. Spend their trip on the loo or, worse, stuck in traffic watching cows wobbling about the place. Truth be told, he made the place sound like one giant, spicy farm and so she grudgingly settled for the familiarity of the Greek islands for an easier time of it. Rhodes and Corfu were like well-worn slippers by the late seventies and, one year, when Jimmy was feeling particularly prosperous, they even ventured as far as the island of Crete.

The problem with life, though, is that it remembers the choices you don't make as well as the ones you do, and it bothers her now, as she sits in front of the Bollywood movie on a quiet Saturday morning, reminiscing about Em and Angelo. It bothers her that she's never had the chance to experience India because Jimmy is reluctant to explore.

'Oh well,' she commiserates, contemplating her first cuppa of the day. 'In the next one, Ev.' And she chuckles at the absurdity of the statement, because *this* life is it.

Many things tried and failed to spoil Card Tuesday. Surprise babies, Emiliana's arguments with Theo and then, later, with Angelo. Hospital appointments and unexpected cancer diagnoses. Family dramas, secret lovers and distraught daughters, but like she's always told Jimmy, the show had to go on. She reminds him of this now as she buttons up her dusky pink blouse and paints her lips the same, sticky colour. 'The show must go on, love.'

He stands in the doorway of their bedroom, staring, fish-mouthed, as she spritzes rose and bergamot perfume into her giant bosoms and teases her blonde hair into a fabulous golden halo. She can't help but wonder, as she sprays, spritzes and presses her lips into a tissue, how long it will be before she is unable to style her hair. Before it starts to falls out again and she has to go back to wearing her scarves.

'I'm worried about you, Ev.'

'Well, don't be, love.' She's making the most of the time she has left, she replies, barging past him to flounce into the bathroom. Isn't that what you're supposed to do? She scrubs stubborn foundation stains from her fingertips and peers into the mirror to check her blusher. Turning her head this way and that, because it wouldn't do to overdo the Warm Hibiscus on top of everything else.

Jimmy pats his trouser legs for the car keys. 'I'll drive you over, then.'

'Don't bother, love,' she tells him from halfway down the stairs. 'It's a nice enough evening. I think I'm going to walk.'

She slips on her shoes with the sensible heels and snatches up her handbag from the coat hook. She reminds him that a ham is crisping in the oven and that there's salad in the fridge and slams the door behind her. She's emphatic as she bobs along Addison Avenue in the twilight and then, as she turns the corner onto the main road, slightly ashamed, too. Perhaps she's trying to prove that she can still do the things she's always done despite the terrible news, but, as traffic rushes around her like waves breaking against the shore, it just feels good to be alive.

She's been looking forward to tonight all weekend. She's been playing cards with Em on Card Tuesday for nearly thirty years and there's something about being in the company of her best friend that comforts her in a way nothing else can. Her Jimmy is a bit like a lamp-post. His long, bony arms digging into her in all the wrong places while Em's squeezes are soft and womanly. Enfolding her in a bosomy reassurance that her husband can't provide.

'It's just different with a girl, Mum,' Despina confided after it all came out about her Sarah, and, in some ways, Ev agreed with her.

She arrives ten minutes early. It's part of their long-established custom and, when Emiliana opens the door in her lovely grey dress from C&A and thrusts a gin into her hand with her customary 'ta-dah!', bubbles of excitement pop inside Ev's chest.

'Wonderful! Stuff the pills, my darling.' She reaches out and grabs the drink gratefully. 'This is exactly what Mr White Teeth ordered,' she chuckles. 'He just wasn't allowed to say it in the hospital.'

She slips off her sensible shoes, aligning them neatly with the wall in her friend's hallway, and wanders into the front room with a huge grin on her face. She's pleased to have this time to unwind on the broken sofa before the cards come out.

'How you feeling, Ev?'

'So-so, my love.' She doesn't want to talk about it, not tonight, but she reaches across and pats her best friend's knee to mitigate her refusal.

Em takes the hint graciously – 'Of course, my darling' – pulling a packet of cigarettes out of her dress pocket to complement the booze.

~

In the early years, when Emiliana was still upstairs getting ready for their session and Theo was working late at QCH, little Angelo would open the door for her in his pyjamas. 'Aunty Ev's here, Mamma!' he would cry out excitedly, before following her into the front room to sit on the couch beside her. He was an intense, precocious little boy with pale skin and intelligent dark eyes that would constantly search hers for answers.

'What's it like when we die, Aunty Ev?'

'When we die? Hmm, I don't rightly know, my darling,' Evgenia replied, careful not to sound too disturbed at the thought. 'It's not something I think about very often.'

'It's something I think about *a lot*. Mamma says I shouldn't but I can't help it.'

'Can you try to think about something else, perhaps? How about your favourite toy?'

'Socrates is my favourite toy. He's a skeleton, which means he's *already* dead.'

'Oh! I see . . .'

Fortunately, Emiliana would materialise in the doorway at the crucial moment, her curly hair still damp from the shower and her dark eyes emphasised with eye-liner and mascara.

'Bedtime, Angelo. Go upstairs and stop bothering Aunty Ev.' Little Angelo's eerie questions would haunt her all the same and she would wonder afterwards, on her tipsy walk home along Seven Sisters Road, what it might actually feel like to be dead.

'He's a peculiar one, that's for sure,' she would remark to her Jimmy as she unpeeled her coat from her shoulders and looked for a space on their overburdened coat hooks. 'All that talk of death and decomposition. I mean, it can't be normal for a boy of his age to think like that, can it?'

'Told you they were nutters,' Jimmy would say, still nursing his ancient Greek grudge and happy to have been proved right in the end.

After Emiliana's drunken disclosure, everything changed.

'Are you OK, Aunty Ev?' The poor child was still oblivious to the truth. 'Do you want to play with Socrates on the sofa with me?'

'It's getting late, my darling. Perhaps you'd better do as your mother says and go upstairs to your room?'

Through the bannisters she would watch him drag himself reluctantly up the stairs, his bottom lip quivering with his childish disappointment, and perhaps she did blame Emiliana for the guilt she'd introduced into their previously innocent relationship.

~

'Bastra tonight, Ev?'

'Why not, my darling. I quite fancy a bit of fishing – for matchsticks, though; my concentration is in scant supply.'

Emiliana reaches behind her and switches on her jellyfish-shaped lampshade with a click, and Ev is transported twenty-five years into the future where there is no little Angelo and she's suddenly sixty-three. *Tempus fugit*, she thinks, glancing down at the backs of her dry and wrinkled hands. The knuckles specked with age spots. Time flies, but in many ways, everything stays exactly the same.

'So, the prodigal son finally deigned to visit me at the weekend.' Em's face glows pink as she shuffles and deals the cards. 'Brought me a bunch of dying flowers that he stole from some relative's arrangement.'

'Oh?' Ev smiles incredulously. 'Is he allowed to do that? Seems like sacrilege.'

Emiliana shrugs her shoulders. 'What do you expect from a cheapskate?'

'How is he?' Another game. Like the tricks and the trumps and the poker faces at bridge, Ev knows exactly how he is.

'Angry, moody, righteous. Stomping about the place with his nose in the air and holding his life hostage until I answer his question.' Emiliana shakes her head at the unfairness of it all while fumbling about her person for a cigarette. 'Always that same bloody question.'

Ev places her cards face down on the table and sighs sadly. 'Then I think it might be time to answer it, my love, don't you?'

'What?' Emiliana's dark eyes fix hers with incredulity. She throws her own cards down and picks up her cocktail. She fingers the rim of the glass and it responds with a manic squeak. It's the first time her friend has challenged her authority. The first time she hasn't instantly agreed with her point of view. 'Answer it?' Her shriek reverberates around the quiet of the room. 'What conceivable difference will telling him make, other than raking things up for *me*?'

'What difference? Darling, the difference between night and day. That's the difference. You owe him that much.' Ev lowers her own voice to compensate for her friend's tone. 'As do I . . .'

Emiliana's dark eyes are on stalks. 'What's brought all this on, Ev?'

The cancer, Ev thinks. The Bollywood dancing. Realising that she'll never make it to India because Jimmy's afraid to travel and it's too late to book an airline ticket. Knowing that there are only so many sunrises left to admire over Addison Avenue before Angelo knocks on her door. 'Because I'm tired of the guilt,' she replies. 'It's time to make everything right.'

~

Her parents, whose faces she's rarely recalled over the years, invade her memories like locusts. Not as they were when they passed, worn out by the years in their lives, but as they appeared to her when she was a little girl on Cyprus.

Her father, with his tanned shiny brow and dark trousers, his waist constricted by an assortment of belts. Her mother with her dark, reproving eyes and tightly knotted headscarves. The three of them, cowering beneath the shade of the lemon tree in their back yard to escape the might of the Cypriot sun. She supposes it's because she's nearing the end that she wants to remember again. To go back to the beginning and understand if there was some purpose to it all. Or perhaps it's simply to exonerate herself.

Cyprus, 1934. Evgenia's mother, Sotira, scraped three hot baked potatoes out of their clay oven and, along with a shovelful of ash, tossed them unceremoniously onto a blanket in their yard. She disappeared inside the kitchen and emerged moments later from its cool, shadowy depths with a bowl of freshly prepared salad, a jug of olive oil and a carafe of koumandaria wine, muttering all the while about the intensity of the heat, the abundance of flies and the absurdity of a husband dressed in his best but actually good for nothing.

She dumped the salad next to the potatoes and declared that they should eat before her goodwill ran out and she flung everything into the bin. Evgenia, bursting with hunger and impatience, grabbed at a potato with too much alacrity and scalded herself on its skin. 'Aou!' Five painful blisters bubbled beneath the surface of her delicate fingertips and she received a clip round the ear for her troubles. Her father, Foti, hitherto reclining on his back beneath the tree with a toothpick dangling from his mouth, chose that opportune moment to sit up and pose a curious question to the group. Which was preferable, did they think: the heat of the summer sun or the soothing shade of their lemon tree?

His wife looked fit to stab him with her fork so he redirected the riddle to his only child. Evgenia's teacher sometimes asked similar rhetorical questions. Was she born stupid or did it develop later? Did she actually have a brain between her ears or was it just a piece of cloth? And so she procrastinated at length over the right response while sucking noisily on a piece of tomato. Her mother, meanwhile, grew weary and uncomfortable and attacked the stray hairs hanging in front of her own face by yanking them out of her scalp altogether.

'Well?' When Evegenia failed to answer in the allotted time, her father reframed the question. Which was better, did she think? Toiling like a sunburned peasant or living a life of prosperity in a wealthy foreign country?'

Her mother tutted '*garo*' under her breath, but still loud enough for the whole street to hear, while Evgenia declared that of course she wanted to lie beneath a prosperous lemon tree and enjoy the shade it afforded. 'I wouldn't want to get sunburned, Pappa.'

Foti raised his cup in the air and toasted the clear blue skies in his daughter's honour. 'Then so be it!'

She assumed it was the right answer because her father's face glistened with beads of excitement and his wine-shot eyes nearly bulged out of his head. 'Bravo,' he said, stroking her light brown ringlets and telling her she was right and that she was clever, while Evgenia was pleased to have her childish worth confirmed.

She often wondered how her life might have turned out if she'd answered her father differently that day. If she'd been more patient, less ravenous and not blistered her skin on the potato. If her father had been less drunk on the koumandaria and the heat not quite so intense. If there had been no lemon tree to provide shade, would they still have moved to England?

Of course, she tortured herself needlessly for all those years. Her mother's irritable mood and her father's lemony riddles were not a prelude to his decision-making, merely a nice postscript. A gentle way of breaking the news of their imminent departure from Cyprus to a girl too young to understand.

They arrived at Victoria station in London on the first day of October in 1935, and it seemed like Evgenia's life was beginning again with the changing of the scenery. Gone were the fruit trees, the blue skies and the rays of scorching sun. The Mediterranean Sea was suddenly replaced by an expanse of grey and etiolated skin.

Behind the throng of pale people hurrying past them stood a fat, bald man with a cigar dangling from his mouth. The bald man's name was Mr Karvelas and he appeared to know her father. 'Welcome to England, my Cypriot friends,' he declared, his pudgy hands plucking the unremarkable Foti out from the crowd as his voice rose upwards to compete with the hissing of the trains. He shook hands with each of them in turn, collapsing himself onto a single bended knee to kiss the back of Evgenia's hand. 'Come with me.' He loaded their tattered cases into the boot of his car and drove them all to a place called Soho.

'So-ho!' Evgenia was mesmerised by the scenes

whizzing before her eyes in the early-evening twilight: the disappearing station; the tall buildings and brightly coloured signs; the huge, bell-shaped lamps hanging from brick walls; the important-looking men in suits, scurrying across busy roads and the women with cloche hats pulled over their faces, their bags filled with meat and fruit from the markets. 'Wow,' she exclaimed at it all, and Mr Karvelas chuckled at her childish wonderment in the rear-view mirror while telling his steering wheel and his horn that Foti was brave. That not many men had the brass balls to transplant their families into foreign soil and start again aged thirty-nine.

Her father, unaccustomed to praise of any kind, never mind from the likes of Mr Karvelas, drank the compliments down in one go. He seasoned their outbound journey on the *Messapia* with non-existent spectacles to leverage even more admiration – much to the annoyance of those who had actually been there. 'Such a magnificent ship, and you should have seen the welcome we received at Piraeus harbour. Even the trees came together to bow.'

Trees? In reality, the three of them had spent the week vomiting overboard and not admiring the majesty of the Acropolis or the twinkling stars or the Naples shoreline at all. 'That's why I intend to reward you, my friend,' Mr Karvelas told his car mirror. 'Because such courage deserves recognition.'

They arrived at Number 2 Berwick Street in the gloom. Mr Karvelas parked the Golden behind a row of padlocked shops and retrieved their bags from the boot with a grunt and without any assistance from her flimsy father. He led them through an alleyway lined with metal bins, up a circular staircase that clanged beneath their heels and into the bosom of a warm and welcoming apartment. Smells of coal, sausages and lavender soap tickled Evgenia's nostrils and her stomach lurched in anticipation. 'Your new home,' Mr Karvelas announced, depositing their luggage in an inadequately sized room filled with grey mattresses and an even dirtier sink, and announced that dinner would appear in an hour.

The Great Reward Mr Karvelas had dangled before Foti was a job in his tea shop on the ground floor of the building. Evgenia's eyes widened with excitement at the thought of a caffeinated underworld beneath the squeaky floorboards. 'Under *my* feet?' She stomped around their new room in vomit-splattered shoes, making quite a racket until Sotira yanked her by the hair. 'Aow!' Without the generosity of Mr Karvelas, her father whispered – although it was more of a hiss than a whisper – they would not have been able to enter this prosperous country and live in the shade of the imaginary lemon tree. The man deserved their gratitude and respect. He directed the last part of this speech to his wife with a grand sweep of his arms, while Evgenia yawned to her tonsils and wondered if the mattresses were as damp as they smelled.

The next morning, Foti rose refreshed from his borrowed bed and tried to wash his armpits in the little sink. He put on a clean shirt and a pair of navy trousers and teased his stringy, dark hair across his head with a broken comb. At half past ten, the four of them – Evgenia, her newly coiffured father, Mr Karvelas and Mr Karvelas's wife – trooped back down the clanging stairs to examine the New Place of Employment.

The tea shop was called 'Parks' because Mr Karvelas had bought the enterprise from a man called Reginald Parks and never bothered to replace the sign. 'Besides, "Parks" has a ring to it, don't you think?' Evgenia whistled at the red and gold carpets beneath them, at the round tables and the swirly wooden chairs housing the bottoms of wealthy occupants.

Sugar tongs and silver spoons glimmered as they caught the light streaming in from the windows, and somewhere in the distance soothing jazz played on a phonograph. Waiters in well-pressed uniforms twirled trays and navigated tables like expert dancers, and cups steamed from behind afternoon tea stands piled high with tempting cakes. 'Pappa! This place is like a dream!' Evgenia may as well have been at a royal ball that morning with all the twinkling and twirling, although she couldn't imagine her father parading around with a tray in his hand no matter how hard she pretended.

'Best beverages in London,' Mrs Karvelas chimed in proudly. 'If you can stomach the *Eye*-talians.'

The place was 'absolutely teeming with good-for-nothing *Eye*-talians,' according to Mrs Karvelas. They loitered outside the cafés all day, drinking coffee in their smart suits, 'But don't let the fine clothes fool you

– they're gangsters, the lot of them,' she declared. Ev's father would be joining the two good-for-nothings who already worked for Mr Karvelas, although Mr Karvelas assured the group that neither Sandro nor Manolo were criminals.

'That we *know* of, Ari,' Mrs Karvelas snorted.

In the newly christened Whispering Room, where their hosts were safely out of earshot, her mother would strangle herself with her array of Cypriot shawls and spit at Evgenia hysterically.

'Stay away from the troublemakers, you hear me?'

'Which ones?' Evgenia asked, wrinkling her nose in confusion as she recalled the smiling, courteous waiters at Parks who had offered her tea and chiffon cake.

'All of them. The Italians, the Jews, the Chinese.' She lowered her voice to a menacing whisper. 'And especially the *Eye*-rish.'

'The *Eye*-rish' was in fact Bella Flanagan, Mr Karvelas's wife, although Sotira took considerable satisfaction in explaining that she was not Mr Karvelas's wife at all. The Real Mrs Karvelas was back home in Meneou darning his kids' socks and rueing the day she met him. Bella was his mistress – Evgenia had no idea what this meant, but her mother had been so repulsed by the notion that her spittle had flown halfway across the mattresses.

Bella Flanagan. Everything about her was buoyant. Her brown wavy hair bounced cheerfully around her face and her grey eyes sparkled mischievously. Her huge chest strained eagerly through her expensive blouses to greet anyone in its wake, and so great was its satin wonder that her father would frequently choke on his tongue.

It appeared Mr Karvelas felt the same way, because there would be strange noises leaking from their bedroom across the hall every night. Moans, groans, squeaks and thumps, and Evgenia knew that these sounds had something to do with the bosoms, but she also knew better than to ask.

'She's a gold-digger and he's got gold and that's all there is to say,' her mother would sneer in the Whispering Room, although she knew better than to *actually* say.

Sotira could no longer actually say very much. Her father relished this new dynamic where he was the master, but Evgenia found the shift disconcerting. She tried to coax her mother out for a walk in the same way one might try to tempt a cat out of a tree, but her attempts only pushed her further beneath the bedsheets. Eventually, Evgenia abandoned the vigil, along with the boring paper dolls Mr Karvelas had given her, and accepted Bella the Betrayer's offer of a tour.

Like the satin bosoms, Berwick Street on market day was a wonder to behold. Rainbow-coloured awnings hung over either side of the street and vendors lined the pavements beneath them, promoting their wares at the very tops of their voices: 'Two shillings for a pound of pears, ladies and gentlemen, and you can't say fairer than that!' Tipping their flat caps when the girls walked past and occasionally flinging them an apple. Sausages, bananas, furs and hosiery hung from hooks above their heads and Bella attempted to impress her in her best, broken Greek. Shouting the names of things above the cacophony of people and cars, and buses signposted to mysterious places: Leicester Square, Holborn, Oxford Circus.

'She's my niece!' she exclaimed to familiar faces, pinching Evgenia's arm to elicit her complicity and until Ev was fit to burst with pride. It felt wonderful being Bella's imaginary niece, strolling through Berwick Street Market in London in the centre of the Whole Wide World.

Evgenia loved the ebb and flow of her new life. The market. The huge gas lamps suspended in the streets and lit every evening by a scruffy-looking boy wobbling precariously on top of a bicycle. If Bella had afternoon errands to run, Evgenia would beg to tag along so she could watch him illuminating the cold, misty streets with his glowing stick. She enjoyed spying on the mud-stained kids playing cricket in the courtyards, white wickets slopped on the brick walls behind them. She was captivated by the comings and goings of Parks Tea Shop with its fancy clientele, and by her father's stories in the Whispering Room at bedtime. Stories of spilt milk, red-faced waiters and smashed china. Tales of women refusing to pay and husbands threatening to sue. She relished the smells of the Karvelases' apartment, the waft of coal and bacon mingled with lavender soap and the scent of Bella's perfume.

'Isn't this exciting?' Evgenia ran from window to

window with her arms outstretched, a little aeroplane eager to inform her hermetically sealed mother of the things she saw and heard in the Wide World. The things she was missing while she sulked in bed and fiddled with her eyebrows. Sotira's flower was clearly wilting and the following spring, it was determined by Mr Karvelas that Evgenia should have a friend her own age to play with, so that Bella could focus on her mother.

The new friend's name was Lenny Goldstein, and he came over when he wasn't at school to teach Evgenia how to speak English. 'Boiled sweet, see?' Mysterious objects magically appeared in the palm of his hand while his foreign words swirled around her like the notorious London fogs. Lenny was a Jewish boy with light brown hair, freckles, and ears that were too big for his head. 'Shall we try a ha'penny next? Can you say "hey-penny"?'

Lenny Goldstein already had two jobs and he was not yet twelve. Rising before dawn to sell juice to market vendors from his father's wheelbarrow, and carrying bags of coal up the stairs for rich housewives.

'Proves my point.'

'What point is that, then, Ari?'

'About the Jews ?' Mr Karvelas chewed enthusiastically on his cigar and spat the bits into his dinner plate, to everyone's disgust.

'Leave the boy alone.' Bella liked Jewish people a whole lot more than Mr Karvelas did, and it was all because scary Mr Hitler was persecuting them. Evgenia enjoyed listening to Bella's stories about scary Mr Hitler and his new Germany while succulent sausages from Berwick Street Market sizzled temptingly in her frying pan. She had no idea what any of it meant, not really, and she couldn't picture a place where Lenny wasn't allowed to live; the tales of persecution felt as fictional to her as the baddies in her bedtime stories.

'Scary Mr Hitler will lose in the end, won't he, Bella?'

Nobody was sure. While vile people definitely deserved what was coming to them, the world wasn't necessarily that fair.

Then, a year after they arrived in Soho to live with Mr Karvelas and Bella Flanagan, and a few weeks after she started her brand new school, a man named Jack Christofi waltzed into their lives and turned them upside down.

~

Towards the end of October, when the last of the leaves float from the trees and the world transforms into magnificent shades of golds and browns, they decide to drive to Southend. 'To take the sea air,' Jimmy suggests, although they both know it's because she's on borrowed time. Mr White Teeth had said as much at her last appointment, although he didn't use those exact words. 'Your tumours are growing quicker than we would like, Mrs Theocaris,' which roughly translated to, 'You've not got long left, dear.'

There were still options. They could amputate the bones in her lower leg to buy her a few more months.

Flood her blood with a stronger dose of chemicals, but it would all boil down to philosophy in the end. Jimmy stomped around the house like a bear with a sore head when they returned from the hospital. 'Bloody philosophy, he tells us! What's *that* supposed to mean? Is philosophy gonna cure us of the cancer?' Slamming doors and attempting to smash the bathroom cabinet in retribution for how it had all worked out for Ev and Jimmy.

She called up the stairs that it was all OK to restore some calm to his poor broken soul. 'It is what it is, love.'

Lately, life is just full of aphorisms. 'It is what it is', 'You can't turn back time', 'Make it count' and her favourite, 'When life gives you lemons', and so she happily packs a bottle of fizzy lemonade alongside the Primula cheese and liver sausage sandwiches. They set off in the silver Ford Escort just before noon and while Jimmy heads for the A13, she rolls down the window and looks up at the gathering storm clouds, admiring the ominous shades of greys, purples and blues.

'Looks like it's gonna rain, Ev?'

His eyes were electric blue, so blue they were almost violet. Like two blobs of ink on a piece of tissue, bleeding into his face. She searched for the world in those eyes, once. Ascribed a pathos to them that simply didn't exist.

'Ev? Looks like rain?' Jimmy scratches at the tufts of brown hair sprouting around his ears and regards her nervously, as if she might dissolve like Bisto when exposed to the water. He wonders if they should turn back before the sky splits open but she pats his hand and urges him to carry on. Be better just the two of them, she tells him. There was a time when she would seek out a crowd. When she would have been attracted to its power and vitality and the way that life throbbed within it. Now, she longs only for peace.

They pull into the deserted car park and Jimmy takes the basket and blanket out of the car boot while she grabs the cushions she's packed for the comfort, because the days when she could sit on a shingle beach and enjoy a picnic have dissipated like autumnal mist in the sunshine. They crunch hand in hand through the pebbles, towards the muddy shoreline. Finding a spot he likes, Jimmy spreads the blanket at the foot of the estuary as the first roll of thunder breaks overhead and birds squawk in alarm. 'You hungry?' She is today. Something about the intoxicating smell of the salt-water always makes her ravenous. As though she needs to eat to keep up with the elements. 'Very hungry.' She bites into her liver sausage sandwich with relish.

He was beautiful and charismatic, and it wasn't just Evgenia who thought so. Bella Flanagan purred like a kitten when Mr Karvelas first brought him up to the flat, and even her mother crept out from beneath her duvet to meet the young stranger who spoke Greek like an American. His name was Jack Christofi. He was Mr Karvelas's brand new waiter and what a sight he was.

His eyes were so blue and his quiff jet-black. When

he smiled, dimples danced around his cheeks. He stayed for dumplings, that first evening, and they were all fixated on him as they slurped the broth from their spoons. Bella cooed and gurgled and her mother scrutinised from beneath her cactus-like brows. Her father dabbed at his sweaty forehead, barely able to contain his admiration from dripping into his stew, and Mr Karvelas slapped Jack on the back in the same way he'd welcomed her father on that very first day in October. 'He's really something, this one,' he said – and he really was. But the most thrilling part of all, the *really* exciting bit, was that Jack Christofi only had eyes for her. Little Evgenia, in her navy blue skirt and her burgundy school sweater and her short frilly socks.

Afterwards, her mother brought the thing up in the Whispering Room when her daughter was supposedly fast asleep. Didn't he think it was peculiar? she asked her husband. The way the young man had gawped at Evgenia all night and she still wrapped in her school uniform and barely eleven years old?

Her weary father grumbled into his filthy pillow. 'You think everything's peculiar, Sotira.'

'And his story made no sense.'

'Which part?'

'Well, all of it. None of it.'

'There you go then!'

Although he claimed to have his own place, Jack Christofi became a fixture in the flat when the tea shop closed for the day, at one with the sofas and the armchairs and the skinny lampshades in the corners. Bella was delighted, thrusting her magnificent bosoms into his cheek at every opportunity, but by the middle of 1937 it had become obvious that he was no more interested in Bella than he was in Mr Karvelas's tea shop.

He complimented Evgenia. He liked her school clothes and the way she started letting out her baby braids and pinning her wavy hair at the sides with shiny clips like Bella's. The hints of green in her sparkly brown eyes.

'They're hazel,' she explained, proudly.

'Hazel?' A colour as beautiful as she was.

He liked the way her cheeks turned pink when he paid her attention. The formal way she spoke to him. 'Please, call me Jack.' The way her tongue poked out of the side of her mouth when she was concentrating on her schoolwork, and how her face brightened when she found the answer she was looking for. He liked *everything* about her. 'My sweet little Evgenia.'

She, in turn, could barely contain herself. His voice was deep and gravelly, the way treacle might sound if it could speak, and, when his hot breath tickled her ears, her tummy turned somersaults.

'You're welcome to him.' Bella meant for it to sound nonchalant and light-hearted, but she started to treat Ev differently from the moment Jack arrived in the flat above the tea shop. There were no more trips to the market, no more errands to watch Bicycle Boy lighting his lamps with a stick. She grew colder towards Evgenia than the ashes in her burner and her tone was better suited to a rival.

Jack Christofi was many things, but above all he was a Man with a Plan. Her father revealed as much in the Whispering Room towards the end of the year. Jack didn't want to be a waiter in Mr Karvelas's tea shop forever, twirling a tray around and at the beck and call of every stuck-up bitch from Berwick Street to Holborn. He had set his sights on brighter, shinier dreams.

He wanted to open a Greek restaurant and sell cocktails and colourful lamb and pepper skewers to London's elite. To Laurence Olivier and Vivien Leigh and Neville Chamberlain. He wanted to serve yoghurt and mint platters to singers, and zivania to royals in crystal shot glasses.

'Royals?' her mother would scoff into the darkness. 'Pah! Ridiculous! The man is out of his mind. Where's he going to find money to open a fancy restaurant? He's a waiter in a tea shop, for God's sake!' Evgenia would beg for sleep to steal her away, then, because she knew exactly where Jack was going to find the money, although she'd promised she wouldn't tell. What was another promise, really, among all the others she was keeping in the Alley of Secrets?

It begins to rain heavily and Jimmy untangles the black jumper from around his waist and holds it above their heads like a soaking parapet. The wet pebbles glisten in the hazy, afternoon light and the vast, blue-grey waters of the Thames Estuary blur into the elusive horizon. In the distance, a small sailing boat is silhouetted against the sky and everything seems so beautiful, suddenly. This mournful, misty view before her. Cherished while slowly passing.

~

The Alley of Secrets behind Parks Tea Shop was where Evgenia spent most of her thirteenth year with the handsome Jack Christofi. A steam-filled passage where winding stairs met foul-smelling bins and an assortment of vicious rats, and where shopkeepers sporadically appeared from their premises to toss out buckets of filthy water that splattered grey muck up her socks.

She would arrive shortly after school, her cheeks flushed pink and her woolly hat pulled down over her eyebrows, and Jack would dart out from behind the piles of stacked crates to ambush her with a tickle. He twirled her around and around until her head was fit to explode with happiness. 'Stop, Jack, please!' Little shiny stars popped behind her eyes and she wondered, in those incredible moments, which sensation made her dizzier: the feel of Jack's arms spinning her around like a tea tray, or the honour of being confidante to his aspirations.

In November of 1938, as Jewish homes and synagogues burned in Scary Mr Hitler's Germany, a Frenchman named Monsieur Laroche put his property up for sale. Number 11 Dean Street. That very day, Jack's dreams grew even wilder. 'I'm gonna buy it, Ev, and I'm gonna turn it into the finest Greek restaurant

anyone's ever seen!' Evgenia believed it, too, this idea
that Jack would achieve everything he wanted, because
his blue eyes pierced holes in her soul and his dimples
danced about his cheeks as he spoke, and didn't beautiful people, already blessed, continue to attract good
fortune?

She had an important role to play after Scary
Mr Hitler burned Germany: eavesdropping on her
parents' conversations in the Whispering Room and
disclosing the information in the alley. It was a promotion, a step up from Jack's confidante to his special
accomplice. 'Like a wartime spy, Ev!'

Did her father have any money? Where was he
stashing it? How long did he plan to live with
Mr Karvelas and Bella the Bitch in the flat above the
tea shop? Did Foti like being a waiter or did he, like
Jack, want more than a monkey's life? A life of placing
cake in front of rich bitches and watching them stuff
their faces?

He compensated her for her intelligence with
beaming smiles that sent her heart soaring into the
clouds – or sometimes, with a delicious kiss on the
mouth. An actual kiss! What did she do right? she
wondered, at the tantalising moment his lips met hers
and her legs buckled beneath her. What did she do to
deserve *all* of this happiness?

At dinner, Ari Karvelas, his big brown teeth clamped
around his cigar, excoriated Scary Mr Hitler while they
nodded, slurped or chewed their food in unison. 'All that
culture, razed to the ground!' he boomed into his spoon,

and Bella, who had always seen things in Mr Hitler's character that others apparently hadn't, would stretch her flimsy cardigan across her bosoms and declare the man a maniac.

'I told you he was crazy, Ari.'

The Night of Broken Glass, the newspapers were calling the fires, and everyone, with the exception of her father, had an opinion to venture.

'Foti! What do you think of this deplorable nonsense? This burning by Hitler?'

Summoned by his landlord and employer to express a view worth hearing to the rest of the dinner group, Evgenia's father shrank, sweating, into the collars of his shirt and waved his hunk of bread at Jack. 'Save me,' the hunk pleaded. 'I have no idea what's going on.' He was a man about to drown, and the pressure was all too much. What did flimsy Foti know about politics of this scale and magnitude? About the poor, persecuted Jews of Europe and the flames of racial hatred? All he really cared about was his toothpick and the soothing shade of the lemon tree!

Jack half rose from his seat to toss her father a life ring and Mr Karvelas contemplated each of his employees with a curiosity that hadn't been there before. 'I think Adolf is destined for glory, personally,' said Jack, half slurping and half burping his words, while Evgenia's mother wrinkled her nose at his table manners. 'Playing the long game.' For what were the fiery synagogues and shards of broken glass, if not the symbols of his potency and ambition? He gave Evgenia a sneaky blue wink while Mr Karvelas coughed up his incredulity along with more gelatinous blobs from his cigar.

After the Night of Broken Glass, the hushed voices in the Whispering Room were particularly active in the darkness. There was lots to share with Jack in the Alley of Secrets. Her father wanted to find his inner Hitler too, it seemed. 'He doesn't want to be a monkey either, Jack. He wants to prosper beneath the shade of the lemon tree in our old garden.' Evgenia's voice sounded muffled and laboured as she swung upside down on the swirly staircase rail.

'Does he now?' Jack Christofi rewarded her cleverness with a creeping, upside-down smile.

There was one last thing to confide in the alley as the sun sank behind the London rooftops, taking the steely light with it. Evgenia's father was saving the money from the sale of their Cypriot home for an investment worth investing in.

'That's exactly what he said, Jack! He doesn't want to live with Mr Karvelas and Bella the Bitch, either.'

Jack's pretty face lit up like a torch. He grabbed her by the ears and smothered her mouth with his. 'An investment? My sweet little Evgenia . . .'

It was the longest, and, as things turned out, the very last kiss he would ever place on her childish lips.

One by one, the people in Evgenia's life began to disappear. Jack Christofi evaporated into the London mists one night, never to be seen again. Her mother melted into the mattresses lining the Whispering Room floor and her long-suffering father lost his last few marbles.

'Where did Pretty Boy go?' they all wanted to know. 'He was here just a minute ago!'

Mr Karvelas, bemused by the turn of events that had turned one waiter into the Ghost of Christmas Past and another into a dribbling wreck, sent his finest *Eye*-talian to investigate. A young woman answered the door of Jack's supposed flat. She told Sandro Sterlini that she had never heard of a pretty boy who sounded like an American film star, but he would certainly know about it if she did.

Monsieur Laroche didn't know him either. 'Ooooo?' Newly remunerated for the sale of his property and preparing to float back to France to eat nicer cheese, he'd never come across the man. He'd certainly never enquired about Number 11 Dean Street and so this imaginary restaurant could never have existed. 'A Greek restaurant? *Mais non*. Number 11 will be turned into *une épicerie, je crois.*'

This final confirmation of a daylight betrayal so flagrantly schemed and executed pushed Foti into a state of catatonia. For when Jack vanished into next Christmas with his false promises and his lemon trees, there was more than just her father's pride in his briefcase. Jack had conned him out of their life savings. Every penny. Money from the sale of their property on Cyprus, an inheritance that Evgenia's grandmother had bequeathed to her mother. Money Foti was saving for a fresh start in England, a house, a car, a dowry for Evgenia.

Sotira had just one question for her newly destitute husband and she delivered it through the locked bedroom door in case the temptation to slit his throat overwhelmed her. 'How could you be so stupid?' If there was ever an answer to his wife's question, her father took it with him to the grave.

Evgenia knew the answer. She knew that the machinations in the Alley of Secrets had caused her father's downfall. The plotting, the scheming, the delicious kisses. She was to blame for all of it. 'It was me,' she wanted to shout from the Soho rooftops. To the market vendors and the shoppers and to the man who sold *The Times* beneath their window. 'It was *my* fault; I was Jack's accomplice.' But what difference would it have made, now that Jack had vanished into the mists of time and there was to be no new life for her family? When her father was condemned to an eternity of twirling trays in someone else's tea shop with no tree to shield him from the sun?

She felt mucky. Mucky and dirty. She scrubbed at her skin with Bella's lavender soaps until she shrank the purple bar to a pebble, studying her face in the mirror to see if she looked as filthy and as gullible on the outside as she felt inside. Pulling at her cheeks to check if the hazel eyes he'd once admired exuded a special kind of filth that marked her out. For the first time in years, she wanted her mother, who had been there all along but didn't seem to exist any more. Who now passed through Evgenia as if she lacked real substance, like a waft of smoke or steam from a cooking pot.

She thought about Lenny Goldstein instead. Kind, uncomplicated Lenny who'd tried to teach her English using just the palms of his hands before Bella had enrolled her in school. She thought about his light brown hair and his freckles and his protruding ears, and not because he had been a particularly close or valued companion, but because he'd meant her no harm. She saw him one last time in the autumn of 1940, and it was as if she had dredged him out from the sooty crevices of London, and from happier, simpler times.

There had been a series of air raids in Soho that September. Banshee sirens that shrieked their warnings into burnt orange skies, and, that particular night, she grabbed her coat and ran towards the underground without waiting for her family. She descended breathlessly down the interminable stairs, but lumps of blankets already covered the platforms and there was no space for her to lie down. Somewhere in the distance, a child whimpered for his mother.

Evgenia drew her knees to her chest and concentrated on the posters plastered on the walls. Posters she knew by heart. 'Dig for Victory!', 'We'll Defeat Hitler!', 'Support our Boys!' They sounded like the things Jack would pour into her ears in the alley and she wondered if the exclamation marks made the words preceding them more or less convincing.

The explosions began immediately. Muffled thuds rocking the signs overhead and causing showers of silt to rain down into her uncombed hair. Hair she no longer had any regard for because the waves and the clips reminded her of *his* compliments. Some people cheered while others sobbed, quietly. The lights blinked once, twice, before switching off and then on again with a buzz. Applause filled the tunnel as another air raid passed without incident and there was Lenny Goldstein, suddenly, in the middle of it all. Navigating the crowded platform with a tray of sweets dangling from his neck. She could almost hear Mr Karvelas sneering in her ear as he called out for customers. 'See, another job! What did I tell you?' Evgenia forced her head between her legs and hoped that the voice would fade. That Lenny Goldstein would walk straight past and back into her memories. That he wouldn't recognise her in the gloomy chaos, among the grey-coloured clothes and the blankets. She didn't want to stand out any more.

Why would he? she thought afterwards, as she emerged, dazed and slightly bruised, from beneath the earth and stumbled back along Oxford Street. Why would Lenny Goldstein single her out from the crowd when she had changed *so much*?

Three buildings were burning brightly: a shop, a church and a café called Ned's. Their roofs were missing and their jagged new profiles pricked the night sky in retribution for their disfigurement. The ARP were shouting for more water and warning people to keep away and a fire engine wailed in the background. The air smelled acrid, of smoke and burning wood, and the intensity of the heat stung her eyes and made them leak.

She blamed herself as she walked towards the flat above the tea shop where, thanks to her complicity in Jack's plan, she and her family were doomed to live forever. She blamed herself for the moon, the stars and the air raids, too. If she hadn't been shining so brilliantly in the sky, Mr Hitler wouldn't have singled her out. Without her light, he wouldn't have noticed her at all.

~

'I've decided I'm going to tell him.'

It's Card Tuesday, and they sit at opposite ends of Emiliana's wonky wooden table while the hostess deals the cards with long, skinny fingers. 'I don't know *when* I'm going to do it. I might wait 'til after Christmas when he's finished renovating the house, but when the time is right I'll do it. I promise.' She moves a bowl of spicy crackers out of the way to lay four cards between them, face up. 'No jack.'

'Pardon, my darling?'

'There's no jack. You go first.'

Evgenia takes a deep breath to steady her racing pulse and pairs a card from the centre of the table with one of the six in her hand. 'I have a pair of aces. I see what you mean now. About the jack.'

Her new ring glints in the glow of the jellyfish lampshade, complemented by red-painted fingernails. A trio of diamonds sparkle in its centre. It's engraved, a gift from her Jimmy's jewellery shop. He surprised her with the little gift box this afternoon, telling her, 'It says "Ev and Jimmy, established 1943", see? Because if there's no you, then there's no me, remember?' Pleased with himself, Jimmy leaned across the torn wrapping paper to plant a kiss on her forehead.

'I remember, my love. I remember . . .'

Forty-five years in the blink of an eye. She'd been barely eighteen when he'd breezed into the smoky candlelit pub she was drinking in with the erstwhile Klara Klaus, her excited friend squealing in her ear as Jimmy winked in the direction of their table.

'Aw! Isn't he splendid? If he's a Suitable Jewish Boy, he's all mine.' Klara's small grey eyes danced mischievously in her chubby face, and her lips glistened like moist slugs at the thought of tasting him.

He stood out that night, she'll give Klara that. Outshining the handsome soldiers on leave, huddled around their pints. Jimmy's cream hat contrasted with the sea of navy blues and khakis, like a shell gleaming on a rock. Jimmy being Jimmy, dancing to his own tune.

'Can I buy you lovely ladies a drink?'

He wasn't a Suitable Jewish Boy and he wasn't wearing a soldier's uniform beneath his leather coat. Klara's face clouded over like a stormy sky once he peeled it off to reveal a plain white shirt and black trousers. 'Sorry, ladies, afraid I've not seen any action.'

His father was a Greek-Cypriot, although he was born and raised in east London. What were the chances of that? he asked Evgenia's left ear. The chances of meeting a fellow Greek in a pub in wartime London?

His name was Jimmy Theocaris. 'Sounds like a song

but it means "God's grace".' He tapped the four syllables out on the table with his beer mat to illustrate the point. '*Dum*-dee-*dum*-dee.' Did she believe in God? Evgenia shrugged her shoulders and stared at the patterned paper on the walls, fiddling nervously with her newly brushed hair and wishing she was older and more sophisticated. That she could puff provocatively on her cigarette like Klara Klaus.

He made jewellery in a workshop in Hatton Garden, apprenticed to an old man named Feldman. 'They're all Jews in the trade,' he said, glancing furtively over at Klara. 'They're very good at it, though, so no offence intended.' He hoped to open his own shop one day because diamonds were the greatest thing after beautiful women. He was a little bit addicted to them. Diamonds that is, not girls. They were the closest thing to capturing stars, he said. Did Evgenia like stars?

'Oh God!' Klara's irritation was now a fully blown member of their awkward group, while Jimmy's brown eyes examined Ev's in the candlelight. 'Put a lid on it, Mr Diamonds!'

'If you must know, I don't like diamonds and I don't like stars,' she said to him afterwards as they waited outside the Red Lion for Klara's father to pick them up in the Austin. She said it to see his reaction and not because it was true. She remembers twirling playfully around a lamppost as she pretended not to notice that he liked her.

'If you say so, Evgenia. Mind if I call you Ev, by the way? Suits you!' He took her in his arms and spun her around before replacing his cap and walking off into the night. She almost expected him to leap to the side and click his heels together in the shadows, he seemed *that* pleased with himself.

'What a blooming liberty,' Klara tutted jealously behind his back. 'I wish my doddery dad would hurry up; the war'll be over by the time he shows up.' She lit another cigarette, this time without offering Evgenia one. 'Suppose you'll be seeing Mr Diamonds again?'

'Him?' Evgenia watched the smoke from Klara's cigarette wafting towards the sky as Jimmy turned the corner onto Argyle Street. 'Never.'

They were married that summer because there was no point in waiting for things – the war had taught them that. The war, and, she supposes, Jack Christofi emptying their coffers. An elderly priest dressed in black and wearing the biggest cross Evgenia had ever seen performed a swift ceremony in the Klauses' back garden. Sotira and Bella baked cheese pastries to furnish the bare tables and, with no Suitable Jewish Boy on her daughter's horizon, Mrs Klaus made her a lopsided wedding cake using her own stash of coupons.

Evgenia's dress materialised from a discarded silk parachute that Bella bought on the black market. Ev tried not to think about its unfortunate former occupant as her mother pulled it tight around her spiky ribs; whether the man had landed in friendly territory, or if he'd been captured by the enemy and shot. 'He's probably in a prison camp by now,' her mother shrugged. 'But who cares? It's silk!'

An uneasy silence ensued in the Whispering Room that afternoon. Sotira sighed sadly as uplifting jazz from the tea shop's expensive new gramophone wafted up through the floorboards to remind them that everyone else was happy. That they had not been robbed of their futures.

'It's where Jack belongs.' The words escaped from Evgenia's mouth before she could squeeze her lips shut. 'I mean, he belongs in prison for what he did to our family.'

This elicited another sigh from Sotira, although Evgenia couldn't be sure whether it was a sigh of sadness, acceptance or regret. Had she been very keen on him? her mother asked, looking like a metal-toothed monster with her scarf fastened tightly behind her ears and long pins sticking out of her mouth.

'Not especially,' Evgenia lied, her shoulders rising up to meet her ears, and that was as far as Jack's epilogue went, because in the months following the arrival of Jimmy hope had battled her guilt and won.

'Get us!' She laughed as they walked hand in hand through the streets of a pummelled London. Oxford Street, Covent Garden, Leicester Square – places immortalised in her childhood tours with Bella. 'We're Ev and Jimmy!' They were a young couple like any other wartime young couple: anxious about what lay ahead of them, but secretly hoping for the best.

The future was the third diamond in Evgenia's ring: a place of hope, but also one of uncertainty. The past was the first stone, and represented memories: the lie

she told Angelo the night before Theo's funeral; little
Evgenia, twirling around the staircase in the Alley of
Secrets, in love with a pervert and a conman. The
middle stone was the present: the biggest and the
brightest of the bunch. A chance to make things right.

'Two queens. I think telling him is for the best, my
darling. He's suffered enough, don't you think?' She
needs to do this for him. She wants her conscience to
be clear when he comes to take her home. No more
collusion. No more secrets. She examines her ring
finger in the pinkish light. 'And you tell him from me
that I want to keep this on when it's, you know, *that*
time.'

Emiliana's mouth falls open and she shoots up from
the table, knocking over her bowl of crackers. 'Oh Ev,
please don't go! Don't leave me!'

Evgenia wraps her arms tightly around her best
friend's shoulders and buries her face in her lovely hair.

～

A few years after her wartime marriage to Jimmy,
Evgenia's father scraped enough money together to rent
a poky flat in Camden Town. The mice may have scurried happily between the damp, crumbling walls, but
her parents lived there miserably until Foti died on the
loo.

Once the earth had been heaped on top of her
husband, Sotira began to hoard. It started with her
refusal to empty her bins, so that newspapers piled up

around the small sitting room and unopened letters bricked up the entrances. When the papers failed to multiply as quickly as she hoped, Sotira actively scouted for miscellaneous jumble to grow her various piles, wandering around charity shops and church fetes in her headscarves collecting strange curiosities, only some of which could be identified. Boxes of buttons and jars full of shells. Cosmological paraphernalia and old-fashioned magnifying glasses. Miniature glass ornaments shaped like enchanted animals that, when held up to the light, projected little rainbows onto the ceiling.

There was no room to stand, let alone sit, and, by the late sixties, Sotira's flat had begun to look less like a home befitting a sweet grandma and more like the Museum of Dusty Dreams. Evgenia wondered with a stab of guilt if her mother's stockpiling was somehow linked to Jack. If Sotira, having once lost everything she owned, was determined to hold on to things forever.

Periodically, Ev attempted to unclutter the place, but her mother's mind was no longer with her and she threw insults at her daughter from her rocking chair.

'You're getting fat, Evgenia,' she shouted over the rising rubbish. 'That blonde hair doesn't suit you. You think you're Dusty Springfield, dyeing your hair like that?'

'OK, Mamma. Try to calm down. Did you take your pills this morning?'

'You look more like Myra Hindley than Dusty Springfield!'

Usually, though, her indignation was reserved for

Jimmy Theocaris. For in sickness, Sotira discovered a new hatred of her son-in-law.

'Evgenia! Your husband is a damned fool! If there had been a competition for fools, your father would have won it, but your Jimmy would have come in second, mark my words.' Ev wondered if this contempt had always been lurking in the shadows or if it had been conceived by her mother's ailing mind.

One morning, when Evgenia went round to free her mother's fridge of the greenish bottles of milk that dated as far back as the death of Winston Churchill, her mother caught her by surprise, creeping up behind her with a pot and a spoon and banging them loudly in her ears. 'Evgenia! Your husband is a pervert! He means to hurt you, child – oh *please* be careful!'

'Mamma? You're scaring me!'

Sotira wailed for so long afterwards that Evgenia was quite shaken by the event. 'Thank God for Card Tuesday,' she said to Jimmy when she returned home and peeled her coat from her shoulders as if it were a painful scab. Something to look forward to, because her mother was getting worse.

'A funny turn?' he frowned. 'About what, love?'

'Who knows?' she lied. 'Poor woman invents things in her sick mind.'

Her mother gave up the ghost in the early eighties and the shock of it was not the ghost's floating away but how it had managed to cling to corporeality for so long. Evgenia returned to Sotira's flat one last time after that, to relieve the groaning surfaces of their dusty burdens with long, sweeping movements of her arms. Papers, ornaments, shells, jam jars, all disappearing into mushroom clouds of silt and cobwebs and into waiting bin bags. The air smelled stale, as if time had long ago abandoned it for a better life, and Evgenia was suddenly envious of its ability to move on to pastures new without a second thought for what had been.

With a sigh for what actually *had* been, she gathered up letters and photographs and set them aside along with an assortment of gold crosses and her mother's stack of recipe books. She had been an accomplished cook before Number 2 Berwick Street had robbed her of her freedom, jotting things down in notebooks in the hope of a second chance at making things better. Hints and tips that had occurred to her randomly throughout the years. 'Next time, grate a handful of halloumi into the béchamel and mix in well.' Words and sentences overlapping, as modern ideas replaced more traditional ones. 'Add a sprinkle of mint into the cheesy filling for a lighter and more refreshing taste.'

Evgenia sat down in the old rocking chair and thumbed through the time-faded pages as light from the newly cleaned windows flooded the room. 'Throw a handful of chopped parsley into the kofte mix for a more peppery flavour.' The things her mother had scrawled intrigued her, as if someone else was now emerging from these lines to instruct her in her future. Someone new. 'Add crushed chestnuts to the livers and rice, and, for a sweeter taste, sprinkle lightly with cinnamon.' Someone with the confidence and authority to leave these notes behind, and not the woman Evgenia remembered.

She resolved to take the books back to Addison Avenue and practise the recipes in her own kitchen, imagining Jimmy's delighted face as she relieved their oven of a magnificent moussaka or a tray of delicious biscuits soaked in orange juice to dip in his tea, but something stopped her. When she reached the last page, 'Grandmother's Recipe for Turkey Stuffing', she realised she didn't deserve it, to be part of this important legacy established years ago and handed down from grandmother to mother in a pile of dusty notebooks. She wasn't worthy of weaving the tapestry.

They were not her recipes to follow and so she hid the sepia-tinted books away from view and from memory. She lost the right to relieve her oven of anything, she determined back then, when she colluded with Jack Christofi.

~

When she returns from Emiliana's, Ev slips off her sensible shoes and places them neatly alongside her Jimmy's on the mat by the front door. She pads tipsily into the kitchen, careful not to disturb him and elicit a barrage of concern, and pulls open the drawer beneath the sink. She pushes sponges, candles and old coins aside until she finally finds what she's looking for in the gloom.

'It wasn't my fault, of course it wasn't. I was just a child . . .'

It's on the very last page of the very first book, surrounded by Sotira's instructions.

It's time to make a list.

'I want to invite Dezzy.' Evgenia hoovers enthusiastically beneath Jimmy's battered slippers, raising her voice over the cacophony of whirring and moaning.

'So invite Dezzy.'

'Dezzy *and* Sarah. I want to invite them both.'

Jimmy lifts his big clumsy feet in the air so that Evgenia can scrub out their imprint. 'Sarah?' His eyebrows shoot up over his crumpled newspaper. 'The boy's not gonna like it one bit, I'm telling you now.'

'Well, the boy can lump it. It's my Christmas this year. My Christmas, *my* way.'

The whining gradually fades into blissful silence as Evgenia pulls the plug. She dabs at her sweaty forehead with the edge of her pink sleeve before Jimmy notices the beads of perspiration and scolds her. 'You're doing too much, Ev. Leave the bloody hoovering.' Truth is, there's nothing more satisfying than a newly hoovered carpet, whether she's up to it or not; the comforting *clunk clunk* of unspecified debris being sucked up the nozzle on its way to certain death in a bag of oblivion. It's like cleaning the day itself, in a way, and starting all over again.

'Hoovering? What would Mr White Teeth say, Ev?'

'I don't care what he'd say. Probably that my tumours

are growing faster than he would like but that he's going skiing in Aspen. Carpet's marvellous, though. You can play boules on that.'

'And what we s'posed to talk about with this Sarah woman? We barely know her.' Jimmy's feet still stick up in the air as Evgenia leads the hoover by its hose into the cupboard beneath the stairs.

She barks at him from inside the musty hole. 'I think that's the point I'm trying to make, love. I want us to get to know her. She's Dezzy's special friend and I think it's time we made an effort.'

Looking back, there had been signs. Quite a few, in fact. Sotira's insinuations, for one. The time they all drove down to Margate for Cousin Cara's wedding and Dez danced cheek to cheek with the blonde girl from Greece. Their amorous display, soliciting unwelcome attention. 'She's making a show of herself, Ev,' the grannies warned. 'And of you.'

She and Jimmy dismissed the whole thing as a drunken lark. 'Too many rum and Cokes,' Jimmy laughed unconvincingly while patting his pockets for his car keys so they could speed back up the M2.

Then there had been the time she and Dezzy were having breakfast in their favourite café near Finsbury Park station. Evgenia watched the young mothers cooing over their little ones and wondered if her Dezzy had her eye on anyone nice. Didn't she think it was time to settle down? she asked innocently, in between slurps of coffee. Marry? Start a family of her own?

Poor Dez choked, spraying Nescafé all over their tray.

'I don't like men, Mum. I thought you knew?' Her eyes had been wide with a mixture of surprise and, looking back, worry. Ev can see it now. Dez had been waiting for her mother's approval, her reassurance that it was all right to be different and to like girls instead of boys, but Evgenia was clueless. Plenty of women didn't like men, she reasoned, but it didn't make them *lesbians*.

Turns out Despina was a lesbian. Sarah was a special friend, not a reliable roommate, and the thing came out in the most unfortunate way on Dezzy's fortieth birthday.

Evgenia had planned a small surprise party for her daughter at the house. Nothing too fancy, just the three of them hiding behind sofas with a few half-blown-up balloons, waiting for her to burst in through the front door so they could jump out with a wonky cake and shout 'Happy birthday, Dez!' Only Dez didn't show up by herself, and, finding the house appealingly empty, she shared a furtive kiss with her special friend on the Theocaris welcome mat. They *all* knew, then. James-Dean walked out in a silly sulk and Jimmy crammed himself into the narrow space between their sink and their toilet and cried tears of fatherly humiliation. 'What we gonna do, Ev?' Rocking back and forth like it was the end of the world, and, while she supposed the whole thing had been a bit of a surprise, Ev did think his behaviour rather ridiculous.

'She is who she is, love. Now grab a tissue, wipe your nose and pull yourself together.'

Aunty Maro found out of course, although God knows how. Slithering round the next day to revel in

Jimmy's misery, she almost choked on her forked tongue when Ev confirmed that it was true without a trace of maternal disappointment. 'You're a much better person than me, I have to say . . .' Aunty Maro declared, and Ev responded by throwing her out of her house by the strap of her bag and wiping her hands on her dress for good measure.

She doesn't think she's a better person than Aunty Maro – or anyone else, for that matter – but in the past few weeks she's been thinking a lot about her lovely, gentle Dez. Living in her flat all the way over in Cricklewood with an invisible special friend. Shame on them, her and Jimmy.

'Well, if you say so, Ev,' Jimmy says now.

When you're facing death, people are nice to you. It's something else she's learned since Mr White Teeth's bleak prognosis, so she gladly seizes the opportunity to paint Sarah into their Christmas Day proceedings. Any other year and she would have had a fight on her hands, but this year is different because it might well be her last.

'Well, I do. And I want Em and Angelo there as well.'

'Em and Angelo? God give me strength!' Jimmy chuckles incredulously into his newspaper, imagining the chaos that will be their Christmas dinner, while Evgenia takes the carefully folded list she's been carrying around in the pocket of her blouse and wonders when she should start the shopping.

Christmas Day 1988. She finishes decorating the Christmas tree with a *humph* and they sit beneath it in their slippers and dressing gowns. There's not much to admire this year. The tree's red, blue and green lights are outperformed by the steely brightness of their living room, and the silver tinsel hangs limply from its branches as if it knows it's part of a charade. James-Dean cocks his head to the side and offers to re-dress it, but Evgenia refuses. 'It'll look better later, love. It'll glow more brightly when it's dark, you'll see.' The tree isn't important and it's enough that he's made it home to be with them on this special day.

He came hurtling in through their front door on the twentieth. A damp, overexcited dog leaping into her deflated bosom and wrapping himself around her for hours. They both knew why. 'It's OK,' she told him, rubbing his long, bony torso loosely draped in his signature baseball shirt, surprised by his new physique. The sharp, jagged feel of him beneath her wobbly arms. He was morphing into his father, she chuckled. 'Have they run out of food in Brighton?' His response was more of a sob than a snigger. She thought he smelled like wet leaves on a dewy autumn morning, sweet and musty, and, when she removed his Giants cap to stroke his light brown hair, she collected a handful of goo for her troubles.

'What's this?' she asked, the greyish gel sticking her fingers together. 'Egg whites?'

'New Kids on the Block, apparently,' Jimmy snorted from the vicinity of the television, referring to their son's slimy curtains. 'It's the new office fashion, he says.

Though what would us old codgers know about trendy pop stars, hey Ev?'

'New Kids?' she chuckled. 'I see.'

A traditional kebab dinner followed his arrival and, as the three of them sat around the table in their dilapidated kitchen and bickered over Zeus's finest doner drizzled with juice from a plastic lemon, she grew misty-eyed at the realisation that she would soon be erased from these scenes. She must have sighed a little too obviously because James-Dean pushed the hummus pot out of the way to grab her hand. 'Be OK, Mum,' he reassured her. 'You'll see.'

Her ring glinted beneath the kitchen lights along with flashes of long ago Welcome Home dinners and the ghosts of holidays past. Early Christmases when Dez was a little girl and they were still basking in post-war victory. When they didn't have a Christmas tree to decorate, but stuck paper angels to their walls. Baby James-Dean, jumping up and down to Jimmy's Rolling Stones records, as surprised as anyone to have been born into the world, never mind into the Swinging sixties. Emiliana, Theo and Angelo, dressed to the nines at Emiliana's Moon Landing party. Memories that reminded her that her life *had* been a happy one. She was lucky, she thought, wiggling her diamonds. Not many people could sit there and say the same.

Jimmy helps her up from beneath the wilting tree and Ev abandons the boys to their Christmas Day tradition. The *Top of the Pops* special on the BBC. She pads into the kitchen in her favourite pink slippers and takes the bowl of rice, liver and chopped chestnuts out of the fridge, then unpeels the cling film and brings the bowl up to her nose, smelling the spices and recollecting her childhood. She takes a spoon out of the drawer, scoops up a dollop of the mixture and thrusts it into the heart of the turkey, careful to fill all its dark spaces so everyone gets a taste. Her grandmother's recipe for stuffing, resurrected from the back of the drawer for her beloved friends and family because it's time to let go of the past. Vaporising Jack Christofi back into the Nobody he always was, and making things right with Angelo.

'I'll tell him soon, Ev,' and it's just as well, she thinks, setting the timer on the oven. It's just as well.

Outside, it begins to rain. Gradually at first, and then more determinedly. 'It's raining cats and dogs,' her father used to joke, in an attempt to sound less like the foreigner he always felt himself to be. 'Isn't that what the English say?' Evgenia sighs as she recollects him in old age, sitting in his broken chair and staring wistfully out of the window. What could he have been thinking? she wonders, as he stared out at the world towards the end. Was he recalling his wife, shovelling potatoes out of their clay oven and dumping them onto the blanket beneath their lemon tree? Was he remembering the tree's long branches and the shade it offered from the excoriating Cypriot sun? Did he still think the infamous lunch in their back yard had been the beginning of a promising journey? Nobody knew. For with her father's death, resolution was no longer possible.

Evgenia unlocks the back door and pushes it wide open to breathe in the earthy scent of the world, the smell of water pelting their concrete garden and washing it clean. Cliff Richard croons passionately from the front room amidst a faint burst of applause and she calls for James-Dean to turn the volume up so that the sound of it can mingle with the rain.

The middle stone of her diamond ring glimmers happily in the fading wintery light, and there is peace. In this moment, awaiting the arrival of her beloved guests while her grandmother's chestnut stuffing turns to gold in the oven, there is only peace.

Angelo

April 1990

EVERY FUNERAL HAS its own unique feel and this morning the atmosphere is charged, electric. Evgenia Theocaris's personality has dispersed into the gathering mourners and shaken them from their grief. People wear bright colours for her grand finale. Yellows, pinks and greens instead of the usual blacks and navy blues.

She died last week and Uncle Jim asked for him personally. It was just as well, his mother sniffed over the telephone, her own voice wet and shaky. 'Imagine going somewhere else!'

'I'll take good care of her, Uncle Jim.' He placed a reassuring hand on the man's shoulder and bowed his head respectfully as he trudged up the stairs to the room where she lay, followed by his faithful apprentice, Stel.

The door creaked open at his bidding and he looked around at the space she'd once occupied for the very first time. Aunty Ev's inner sanctum. He was hoping to steal a glimpse that would later inform his presentation of her; a special vase or a meaningful photograph, a message on a card, a colour that stood out from all the rest. Jimmy, brushing away a tear with the tip of his thumb, followed his gaze in the gloom. He sighed at the picture frames and holiday ornaments. At a single, fuchsia slipper. A fluffy pink robe hanging behind the bedroom door. A life interrupted.

'She really loved colours.' His voice, along with every other part of him, was devastated by his grief.

'Yeah, I remember.' Angelo cleared his throat, surprised by the emotions that threatened to spill tellingly from his eyes and jeopardise his professional composure; the human side of him attempting to break free from the practised facade. 'Um . . . the trinity ring my mother mentioned. Is she wearing it?'

'I've got it here.' Jimmy retrieved a small brown envelope from the pocket of his dressing gown and placed it at the foot of the bed. 'I thought I'd better slip it off now, before . . . you know.' He retreated hastily, closing the door behind him and leaving Angelo and Stel alone with her. Angelo supposed he didn't want to think of his wife like that. Lying in the light of a forever day.

The burial of a loved one who was also a personally loved one bordered on sacred, and, back at the shop on Holloway Road, he told his embalmer that he would dress her himself; 'Aunty Ev was family.' He pulled a pink blouse and a long black skirt from the bag Jimmy had thrust into his arms and slipped the diamond ring back on her wedding finger. He brushed what was left of her hair to the side, remembering her big, bouffant hairstyles and her long red fingernails.

'The Queen of Hearts!' his mother used to shriek from the top of the stairs. 'You've come dressed as the bloody Queen of Hearts again, Ev!' And Evgenia would chuckle good-naturedly.

On Card Tuesday she would let him sit next to her on the sofa in their old house while his mother was upstairs fixing herself up, scrunching her hair between her long fingers and painting circles around her eyes. Aunty Ev would rummage around in her giant handbag for cigarettes while he talked about ghosts and ghouls and things that went bump in the night.

'Seems your mother has turned into a ghost, too!' she used to joke, until Emiliana eventually wafted down the stairs like Queen Cleopatra to take his place, banishing him to his bed so they could gossip in private.

'Piss off, Angelo, it's adult time,' she'd say, her hand already reaching for her own fags.

She loved him, his Aunty Ev. He could tell by the way she listened patiently to his stories and blew raspberries on his tummy, lifting up his pyjama top so that they would really tickle. She loved him until he was six or seven, and then something changed. She became awkward and self-conscious in his presence. Anxious, even, and he thought, at first, he might have scared her, going on about his ghosts. In his childish mind, he thought he'd frightened his Aunty Ev away and it was only that night, the night before his father's funeral, that he'd realised she known all along. That that adult time had not been for cards or cocktails but for whispering things about *him*.

'Who's on today?' Outside St Sophia's Church,

Angelo and Stel wait patiently for the funeral service
to finish.

'Pater Avram.' They're leaning but not slumped
against the newly polished hearse and Angelo imagines
the young man groaning inwardly at the mention of
the clumsy old-timer.

'OK, boss. Sweet.' Pater Avram's ceremonies are
notoriously long but Stel's face stays poker-straight and
his green eyes search the skies for extra stoicism.

He's taught Stelio well, he thinks proudly. Bantering
is banned on funeral day – it would be inexcusable for
the families of the deceased to find the pair of them
pissing about outside the holy church, laughing and
joking about last night's Arsenal game, who they
fancied for the World Cup in the summer, what their
girlfriends were cooking for dinner.

'It's a process of transformation,' he explained to Stel
on his first day in the office. 'When you put on the suit,
you're playing a role for the relatives, yeah?'

'I get it, boss,' Stel said, nodding solemnly, already
performing the part.

Pity his mother doesn't 'get it'. He can see her now,
in his mind's eye, tutting and cursing on her pew.
Fiddling with her grey curly hair and wondering why
her son has chosen to remain outside on such an
important day when they *both* loved Aunty Ev. 'I even
saved you a seat, Angelo.' He's told her before, many
times: he has a job to do, and he can't just drop the act
whenever she feels like it.

'You don't get it, Mum.'

'You're right, Angelo. I don't.'

Maybe she's right. Perhaps today, of all days, he should have left Stel in charge and joined Ev's entourage, but he can't afford to get distracted by the memories. Especially when he knows what lies ahead. What his mother will want him to do afterwards.

He unbuttons his blazer and thinks, instead, of Priya. Princess Priya, perpetually floating in her soapy bath. Her cinnamon-coloured skin contrasting with the delicate foam and her long black hair fanning out beneath her like an open parasol. He's never met anyone who washes more than she does or has more time to go shopping for handbags.

'Nice life if you can get it, baby,' he teases her.

'Tear yourself away from death and you could join me?'

'In the bath or at the shops?'

She came round last night to cook them a curry because Ash was away. He sat behind her at the kitchen table as she peeled prawns and grated pieces of coconut into a frying pan, the smells of turmeric and coriander filling the room as she hummed along to Sinead O'Connor: 'Nothing compares to you . . .' She turned around and smiled at him, and he wondered, in that moment, as he often did, what he would ever do if she stopped returning his calls. Settled for her traditional life with Ash.

'They've finished.' Stel coughs twice into the palm of his hand and nods towards the church. Angelo climbs back into his professional skin, refastening his jacket and straightening his tie until it lies directly in between the starchy collars of his shirt. The mourners flinch when the pair of them walk up the aisle towards the coffin, their heads once again bowed. Nobody wants to get too close to the undertakers for fear of being next. Their clipped footsteps on the tessellated floor reverberate around the hushed room, a room that today smells like the inside of a pocket. Like used tissues, runny noses and dry, stale bread. People form a queue to kiss the top of the coffin and mutter their condolences to Jimmy. 'O *Theos na din Makarisi*.' A prayer for immortality. Jimmy nods in agreement and shakes proffered hands.

Angelo stands respectfully to the side and waits for the end of proceedings. He can see his mother hovering in the shadows, her handsome square face streaked with tears and the only one of the mourners who ignored Jimmy's wishes and decided to show up in black.

'You look like a bloody crow, Mum.'

'It's a funeral, Angelo, not a party. People wear black at funerals, in case you hadn't noticed.'

He wonders why she never told him that his Aunty Ev had lost part of her leg to the cancer. He remembers the surprise of peeling back her bedspread and seeing the amputation for himself. The slight recoil despite the years of training and discipline. Why did she decide to keep this detail from him? His mother, always with her secrets.

He didn't slip a shoe onto her remaining foot. It had been another last request. After everything that she'd been through with the treatment, Jimmy explained, she just wanted to walk free.

At New Southgate Cemetery in north London, Pater Avram pours three drops of olive oil into Aunty Ev's grave. He throws in a handful of kolifa seeds to symbolise life everlasting and smashes a plate over the top of the casket to divest the soul from the perished body. 'Amen.' The formalities dispensed with, mourners step aside to nibble on bread and halloumi in Evgenia's memory. The atmosphere lifts as the ceremony ends and the sun peeks out from behind thin veils of cloud. It's an April morning, bright but not too breezy. 'Conditions,' as Mike Sedaris used to say back in the day, 'are optimal.'

Angelo looks up at the sky appreciatively and with a sense of relief. The recently bereaved welcome the sun, inferring messages from their loved ones from its warm, yellow rays. He's pleased that it's chosen this very moment to make its celestial appearance. Pleased for Jimmy, for their kids. He doesn't believe a word of it, personally, he's seen enough corpses to recognise the twisted reality of death, but he nonetheless admires man's willingness to look for meaning in the smallest of things. A drop of dew on a desiccated leaf, a rainbow over a sea of black umbrellas, the tweeting of a distant bird rising above the sounds of the traffic. He admires it and, some days, he envies it.

He watches the group from a respectful distance and with his hands still crossed in front of him. He refuses to partake in the graveside wakes. It's not the under-taker's place to hover around the fold-out tables and commiserate with the family. Ask for a pastry on a paper plate and hold out his cup for a large koumandaria. He knows where to stand so as to minimise and not emphasise his presence, and it's lessons like these he tries to instil in young Stel.

'On the day of the funeral, know your place, yeah?'

'Yes, boss.' Stel fingers an imaginary cap.

'Write it down if you have to.'

'I got it, boss.' The young man taps the side of his head. 'It's all up here.'

The protégé, as Angelo affectionately calls him. His protégé and, the way things are going in his own life, his most likely successor. A good-looking man with perturbingly green eyes and a gift for charming the widows. Adept at reading Angelo's moods, his grunts and growls, and, more importantly, when to step back and leave him alone. 'Shall I take a message, boss?' as Angelo slams doors in his face and escapes to the privacy of his dark, shadowy office.

He is the complete opposite of his mother, who is insensible to his moods. He can feel her stare boring into his cheeks as his own eyes process the scene, searching for the simple grey cross that belongs to him among all the black, white and grey crosses scat-tered across the old Greek Orthodox section of the cemetery. He knows that today, with his mother in attendance, he won't be able to escape him.

'Have you put flowers on it yet?' Emiliana will ask, tutting and sniffing. 'It won't make any difference, you know, abandoning him now.'

He knows the inscription by heart, having sat in front of it many times in pursuit of his own answers. Looking for them not in the beams of sun or the clouds, but in the glass cabinet, the candle and the black and white photograph. In the epitaph that reads: *Here lies Theodoro Angelides. Loving Husband and Father.*

'Place is a total dive, boss.'

Stel prefers the pubs at the top end of Holloway Road. The ones with low ceilings and shady, candlelit alcoves. Bars where overpaid City boys loosen their ties and splash money around after work. 'A *proper* dive.' The Dog and Damsel is loud and bright. The pints are weak and taste like piss and the toilets smell like dog shit, but it's alive and, after a day dealing with death, Angelo likes to feel a pulse.

'It's fine, relax.'

He suspects Priya was heading to one of Stel's classier places the night they first met. The look of confusion on her face as she surveyed the lumpy orange chairs and red carpets still raises a smile. Wondering why she'd been summoned to a dump she wouldn't usually be seen dead in. Where the furniture cost less than her clothes.

'I'm supposed to be meeting someone but I think I might be lost.'

'*Someone?*' 'Temptation' by Wet Wet Wet was playing

on the jukebox as she coiled a strand of hair around her finger and let him buy her a drink.

'She's one of them, then, your aunty's daughter?' Stel and Angelo sit at the back of the pub with their ties in their pockets and their top buttons relieved of their formal duties. Angelo swills his Scotch around so the ice cubes clink happily against the glass.

He sat next to Dezzy's girlfriend at his Aunty Ev's Christmas party the year before last, a shy older woman with grey-blonde hair and eyes that darted around the room. The eyes were grateful to be there, among Dez's family; he could tell by the way they sparkled. Dezzy's, too, and it was the first time Angelo had ever seen her happy. Or at least, as happy as she was that afternoon.

'So?'

'Just asking, boss. She was wearing a man's suit so I figured she must be.'

'Yeah? Well, don't.'

Stel shrugs apologetically as his hand rummages around, crab-like, in a bag of smoky bacon crisps. His green eyes are highlighted by the hallmarks of inebriation. Angelo braces himself for the young man's inevitable descent into broken, drunken Greek. The expletives of his teenage years. *Pousti, garo, pesevengi, malaka.* Manoeuvring his eyebrows into approving arches as he recalls exchanges with female mourners in skin-tight clothes.

'She was nice. The girl at the funeral we did last week. The grave next to your aunty.'

'The wife?' Angelo teases, finally relaxing his tone. 'Weren't she a bit old for you, Stel?'

'No, *malaka*, the daughter.' A snort of incredulity from Stel. 'What do you take me for, some desperado granny-snatcher? Don't remember the girl's name. Lina, maybe . . . ?'

It's Angelo's turn to shrug. He has little interest in other women – Princess Priya is more than enough for him, and he suspects she's enough for any man. Besides, he makes a point of forgetting the families after the big day, after their loved ones are dead and buried and their names consigned to his filing cabinets. Keeping in touch would be weird. Like a shopkeeper taking his customers' phone numbers and calling them up for a chat.

Except Aunty Ev, of course. He could never forget his Aunty Ev.

'Another shot?'

'Yeah, go on then, boss.'

Nor Theo. Angelo sighs. He's in a hurry to throw another drink down his throat before his mood spoils another night.

'Burnt or buried, by the way, when the Grim Reaper knocks on the door? Cos I've been thinking about it and I'd rather be cremated so you can snort me after. Get it, boss?'

'Yeah, I get it, Stel.'

Angelo fiddles with the collars of his shirt to buy himself a few vertical inches and marches over to the bar. She couldn't see him until the following Tuesday.

Ninety-six interminable hours because Ash was returning from New Delhi and what was she supposed to tell him? That she had to go out designer handbag shopping with her friend when he'd been travelling all week?

'Not my problem,' he growled down the phone. 'I thought we agreed that your shit with Ash is not *my* problem?'

He regretted it afterwards, because it wasn't her fault that he needed to see her. That today has been emotionally gruelling and that he craves the feel of her soft skin beneath his lips. That he is desperate for the distraction. That burying a loved one is the greatest honour you can bestow on a funeral director but it's not without its personal burdens. The memories it evokes. Theo's funeral and his lonely grave, needling him from across the cemetery.

He didn't lay his mother's stupid flowers in the end, and she'll no doubt insult him tomorrow.

Here lies Theodoro Angelides. Loving Husband and Father.

Except the inscription is wrong no matter how many times he runs his finger over the stone. Theo Angelides was not his father.

It's almost five o'clock in the morning. A shaft of light divides Angelo's bedroom in half; some objects are newly visible while others are still hidden by the darkness. He props himself up against his pillows with a groan. The curly hair on his chest is damp with sweat and he dabs at it with the shiny satin sheets Priya insisted he buy when they first started fooling around. They smell faintly of her body lotion, of apricots, milk and honey. His stomach growls; he's hungry, but not for apricots. For bacon, eggs and fat, greasy sausages.

Recollections of the night before unpeel themselves like the layers of an onion as he contemplates breakfast. It was a heavy night: one too many shots in Stel's trendy bar; a spilt pint and a near punch from a drunk City boy whose breath stank of puke; Stel abandoning him for a girl named Gemma whose ears stuck out like the wing mirrors of a car. 'Looks like I've pulled, boss. Do you mind if I shift?' Blinding headlights and garish takeaway restaurant signs flashing in the dark as he tried to navigate unfamiliar streets using only his memory.

A young couple sharing a bag of chips. 'Watch where you're going, arsehole!' The girl sniggering at the state of him as he almost collapsed into her boyfriend. The security light above the front door flicking into life while he hunted for the house keys. Patting himself down like a pervert for what seemed like hours.

He tuts at his own stupidity as he throws back the covers and pads down the hallway to the bathroom. The embarrassing loss of control that was so out of character for him. He turns on the shower and the white tiles quickly mist with condensation. They're new, like the rest of the house; he purchased a dump in an expensive neighbourhood and renovated most of it by himself. He welcomed the hard work and the solitary evenings, the carousel of excuses to avoid seeing his mother. 'Sorry, Mum, I've got to nail my balls to the ceiling tonight.'

'Charming, Angelo.'

It's a black, white and silver goldmine now. Worth much more than he paid for it three years ago, although there was never any pleasing her.

'The colours of your bloody gravestones,' she mocked when he revealed the newly renovated rooms to her for the first time. 'Why buy a house this size – you going to live with your stiffs and your spooks?'

For the same reason other people buy expensive things, he replied, refusing to let his mother rile him on what was supposed to be a proud day. For the same reason he bought himself the Rolex and the Jaguar when the money started to roll in from the business. A show of wealth. There were no grand-children for her to brag about to his Aunty Ev, but this was much better. This was the kind of success people envied.

He buttons up his white shirt in the mirror and pulls on a pair of designer navy trousers. He combs his thinning black hair and decides that his nose takes up far too much space on his face; it's big and crooked and his small dark eyes sit too closely above it. He looks like a hungry hawk. An unfortunate quality for an undertaker to possess, he often thinks, but Priya seems to like it.

'What I admire most about you, Angelo, is your ambition,' she once said.

'Isn't everyone ambitious?' he replied, confused by the compliment. 'Isn't everyone after the same thing at the end of the day?'

'Everyone? Have you not met my lazy brother? We don't call him Handout Hari for nothing, you know.'

Of course he hadn't met her brother. That was the whole point of their relationship. They didn't delve into each other's personal lives. It was one of the many implicit rules.

He flicks the switch on his fancy kettle and fries three rashers of bacon in a pan. He cracks two eggs over the top. They stare back disinterestedly, a pair of cold, gloopy eyes. He likes Saturdays. He looks forward to them. After calling in on his mother and swinging by the shop to check on Stel, the day is a gift to him and Priya. She tells Ash she's heading into Bond Street to spend his money before taking a cab to his place, arriving in the afternoon with a bottle of expensive wine sticking out of her handbag. 'I stole this from his stash.'

They strip excitedly and enjoy it in bed. 'Watch the sheets, baby,' warns Angelo, his constant desire for orderliness always a priority, even over Ash's Margaux.

Afterwards, she drapes his black robe over her shoulders and cooks them both a curry, blasting the radio to compete with the sizzling of the onions and the garlic. Angelo loves her best in these moments, when she's tipsy and carefree. When she's dancing half naked to Soul II Soul while the delicious smells of her cooking fill his kitchen.

He doesn't allow himself to wonder what happens when she returns home to Ash. Whether he waits up for her and if she goes to bed with him then as well. He closes the door on her other life and lets her get on with it. It would drive him crazy otherwise, this continuation of her night without him.

Saturday morning traffic along Seven Sisters Road moves like blood through a clogged artery. There are so many sets of traffic lights that Angelo considers abandoning the Jag and dropping the car keys down a drain. Washing his hands of the bloody thing as he walks in and out of the cars, ignoring the ensuing expletives. 'You can't leave it there, dickhead!'

He smashes his fists into the leather steering wheel as Depeche Mode blares over the stereo. 'Come on, *move, gamoto!*'

'Why are you always so angry, Angelo?' He imagines his mother despairing at his temper. 'Or is that my fault, too?'

When he pulls up outside her flat twenty minutes later, she's twitching at the front door like a wind-up doll. 'I thought you weren't coming.' She looks pale and gaunt, the clothes wearing her and not the other way round.

'What's wrong, Mum?' He hastens his steps up her pathway, surprised by his sudden filial concern.

'Boiler's broke and there's no hot water.' She claims she doesn't know any plumbers and can't find the *Yellow*

Pages, and he's not surprised she's lost the book given the state of the place.

'It's a car crash in here. You could lose a bloody elephant.'

'Don't chide me, not today.' She's coming down with the flu, she says. Her head's like fog and she can't think straight.

He capitulates. 'Fine. I'll sort it.'

'When, Angelo?' She wipes her runny nose on the sleeve of her cardigan and although it irritates him having to pander to her when he has enough on his plate already, he thinks of his Aunty Ev and makes allowances. It's the day after her best friend's funeral, for God's sake. The least he can do is be kind.

He forces composure into his voice. 'Soon as I get to the shop, I'll ask Stel to call Coz Gee.'

She's momentarily appeased and he follows her into her kitchen to switch off the radio: 'It's aggravating my migraine.'

'It's called "life", Angelo. We don't all want to live in a mausoleum.' Her curly grey hair trails behind her as she navigates the secret nooks of her tiny kitchen, opening the fridge and reaching deep into cupboards for things only she could know about. 'You want one?' She's making a honey and lemon drink for her throat. Her tone seeks his sympathy or, at the very least, an acknowledgement of her interminable suffering. His mother was once very beautiful and could wrap men around her little finger – not just Theo, but any man who met her – and she still felt entitled. It was just one of her many problems.

'Just a black coffee. I'm hungover. Heavy night with Stel.'

'Ah! The sexy Stelio,' she teases. 'Such a handsome young man.'

She bends down to pull a pile of wet clothes out of the washing machine while the kettle is whistling, and the pernicious smell of damp permeates the room. He wonders how long they've been decomposing in there, the clothes. Moulded together like one giant, swollen lump that now refuses to evacuate the drum. Is he the only undertaker who sees *memento mori* everywhere, he wonders. In kitchens, in bins, in the meat section of the supermarket?

'Did you visit his grave yet?' She tugs the pile with both hands and almost sends herself flying across the kitchen.

'No, but I will.'

'When?'

'Today, after I finish up the paperwork.' Another lie because this afternoon is Priya time, and it's so transparent that she insults him in Greek.

She finally abandons the washing ball to stand upright. 'Oh, Angelo.'

Something has shifted and he can see it, whatever *it* is, in her eyes. He can feel the change in the air, too. Like a warm breeze or an electric current and he wonders if this is her grief filling the space or if she is finally going to tell him the truth.

He takes a deep breath and asks again because if there is ever a right time, this moment between them is it. 'I need to know, Mum. If not him, then who?'

∼

Limassol, 1960. Little Angelo sat on a long wooden dock stretching out to sea while his mother dangled her pretty tanned feet in the clear waters of the Mediterranean.

In the distance, the sounds of music and laughter floated in the air like children's balloons. People enjoyed drinks and ice creams beneath large, colourful parasols. The sun blazed brightly in the sky and the skin on the back of his neck felt hot and tight. His mother placed an arm around his shoulders and although her hand smelled homely, of roasted meat and onions, he flinched when she touched his sunburn.

'Listen carefully, Angelo.' She said she had something to tell him and that it was going to change his life. 'We must leave Cyprus soon. We have to move away for Pappa's work, you understand what I'm telling you?'

He looked up to study the side of her face. 'Where are we going, Mamma?'

Her long black curly hair blew in the salty breeze as she spoke not to him, but to the sea. 'We're going to the moon, Angelo.'

He still remembers the way his childish body reacted to her words.

∼

The black and gold letters on the sign announce 'Angelo Angelides Funerals' to Holloway Road. No son, no father, no limited and no fictional, silent partner. Just Angelo.

He opened the shop six years ago and the inauguration is immortalised on his Wall of Fame. Angelo, snipping a ribbon with a huge pair of scissors while an attractive journalist named Vicki Varnavas interviewed him for the *Foni*. She threw him off balance with her sexy fishnet tights and chili-red hair; the proximity of her lips to his face and her list of non-sequential questions. 'Do you remember your first dead body?' 'Why is it that you never see a hearse, when death is absolutely everywhere?' 'What does death look and smell like?' 'Why open a funeral parlour in the middle of Holloway Road?'

Her perfume made his head spin and he made up some crap joke about double yellows. How parking spaces were the perennial problem of all north London Greeks, even those in mourning. He regretted it afterwards. He was spouting shit because he fancied her and it showed in the tone of the write-up.

He creaks around in his leather chair in search of the embarrassing clipping but it's been eclipsed by more recent mentions. Funeral directors seem to be a constant source of fascination, at least to journalists. There is a piece about Greek-Cypriot entrepreneurs with his portrait alongside, his big nose exposed in profile. A story about the leading causes of death in younger men, with a few choice quotes but no portrait. An article about the evolution of religious burials with his shop splashed across two pages.

He was particularly proud of that one because it was for a national newspaper and a photographer had come inside to do fly-on-the-wall stuff: a smartly dressed Angelo sitting behind his desk; his arranging room and chapel of rest, branching off from the reception desk like a pair of soft pink lungs; his afterlife, aka the mortuary and sluice rooms; a portrait of his lanky embalmer, Robert Hawking, whose basement sovereignty made him both untouchable and unpopular.

Not that Rob had time for banter and booze. He was too busy re-inflating the dead. Injecting formaldehyde into discreet openings. Washing and combing their hair. Trimming their beards. Plumping up their sallow cheeks with cotton wool and using pictures to capture their former faces before the families came in for the viewings. Death, an enduring taboo – even in a funeral home.

He poached Rob from Mike Sedaris because he knew he was the best in the business. He was right, too, about Rob; he's managed to restore all but one of the loved ones that has passed through these doors, and she still haunts them both. The body of Tracy Savides wasn't fit to be viewed in the end. There were no rays of sun at her funeral. In fact, it rained all day and he felt like he'd failed her family twice.

Tracy Savides. It had been impossible to go into a petrol station or a coffee shop without seeing her picture on a poster. The girl with the long brown hair and sparkly eyes, the smile that didn't know what lay in store. Her disappearance made the newspapers, the locals and then the national tabloids, because the story had all the right ingredients, the lurid details people liked to read about over their breakfast cereal. An attractive young woman who'd led a seemingly normal life until she'd vanished after a night at a bar.

There had been other, well-publicised disappearances in the years leading up to Tracy's. A lawyer who never made it to a meeting in west London and a receptionist who went missing in her lunch hour. The three women looked similar; they were all nice-looking and had the same colour hair. People speculated that there was a serial killer on the loose, one with a fetish for brunettes.

Tracy's husband addressed the press and made a mess of it. He may as well have been wearing an 'I Did It' T-shirt as he smirked his way through the conference and Angelo, along with everyone else in the country, wondered how long it would be before the police came knocking at the door. He didn't have to wait long for his arrest but it would be weeks before he cracked and revealed where he'd buried her. By then it was far too late to prettify her remains for the burial.

The tabloids nicknamed him 'Mad Mario'. He was a thug, a brute; some of them emphasised the fact that he'd served time for GBH, others that he was a Cypriot – it felt like this prejudice was seething beneath the surface of the story the whole time. The ungrateful foreign man who'd killed his nice English wife. The tone of the headlines made Angelo uncomfortable but he still enjoyed thinking of Mario in a cage, locked up like a wild animal while the world carried on without him. Contemplating the things Mario would never touch, feel or fuck again. Savouring every last drop of Scotch before raising the empty glass to justice.

He'd seen terrible things before; it went with the territory and he was inured to it. Dead fathers carried out of their homes in body bags while the kids cried downstairs. The elderly, dying in front of their television sets and lying undiscovered for months – and once, even years.

The appearance of Tracy's remains didn't shock him, and the coroner's report of how she was killed didn't disturb him either. What upset him was the fact that she couldn't be restored. That, as with Theo, her burial did not offer her family a resolution. That's what got to Angelo the most.

Still, Angelo is good at what he does. Some would even say he's renowned in the tight-knit Greek community of north London, although he isn't one to gloat. Recommendations are rife and he's a successful man; everyone loves Angelo, and he has an award to prove it. An upside-down glass tear balancing on a thin wooden stand. The prize declares him the Local Businessman of the Year 1990 and he shifts it between his palms, enjoying the weight of his success.

'You deserve it, boss.' Stel looked like he was about to bear-hug him that Monday morning, but thought better of it. 'You should be bloody proud of what you've achieved here in the last few years.' The latest article clipping credits him with 'modernising the landscape of death'. What does that even mean? he wonders, shoving his biro into his mouth. Surely, death is always just the same?

There's a tentative tapping at the door of his private office where nobody, not even Stel, is allowed to enter without his permission. It's a large, gloomy room sparsely furnished with metal filing cabinets and decorated with the aforementioned clippings. The only noises are the creaking and squeaking of the black leather chair as it completes its rotations in front of his desk.

'What?'

Stel's disembodied head floats around the corner to greet him. 'Boss? That girl from the funeral we did last week's just popped in with a card for you.'

'I'm in the middle of something, yeah?'

He dismisses his protégé with a flick of his wrist. The younger man's head nods respectfully and drifts off in search of a body.

Angelo flings the biro at his Wall of Fame. 'Fuck's sake!' He's ashamed of himself.

'Don't bring your problems into work with you.' Mike Sedaris taught him that in the early days, but it was hardly rocket science. The recently bereaved didn't want to hear about their undertaker's issues – his argument with the missus or his parking ticket on Ballards Lane. They had enough problems of their own. 'Leave your shit at the door,' Mike would say. 'Or better still, shit in your own toilet.'

Angelo twists around in his chair, although this time the semi-rotation sounds more like a wheeze. 'Oranges, Angelo.' He thought she wanted him to squeeze them into her hot drink. 'No, I was an orange, that's how the bloody thing started. Come round next week and we'll talk properly.' She claimed it was the right time. That it's what Aunty Ev would have wanted and never mind what he's needed to hear all these years. As if it was her death and not his needs that had finally earned him validity.

Angelo emerges from the shadows to find Stel slumped over the front desk, reading the obituaries. He pats him on the back. 'All OK, yeah?' It's simpler with men. A handshake, a half-arsed apology. Priya would be sulking for days if he'd snapped at her like that. His mother, probably years.

'All good, boss. She left this for you.' Stel slides a white envelope towards him through the decorative plastic bouquets.

'Who did?'

'The girl from the funeral we did last week. She said her name was Melina.'

~

There were arguments. Big, noisy ones that sounded like fireworks exploding in the sky. His mother enjoyed the status of a doctor's wife but not the reality of his life. Theo's eminence kept him away for most of the week, leaving her stuck in the house with Angelo. She used words like that a lot, his mother. 'Stuck', 'dumped', 'lumped' and sometimes 'trapped', and these words suited Angelo just fine because he felt exactly the same way about her.

She admitted these words to his Aunty Ev on Card Tuesday. Moaning and whining about how hard it was to raise a small child by herself while Theo strutted about being special. Evgenia nodded in sympathy and offered to share cigarettes from her bottomless handbag, and Angelo could tell that she didn't like his father very much. That she, too, would happily ram his stethoscope down his throat given a few drinks and half the chance.

He could still remember the first time Aunty Ev rang their doorbell. She'd smiled kindly at him as he stood at the top of the stairs wondering if *this* was the moon his mother spoke of. He was wearing his pyjamas because he'd wet himself in the van on the way to their new house and Theo had changed his clothes. 'Hello, Angelo.' Her red fingernails were pointier than knives.

There had been a man standing beside her, a thin man with a sad, balloon face who'd glanced around their hallway as if he couldn't wait to go home again. 'This is my husband, Jim.' As time went on, they saw less of the sad balloon man and more of his wife, and he could tell his father was relieved to have been let off the hook. 'Man's about as interesting as a roof tile, and with roughly the same IQ.' His mother took the whole thing personally, of course. As though the glum man's reluctance to socialise with them was somehow an insult to her.

Evgenia liked it at their house, Angelo could tell. She came round every week to play cards with his mother and she soon wore the title of 'Aunty Ev' as comfortably as she wore her own skin. Besides, her visits gave them *both* something to look forward to on a Tuesday evening because Evgenia also took a special interest in him, indulging his childish questions in a way his mother never did and asking after his new friend, Socrates.

Socrates was Angelo's skeleton. Theo had borrowed him from the hospital to teach Angelo about anatomy and they forgot to give him back. Socrates had two hundred and six creamy-white bones and Angelo knew this because he was good at counting and he had once counted them all without stopping. Socrates' jaw moved up and down and his shoulders spun round and round and if Angelo pulled hard enough and at just the right angle, his head flew off with a 'pop'.

Aunty Ev had jumped back in shock when he'd first showed her his magic trick. 'Look, Aunty Ev! Look what my skeleton can do!'

'Oh my, Angelo, he gave me quite the fright!'

In those early days, he spent a lot of time flopped out on his bed playing with Socrates. To Angelo, he embodied death. What it meant to die and what it might actually *feel* like. Was dying as simple as closing one's eyes and falling asleep, he wondered, or did it physically hurt to stop breathing?

'How long do you think it takes for a human being to melt into a skeleton like Socrates, Aunty Ev?' Melting was one of his favourite things to think about.

She was taken aback by the question, he could tell by the way she rubbed at her own bones and hiccupped as if she'd drunk something fizzy. She obviously went home and thought about it, though, because the following Tuesday, when his mother was upstairs painting the smudges around her eyes, she lowered her voice to a ticklish whisper. 'I asked your Uncle Jim and he thinks two years at most, but I think longer. In a good, strong coffin, maybe as long as ten. How's that?'

'That's what I think, Aunty Ev!' His eyes were as shiny as dark pebbles on a rainy beach. 'I think the coffin would slow the melting down because it makes it harder for the worms to crawl in.'

'Worms? Indeed, my darling. Indeed . . .'

When his mother had finished transforming herself into a panda bear, she sailed down the stairs so that Aunty Ev could admire her beauty and flapped her hands in his face. He knew it was time for bed when she showed up with her silly eyes and her silly clothes. His little heart would sink. It was their not-so-secret signal for him to get lost. There were others, too. Pinches, nods and blinking eyes that made her seem crazy. Many different twitches that all shared the same purpose of turning him into thin air. 'Bloody kids' usually accompanied his traipsing back up the stairs. 'Who in their sober mind would have them?'

Sometimes, when he was feeling especially cheeky, he pretended not to notice the secret signals and his mother would roar dragon-fire in his face until Aunty Ev stepped in to save him. 'Let him stay up for just a few more minutes, my darling.'

'No. You're too good to him Ev, but I think it's time Angelo took Socrates and pissed off.'

When he got a bit older, his Aunty Ev was just as keen to smoke cigarettes and sip the dizzy drinks as his mother was. The two of them suddenly had something *very* important to discuss and he wasn't allowed to hear it. Angelo grew cross when Aunty Ev stopped sticking up for him and he refused to go into his room. Why should he? It was his house, too. Instead, he hovered at the top of the stairs in the hope of uncovering their new secret.

He heard many things in his little hiding spot, although none of them were especially exciting. His mother and Aunty Ev talked about fashionable clothes, mostly, or actors they fancied from the telly. Sometimes they insulted his father. His mother wished she could run away and leave Theo to roast a chicken all by himself. 'That would teach him!' she would shriek in delight. 'That would teach him a lesson for leaving me stranded me on the moon because I had no other choice!'

~

He needs to see Princess Priya. A slice of her face through a slit in the curtains or her silhouette in the bedroom window. Something, anything, to reassure him that she is still there.

'There have to be rules, Angelo,' she said to him the next morning while they were still lying face to face between the sheets like two halves of an empty heart. Knees and foreheads touching. An affair was a high-stakes game, and she would be taking all the risks while he was risking nothing at all.

'Boundaries, baby, because if he ever found out . . .'

'Yeah, I get it.'

Did he get it, though? Because what he's doing now, driving to her house after midnight in a mood, is trampling all over her boundaries. Breaking the rules he himself agreed to, because Ash stole their Saturday. Or is that actually what happened? he wonders. Did Ash steal his day with Priya, or is Angelo really stealing from Ash?

He stops outside their expensive redbrick semi and turns off the headlights, leaving the engine running on purpose. He looks around him. It's a nice, quiet neighbourhood in an expensive part of London and he wonders how long it will be before someone bangs on the window or calls the police to report him for casing.

He closes his eyes and tries to conjure the inside of her house. She invited him in once, when Ash was away in India. It was white. That's what he remembers about the place. Everything was white. The carpets, the sofas, the curtains, the nice furniture. It was a home she could boast about rather than relax in, he told her.

'That's a bit rich coming from you,' she snorted. 'Living in your bloody marble mansion.'

'It's granite, babe.'

She asked him to leave his shoes by the door.

'This a cultural thing?' He looked up at her from bended knee as he fiddled with his laces. 'The shoes at the front door, I mean?'

'It's a polite thing, baby. My rugs are white.'

He enjoyed the feel of them beneath socked feet. The comfort of her rugs juxtaposed with her hard wooden floors. Like taking a chance and stepping off a ledge.

There was a large portrait of her hanging above the fireplace. Priya, proudly dressed in a red and gold sari with a string of jewels dangling from her forehead. He had never seen her like that before, wearing her traditional clothes. She looked stunning. She was like a droplet of blood splashed on an all-white wall and he couldn't stop staring at her. She followed his gaze and tugged him away before he could ask any questions. 'Come here, baby, I've missed you so much . . .' but he knew, as he stood beneath the shower to wash her away, afterwards, he knew that the picture must have been taken the day she married Ash.

He presses his forehead to the leather steering wheel and exhales slowly. She walked into the Damsel on the anniversary of Tracy Savides' funeral. A year to the day and he was brooding over a glass of Scotch, wishing he'd invited Stel for the distraction. From the back, the similarities were striking. The slender waist, the long dark hair swishing from side to side. He let himself believe, let himself imagine that she was his second chance. By the time she spun round, it didn't matter that she wasn't Tracy. It didn't matter because here was another girl who was lost and confused. Finally, here was someone he *could* save.

~

He loved Theo. He loved him more than he loved his mother, more than Socrates the skeleton, and maybe even more than his Aunty Ev – but only by a *teeny* bit. Theo was kind, clever and tall. So tall that Angelo would have to tilt his head all the way up to the clouds when he spoke in his giant, booming voice. He felt lucky to have a father like Theo and he was sorry for the children in his new class at school, who only had average dads.

On weekends when he wasn't at his important job, Theo would take him to Oaklands Park and teach him how to ride his big boy's bike. The new bicycle was red and shiny, with handlebars that sloped downwards for a better grip, and Theo would constantly remind him that it was expensive and that meant he had to take care of it. 'Money doesn't grow on trees, son.' This would make his mother tut loudly over her stupid fashion magazines and sometimes, when she came with them to the park, she would tut at them both from the bench.

Most Saturdays, though, she preferred to stay at home and read her boring magazines on the sofa, or go to Aunty Ev's to drink dizzy drinks on her sofa instead. On days like these, days when she put on her miniskirt and went to see Aunty Ev, Angelo imagined her poking fun at him. 'He's such an ungrateful brat, Ev, you have no idea,' she would complain, her long, slender legs packed neatly beneath her bottom and her cigarette shedding all over the floor. He wondered what Uncle Jim made of all the whining and moaning. The daytime drinks and the cigarette ash on the carpet.

Either way, Angelo didn't care. He preferred it when she wasn't there. When it was just him and Theo in the park with no moody mother to distract them. His father behaved strangely when she tagged along. He was stiff and uncomfortable, and he didn't laugh like he did when they were by themselves. He spoke to him differently, too. As if Angelo were a little baby and not a great big boy of eight.

When they were alone, his father shared things with him. Grown-up things about politics and wars. About the shooting of Mr President Kennedy and the problems in Vietnam. He used complicated words like 'assassination' and 'Communism' and, although Angelo didn't know what any of these words meant, he always nodded along. After these manly talks, Theo's blue eyes searched Angelo's little dark ones to make sure he was all right. That he could cope with the enormity of it all and that the real world wasn't too much.

Up close, Angelo thought Theo looked like the handsome heroes in his Greek mythology tales. Like

Hercules, Jason and Odysseus. His eyes were the colour of the sea in summer and his wavy hair was a yellowish-brown. When the sunlight caught it in just the right way, it shone like his mother's gold necklace. Angelo's hair was black and frizzy and his eyes the colour of mud. He wondered if he would morph into his father one day; if the black in his eyes would melt into blue and his hair fade into yellow.

'Will I look like you when I grow up, Pappa?'

Theo would smile and ruffle his hair. Tell him that it was time to go home for their dinner and that it really didn't matter what he looked like.

'Yes, Pappa.'

He made Angelo call him Daddy because he wanted them to integrate.

'What does "inti-grate" mean, Daddy?'

Theo explained that it was a complicated concept as he helped him back onto his bike. 'I suppose it means behaving more like the people who live in this country.'

'You mean being more English?'

'I mean being less Cypriot.' Theo told him that it wasn't because he wasn't proud to be a Greek-Cypriot, quite the opposite, but because he wanted to try to fit in. 'Just makes life easier.'

Fitting in was just fine because Theo liked England and English people, and that meant Angelo liked them too. His mother called England 'the moon' because it was cold and grey and miles away from Cyprus. She hated everything about their moony home and wanted to go back to Limassol where the sun shone brightly in the sky and the Mediterranean Sea lapped against the pier. She kept threatening to leave. To pack a bag, steal the car and get as far away from Addison Avenue as possible.

'I've done it once and I would do it again. Don't underestimate me, Theo.'

'This is silly talk, Emi.' Theo offered to buy them a bigger house in a different area so she would be happier. An area with less traffic, more trees, and schools where the kids wore hats. 'We could move to the suburbs and I could commute to the hospital. To Harpenden, or St Albans.'

'Harpenden?' His mother would shake her head when he pleaded with her to at least consider it. 'Where the bloody hell is Harpenden? I have one friend here, Theo. *One.* And you want to take me away from her, too?' Or sometimes, 'Why – is that where *she* lives?'

'Not in front of the boy, Emi.'

At the time, their fights seemed perfectly normal to him. Angelo thought that everybody's mum and dad shouted at each other when their kids went upstairs to play with their skeletons. That this was just life.

Most of their arguments were about England. About his mother feeling 'stuck' and 'trapped' and being forced to care for her own brat, but sometimes they were about private things. These arguments reminded him of Card Tuesday and Angelo called them the Quiet Fights. During the Quiet Fights, he would tiptoe to the top of the stairs and hear his mother accusing Theo of all sorts. 'You're turning him against me', 'He's not even yours', 'I decide where my son grows up!' Angelo had no idea what they were shouting about but these words gave him a funny feeling in his tummy.

It was the famous summer of the Moon Landing. One afternoon, while they were all still buzzing about mankind's great leap, Theo returned home from the hospital to announce that he was unwell. They didn't pay him much attention at first; his mother was fiddling with the radio in the kitchen because it wasn't working properly and, along with everything else in the world, the static was getting on her nerves. He was devouring a fried egg sandwich smothered in ketchup, licking his fingers greedily and wiping them on his T-shirt.

'Angelo, that's disgusting. Get a tissue!'

She was tutting and he was sucking, and then suddenly there was Theo, his face as pale as the surface of the moon. They'd found shadows on his lungs, he whispered quietly, although nobody knew he was feeling ill or that he had even been for an X-ray.

'Shadows, what shadows?'

Angelo didn't know what any of it meant, but there was something about the *way* his father said it that made his stomach twist into a knot. Theo's voice was calm but the knuckles of his clenched fists poked out of his skin like ten uneven sugar lumps.

'Shadows?'

The egg turned to stone in Angelo's mouth and began to grind against his back teeth. When he tried to swallow it, the lump refused to go down and clung stubbornly onto his tonsils.

'Bad shadows?' his mother asked, no longer trying to tune the radio but still only half interested in the conversation until his father replied, 'Shadows are never good, Emi.' Then the radio burst into life but everything else stood still.

Only three days before, they'd hosted a party in honour of the astronauts. Aunty Ev had come round with an Apollo-shaped cake and a bottle of gin, and he and Theo had laughed at the shape of it because it looked more like a dick than a rocket. 'She must have necked the gin first, hah?' his father had guffawed into his bottle of beer, and when she whipped the cling film off with a triumphant 'ta-dah!' the pair of them snuck into the kitchen to piss themselves laughing.

Afterwards, they'd watched the grainy footage from the moon on the news. The *actual* moon, and his father was so proud because he'd spent a year studying medicine in Houston and thought he deserved some of the credit. 'Only great countries do great things, and great men live in great countries.'

'Of course, the *great* Theo!' Aunty Ev, who had never been his biggest fan and was still sore about the cake, rolled her eyes at his comment. 'Doctor *and* astronaut now? Is there no end to your eminence?' Though she'd muttered the last part under her breath.

Angelo couldn't handle his emotions. Teenage boys didn't cry – at least not in the kitchen in front of the fathers they worshipped – so he screamed at his Che Guevara poster until he had no voice left and thought he might throw up on the carpet.

'Why him?'

It was the question on everyone's lips and especially his mother's. 'Why, Ev? He's only forty-bloody-four!' she asked his Aunty Ev again and again as if death might hear them and piss right off. 'He jogs every morning and eats grapefruits for breakfast, for God's sake.'

Aunty Ev nodded and patted her friend's knee, offering more cigarettes from her handbag until their front room was filled with a thick, impenetrable fog and Angelo thought he might suffocate. 'Cancer sucks,' she soothed hoarsely, from behind the curtain of smoke. 'Cancer sucks, my darling.'

In some ways, the world changed forever after Theo's announcement, and in others everything stayed the same. Theo still went to work at the hospital, and when he came home his mother still plonked burnt roasts onto their plates that sent them sniggering to Charlie's Fish and Chips. They still went for walks around Oaklands Park and talked about the things that mattered to his father. President Nixon, the threat of nuclear war and the war in Vietnam, but, while there was lots to say, there was also a grief for the things that would never be said. The things that Theo would never get to see or experience. Angelo's exam results, his first girl-friend, his wedding and his children.

'I'm sorry, son.' Everyone said they were sorry but, in those last few months of 1969, nobody was sorrier than Angelo.

Winter came quickly and claimed the last of Theo's energy. Their walks became less frequent. When they did go out, they spent longer sitting on the benches peppering the paths than they did walking between them. Eventually, they talked by the light of Theo's bedside lamp because the shadows had taken him over. The day that Theo took to his bed for the last time, Angelo tore his Che Guevara poster off the wall. He tore him into little pieces and flushed him down the toilet, because Che didn't deserve to preside over his bedroom when Theo was drowning in himself.

Towards the end, there was something Theo wanted to say. He would begin conversations he couldn't finish, pulling himself up against the pillows and rasping into his son's ear but falling asleep before he could breathe the words out. 'What is it, Dad?' Angelo asked, carefully pouring drops of water into his mouth in the hope that the cold liquid would free his tongue. 'What's wrong?'

After he died, his mother finished Theo's sentence and he was so angry with her, so full of hot, salty rage, that for a long time afterwards he wished it was *her* who had died.

The night before Theo's funeral, he stood outside Ev's house in the pouring rain, frantically pounding on her door with his fists.

'Aunty Ev?'

It was late and, when she finally answered, she was in her robe and slippers, her short, bleached hair twisted round rollers.

'Angelo?' She glanced furtively behind him and at the partially lit street. 'What are you doing out here at this hour? What's happened, is it your mother?'

He'd been marching up and down Addison Avenue for hours, trying to make sense of the news and wondering what to say to his Aunty Ev. He was wet and shivering, his face slimy with snot and his hair plastered to his forehead.

He decided to come right out and ask her. 'Is it true, what she just told me?' He could feel the veins in his neck bulging beneath his skin as he croaked his hoarse words.

'Angelo?' She instinctively reached for him, but he backed away as if her hands meant not to soothe but to burn him. He stepped out from beneath the shelter of her doorway and back into the torrential rain. 'Is what true, my darling?'

'She just told me that Theo wasn't my real father. Is it true?'

Aunty Ev's eyes flickered in surprise before returning to their familiar expression, but, in that flicker, he knew that she knew. Memories began to make sense. The way things had suddenly changed. How there had been fewer tickles beneath his chin but many more whispers behind his back. Trivial details his brain had been keeping stored away and now proudly handed back to him in confirmation.

'She told *you* and not me? You knew all along?'

The rain punctuated the silences between his questions.

'Of course not, Angelo.'

There was the sound of creaking upstairs and the upside-down head of Uncle Jim loomed, ghost-like, over the bannister.

'Ev, everything OK?'

'Fine, love. Angelo's come about the funeral arrangements for tomorrow.'

The loyal footsteps lingered for a while before trudging back to bed. Uncle Jim, who had never really liked him, making late-night allowances because his father had died. Poor, pathetic Angelo. Someone to be patronised and pitied. Perhaps he knew that Theo wasn't his real father, too.

'Look . . .' Ev lowered her voice to a murmur. Fiddled nervously for a cigarette in the pockets of her robe but couldn't find a lighter. 'You should go home and talk to your mother.' She pointed the unlit cigarette in the direction of their house and he could see that her fingers were trembling. That he'd got to her. 'But whatever's going on, whatever she's just told you, I know that Theo loved you like his own.'

Those had been his mother's exact words only hours earlier. 'He wasn't your real dad, Angelo, but he loved you like his own son.' She'd come into his room

to ask if he'd ironed his black suit, but there was something preying on her mind, he could tell. When she
sat down on the bed next to him, the mattress sagged
beneath her. A sad, ominous groan that almost gave
her away.

She looked around at his bare bedroom walls as if
seeing things clearly for the first time. 'Where's Che?'

'I tore him up when Dad got really sick. I tore
everything up. All my photos, too.'

Hearing him say it, calling Theo 'Dad', somehow
gave her permission. She exhaled deeply, as though
she wasn't the sole creator of his misery, but the reluctant bearer of bad news. As though none of it was her
fault.

He should have known. She never came into his
bedroom unless it was to tell him that it stank of
armpits or to put his dirty clothes in the washing basket.
'There's something you should know before the funeral
tomorrow, Angelo. Something I've wanted to tell you
for the longest time, and it can't wait any longer . . .'

He looked up at the side of her face and for a few
brief moments, he was four years old and they were
sitting on the pier in Limassol. 'Theo wasn't your real
father, but he always loved you like his own.'

Lightning slashed the sky above Aunty Ev's doorstep
and she exclaimed in surprise at the force of it. 'Oh my,
it's so close! Angelo, please go home – you'll catch your
death out here! I'll see you at the church tomorrow.'

Betrayed twice over, he turned to leave, but nothing
was ever the same after that night in the rain. The man

they lowered into the ground the next morning wasn't *his* Theo. The father who took him to the park to ride his red bike, or the father who lectured him on American politics. The man in the coffin belonged, like he'd always done, to Emiliana. His funeral was her resolution. There was to be no closure for him. No matter what she did afterwards, she could never make it right.

~

The first and last names of the woman in his arranging room clash like symbols.

'I just want to lay my son to rest, Mr Angelides.' Her accent tells him that she's lived here for many years, but not enough to disguise her ethnicity.

She appears familiar to him, as though he might have known her in some former life. A life when everything around him was hazy and distorted. 'Please, everyone calls me Angelo.'

She nods respectfully, dabs at the corners of her black eyes with a tissue. 'It's a beautiful name. An angel's name. He's been with the coroner a long time, An-ge-lo, but they've concluded their investigations and I would like him to have a proper burial. A Christian burial.'

'Of course. I understand.'

She tells him that her son's life veered off the rails many years ago and that his tragic death, although premature, was not unexpected.

'I lost him, really, at sixteen. He left home, fell in with

a bad crowd and I lost him to the temptations of the world.'

'I'm sorry to hear that.' He reaches across for another box of tissues with a practised hand and places them on the table in front of her.

He knows what Mike Sedaris would have said to the woman whose names didn't fit together. Mike would have told her he was very sorry for her loss, guessed what she was hinting at and recommended somewhere else. A funeral home *better suited* to her financial situation '. . . and here's our *bro-chure* for next time.'

Angelo wants to help. To offer this grieving mother the closure she craves, regardless of the hit on his commission.

He clicks the end of his pen. To fill in the silences more than anything else, to give her the space to compose herself. 'I can speak with the coroner and arrange to have him released to us. Can I take some details first? What was your son's name?'

When she tells him, his pen freezes in mid-air. The name Nicky Martinez propels him back to a time pervaded by Theo's loss. A time filled with strange moon faces and his own vivid, drug-fuelled dreams.

~

They called him 'Nicky Black Eyes' because his irises were darker than his pupils. Never to his face, though. Never to his face. He sold weed, speed and pills from a bedsit on the Raleigh Road Estate. He was a small-timer. A wannabe top boy who occasionally stole some cars, but to Angelo and his friend Zane, he was Al Capone.

When Nicky was in a good mood and his pockets stuffed with cash, he let them smoke freebies to celebrate. Angelo loved skipping school, getting stoned and spending the day staring at the mould on Nicky's ceiling. At the naked lightbulb that swung backwards and forwards despite the absence of a window. 'Place is effing haunted, man.' Maybe Zane was right, but being with Nicky was the only way to forget about Theo. The only way to blot out the pain when, otherwise, everything physically ached.

His mother was relieved. It meant she could disown his teenage anger and watch her telly in peace. Avoid the inevitable question raised by her life-changing revelation.

'If not Theo, then who?'

'It's not the right time, Angelo.'

It never was.

On Card Tuesday, she would play the victim to his Aunty Ev. 'Angelo's a *druggie* now. Looks like a homeless person, too – you would hardly recognise him.' Aunty Ev, sipping her gin and sin while looking nervously in her bag for her fags. 'And his school marks are an insult to Theo.'

She was right, at least about his schoolwork, and the part of him that still loved Theo cringed in embarrassment. All those talks about American politics in the park and he barely scraped two passes. It was a senseless and crushing waste and, at night, he soaked his pillow with the shame.

'Congratulations, Angelo,' said his mother, dripping with sarcasm and fag ash. Dropping bits of herself into his scrambled eggs the morning the O-level results were shoved through the door. 'What are you going to do now, collect people's bins for a living?' The postman needn't have bothered. 'Pick up dog shit off the street?'

Angelo disentangled a curly hair from the yellow mess on his plate and shrugged his shoulders to provoke her. 'I'd make a better bin man than you would, chef, judging by this crap breakfast.'

'That's charming.'

Days when he wasn't buzzing, fizzing or popping and felt vaguely lucid, he took the bus to North Finchley to lurk outside Sedaris & Smith, the funeral home that had handled Theo's burial, and the last place he'd felt any peace. Two and a half years ago, standing next to his father's coffin in Mike Sedaris's chapel of rest. His mother hadn't wanted to go. 'You're much better with these things than I am, Angelo,' she'd sniffed. 'I don't have the stomach for it.' He'd put on his best trousers and gone to the viewing by himself, and he was glad he had, in the end. Glad to have had that private time with him before she'd broken the news that ruined everything.

The man lying in the shiny black coffin hadn't looked like Theo. At least, not the Theo Angelo remembered. The big, strong dad who'd taken him to the park. His lips were too red and his face too pale to have ever belonged to his father. It was as though Theo had vacated his sick flesh a long time before, but left a waxy likeness as consolation.

Despite his eerie look, though, the scene was still and comforting, the dusty furniture, soft carpets and hushed voices of the funeral home conveying just the right amount of sympathy. The chapel smelled faintly of flowers and something else; something sharp and acidic. Angelo wondered, without flinching or recoiling, if it was the *actual* smell of death.

Somewhere in the distance, he could hear the muffled tinkling of a piano. He closed his eyes for a minute, imagining that the soothing music was the soundtrack to Theo's life, to their best bits together. Father and son. It wasn't until Mike Sedaris crept in through the heavy doors and closed them carefully behind him that Angelo realised he'd been in there, not for minutes, but for hours.

'It's peaceful in the chapel, no?' Mike's voice was appropriately deep and hypnotic.

'Very peaceful.'

'Shall we see you tomorrow, young man?'

He wished, as he stood outside the funeral parlour with his nose pressed up against the window, that he'd asked for more time in the chapel that day. That he'd stayed with Theo. That he'd never abandoned him to iron his stupid suit and hear her terrible words.

Mike Sedaris opened the door of Sedaris & Smith and stepped out onto the noisy high street. He cupped his big, meaty hands around his cigarette and waved the pack in Angelo's direction.

'Smoke?'

'No thanks.'

'So.' Mike used the word 'so' a lot. At the start of sentences, at the end, and he sometimes used two together. 'If my memory serves me correctly, we buried your father a few years ago. The eminent doctor?' He had a thick Greek accent and a voice roughened by years of smoking. 'Angelides?'

'Theo, yeah.'

'I thought I recognised you. I never forget a memorable face. Speaking of which,' a knowing smile spread across Mike's lips, 'how's your beautiful mother doing?'

Angelo had no idea how his mother was doing. He saw more of Zane and Nicky than he did of her, but he supposed she was enjoying her cocktails. Toasting his misery in front of *Coronation Street*.

'She all right?'

'Yeah, she's all right.'

'Glad to hear it. So, what about you, young man? Losing your father at such a tender age is a big deal. You OK?'

The question took Angelo by surprise. It had been so long since anyone had cared. He shrugged his shoulders and scuffed the tops of his trainers against the pavement. 'I'm all right too,' he lied. 'I mean, I guess.'

'This comforts you, does it?' Mike tilted his large head towards the funeral parlour behind him. 'Hanging around outside this place every day – it doesn't frighten you? Most people cross the street to avoid us.'

'Nah.' Angelo peered through the glassy shop front

at the flowery bouquets and green carpets, the brochure stands and assortment of collection boxes. If nothing else, it was a place of absolute certainty. You knew where you stood with death. Always. 'Worse things than being dead.'

'Yes?' Mike paused to clear his throat of phlegm, a long, low rasp that sounded more like a laugh than a cough. 'I happen to agree with you. Death, dying, it's all a natural process. But people? Relationships? Life? That's the crazy part, no?' He tapped his temple. 'That's the part that's completely loco.'

'Loco? Yeah . . .' Angelo had no idea what 'loco' meant.

'The dead don't demand anything of you, either,' Mike continued. 'They don't jump out of mortuaries and stab you in the back like your nearest and dearest do.'

Angelo thought of his mother and his Aunty Ev. 'I s'pose not.'

There was a comfortable silence while Mike ground his fag butt beneath his large boot and unpeeled a new pack. The cellophane wrapper escaped from his fingers and sailed off down the street.

Angelo thought the older man looked like the King of Death, standing in the doorway of his funeral empire in his black polo neck and grey flares. Tall and imposing, with jaundiced skin stretched too tightly over his massive, bony face. He looked like an undertaker was supposed to look. Like they did in the films.

'I like coffee, by the way. Especially in the morning when I wake up and I feel like one of those, how do you call them?' Mike cycled his newly lit fag in the air. 'Like one of those . . . zombies.'

Angelo cased the street for a caff, wondering if Mike was hinting that he should go and buy him one in exchange for letting him loiter outside his shop.

'You can make a good cup of coffee, young man?'

He shrugged. 'I make it for my mum when she's hungover.'

'Good. Because Gloria's daughter, she used to make the coffee and tea around here but she ran off to join the hippies. You think you could manage to operate the kettle while she's banging a tambourine and smoking hashish?'

Angelo remembered the stillness he'd felt in Mike's chapel of rest. How he'd been trying to crawl back in there ever since, but instead had ended up searching for peace in the nefarious crevices of the Raleigh Road Estate. In Nicky Black Eyes' filthy bedsit, in the mysterious bags he pulled from his pockets and dangled above Angelo's head like bait. 'Here you go, Angel Face, but first show me the dinero!'

'Yeah, I reckon so,' Angelo replied. He'd been searching in the wrong places; there was no peace in Raleigh Road and no peace in Nicky's bags.

'So, if you promise to smarten yourself up a little bit, we can call the first week a trial.'

'Cool.' Angelo suddenly sounded happier than he had done in months.

'A funeral home?' His mother stood in the doorway of his bedroom with her hands on her slender hips, her nose scrunched halfway up her face.

'Yeah. Sedaris & Smith. They buried Theo.' He could no longer call him his father, at least not to her face.

'I know who they are, Angelo, I bloody paid them. You serious?'

'Deadly.' He couldn't resist the joke and neither, apparently, could she. After a brief moment's hesitation, a tentative smile crept over her lips.

'Very funny, Angelo.' She marched into his room to open his window before sinking into the bed next to him. 'It stinks of socks in here!' Her loose curly hair tickled his bare shoulder and reminded him that they hadn't been this close in years. Close enough for him to touch or feel her against his skin. Her presence seemed dream-like, as though he had woken up in the middle of the night to find her sitting there.

'You freaked out?' Her robe smelled faintly of her perfume, not as flowery as his Aunty Ev's, or as spicy as Theo's used to be, but something in between. Like herbs.

'Not really,' she sighed. 'I mean, it's a bit creepy, but I'm not that surprised.'

Something passed between them in that moment, like the flicking of a switch. The crack of lightning over Aunty Ev's front door the night before Theo's funeral. A moment where her large, dark eyes searched his and they looked like they might spill.

'Why?' he asked. 'Why aren't you surprised?'

Then the moment was gone and the atmosphere was still again, the ripples settling to nothing. 'Because you were always such a morbid kid. Obsessed with dead things. Remember your skeleton, Achilles?'

'Socrates. Yeah. I've still got him in a drawer somewhere.'

'Always bothering Ev with it and trying to shove it in the poor woman's gin. And remember when Theo found that dead squirrel in the back garden and you insisted on sticking your fingers inside it? Full of worms, it was. Horrible.'

'The milky eyes?'

'The bloody milky eyes . . .' She shuddered and it was comforting to feel her breath on his skin. To unravel the past together. To inhale her herby perfume. Until he remembered how much he'd enjoyed burying the dead squirrel with Theo that afternoon; how he'd taught him all about decomposition. 'Don't touch it, just look. It's already full of the maggots that will break down its flesh, see?' Angelo's teenage anger suddenly returned full force. He didn't know who Theo was to him any more. His mother had stolen all his memories and she didn't deserve to be forgiven, no matter how comforting her closeness.

'Well, I guess I should get some sleep. He wants me there at eight tomorrow and the place is in North Finchley.'

'Hint taken.' She got up to leave and blew him a kiss from the doorway of his bedroom, but he refused to reach up and catch it like he used to when he was little. A shadow of doubt clouded her features and he flicked off his bedside light to blot her out.

'Night, Mum.'

'Goodnight, Angelo. Enjoy your corpses.'

Her mood was back to black.

The parlour rooms were big and dusty and decorated like something out of a history book. There were rooms for everything, too: arranging, reposing, managing, displaying, embalming and refrigerating. An entire industry of death in a space once designed for the living.

Mike lived in the company house upstairs with Gloria, a glamorous older woman with ginger hair and lopsided shoulder pads. By day, Gloria was also Mike's receptionist, jumping out from behind the numerous floral arrangements decorating the front desk to steer the bereaved to their rightful places.

'An essential job,' Mike said with a conspiratorial wink. 'It wouldn't do for them to get lost. Wander into the room meant for, say, reposing.'

'Yeah.'

'Might get a bit of a fright in there, so?' He slapped Angelo on the back, and the force of his garden-shovel hands almost sent him sprawling.

Mike liked to laugh but Angelo got the impression it was purely a functional thing. To clear his airways of the phlegm that plagued them and not because he found things funny. In action, he was the very opposite of funny. When he put on his suit, he put on a show. At least, that's how he was back then.

There were professional terms for all things death-related, and it took Angelo months to learn what they were. 'Don't be vulgar,' Mike warned. 'Save "corpse" and "cadaver" for the privacy of the office, and for everything else use some polish.' The grieving families who sought their services were the 'recently bereaved' and their dead relatives the 'dearly departed'. The gravesite was the 'final resting place' and not a hole or a burial plot.

These were the lessons that would inform Angelo's career, but first he had to earn his stripes. There was a hierarchy at Sedaris & Smith and everyone loved to remind him of it. Gloria, with her big hair and piles of random papers. Mike's son, Filip, who occasionally popped his head round the door to tell his father he had no interest in inheriting the death trade. Brian-John Knightley, the embalmer, whose nametag 'B-J Knightley' never failed to provoke a snort from Angelo. He would be starting at the bottom of the funeral ladder, managing his little kitchen area until he was worthy of graduating to car-washing and, if he was lucky, office administration.

He made Mike's coffee – 'Always black, always sweet.'

'Zombies. I remember, guv.'

Satisfied that Angelo could handle a kettle and use a spoon proficiently, Mike let him loose on Gloria's concoction. 'White, hot, plenty of nutmeg.'

'Nutmeg? In a cup of coffee?'

Gloria pulled her glasses halfway down her nose to glare at him over the top of them. 'Did I say I wanted coffee?' If looks could kill, Mike would be even richer.

He was quickly promoted to the icy courtyard, where he would spend hours cleaning the company limos. Plunging his sponge into a bucket of cold, soapy water, he scrubbed until the skin on his knuckles split and bled. 'All done, guv,' he told Mike as his boss emerged from the parlour in his warm fur coat to rub in life's injustices, running his hands along the paintwork while Angelo crossed his fingers and shivered.

'Spotless, young man.'

The reward of administration manager gleamed temptingly back indoors. Angelo accepted the role gratefully, happiest not for the promotion, but for the heaters and the dry trouser legs. Gloria was fit to stab him the morning of the so-called 'big announcement', and Mike squeezed her large shoulder pads in con-solation. 'My dear, there is no competition, no threat to your valued role here. The boy will be working for *you*,' he crooned unconvincingly. 'Besides, you're wasted on your piles of paper when your true talents lie with the bereaved.'

In reality, she was worse than useless. 'Upstairs, she's marvellous, but down here she's a liability. Maybe we should turn her upside down?' Another slap on the back and a raspy cough, but Angelo knew better than to snigger at the guv's missus. You never knew where you were with Mike, when he might jump up and bite you with his giant yellow teeth, and perhaps that was part of the early appeal for Angelo – never knowing where he stood.

'Administration manager' turned out to be a fancy title for answering the phone and scribbling down garbled messages from hysterical relatives. Their voices were often punctuated by mournful sobs and their instructions for Mike frequently involved toilets.

'Mrs Hajimichael called. The husband is still on the loo. Call the eldest son as she's looking for his ring.'

'So . . .' Mike scratched his forehead in confusion while Gloria smirked maliciously. 'She wants me to call the son to arrange the transfer of the body, or to look for her husband's ring in their toilet? Because she might be needing a plumber instead of an undertaker.'

Sedaris & Smith specialised in Christian Orthodox burials, but 'we cater for all religious beliefs' was very much the company motto. Mike was happy to work with anyone who pinged his silver bell. He knew rabbis and imams, temples and synagogues. He was eager to accommodate any ritual no matter how elaborate or exotic. You want to wash your loved one in purified water? No problem! We can get it for you! You need some rice balls? All right! Flowers at the foot of the casket? Of course, whatever you say! Cremations? We have urns!

'You have to diversify to capitalise,' he explained to Angelo over coffee and fags. There was no point in limiting himself to a small sub-section of the city's population when death struck all communities alike. 'Death isn't a racist, hah?'

'Nah.'

Still, the grieving Greek-Cypriots of North Finchley and the surrounding areas preferred to limit themselves to Mike and, when struck by death, they flocked to him. Angelo's second year at Sedaris & Smith was a particularly deadly one, and very lucrative for the business. It was also Angelo's first professional encounter with a cadaver and, like Mike's job offer outside Sedaris & Smith that fateful afternoon, a moment he would always remember.

It began with a phone call and a hastily scribbled note: 'Mrs Galano called for Mike. The husband died.'

A few weeks earlier, the distressed wife had wheeled the dying man into Sedaris & Smith. 'He wants to see the coffins,' she sniffed over the squeaking of the spokes. 'To pick one out before he goes.'

Gloria sprang up from behind a bouquet of fresh chrysanthemums and steered the couple away from the chapel of rest and into the room marked 'Display'. Mike stepped out from behind the caskets to intercept them with a 'So, of course we can help,' and Angelo hovered in the doorway. He would normally leave at this point in the proceedings, excuse himself to make the tea or linger by the telephone, but there was something in the unfolding scene that made him hesitate.

He watched as the terminally ill man dribbled onto his blanketed knees and his wife cleaned up the mess with a tissue. 'You like this one, Mr Galano?' Mike knelt down next to the wheelchair and churned out his sales pitch more rapidly than usual, in case the man died in the process. An indisputable fact made itself apparent to Angelo in that moment. It was the same fact that had informed the window displays he used to stare at with his nose pressed up against the glass. The same fact that hung in the corridors of the funeral parlour like a deathly air freshener. Mr Galano was going to die, and there was no stopping the inevitable.

Mike picked up the message and collected the body in the Sedaris & Smith ambulance later that evening. He wheeled it into the mortuary at the back of the parlour and motioned for Angelo to follow him. 'You want to see what rigor mortis looks like, young man?'

'Yeah,' Angelo nodded nervously as Mike unzipped the black bag to expose the bloodless face of Mr Galano.

'Strange?'

Angelo exhaled slowly, excitedly. 'Very.'

'In some ways, quite mundane.'

'Yeah. Can I touch him?'

'Go ahead.'

Angelo ran his fingers over the stiff cold skin, now stretched too thinly over the face it had once hung from. He stared at the exposed yellow teeth and the vacant blue eyes. They glared up at the mortuary ceiling in disbelief, as if, despite everything, they'd been hoping for a last-minute reprieve. 'He went pissed off, didn't he?' Mr Galano hadn't been ready to let go of his existence.

'I would say so.' Mike's breath literally hung in the cold, mortuary air. 'Wouldn't you be?'

'Yeah.' Angelo was at a loss for words, but he also

learned a valuable lesson that night as Mike slid the body back into the refrigerator in preparation for the next stage of the earthly afterlife.

'Brian will smooth him out. Sometimes they need a little . . . encouraging to go back to their former positions.'

Death wasn't always the graceful event the embalmer would have you believe.

~

He glides the razor along his cheek before dunking it twice in the scummy water. He's glad the weekend is over and done with. Ash, muscling in on his time with Princess Priya. His mother's strange, feverish words.

'I was an orange, that's how the bloody thing started.'

'Why were you dressed as an orange?'

'I was in a parade,' she sighed. 'I was the Orange girl. The one they all came to see.'

'That where you met him, at this parade?'

'Not now, Angelo. Come round next Saturday when my head is feeling clearer. We can talk then.'

He stretches his top lip over his front teeth to shave the hair growing in the shade of his massive nose. He's tired. Tired of waiting for her to throw him a few crumbs from her plate whenever she craves his attention. 'Oranges?' Whenever she feels like reeling him in. 'What you on about now? Just tell me who the hell he is.' It's all he's ever wanted to know. 'Tell me his name.'

At least Princess Priya's back in the picture. She called him this morning, before he headed to work. 'Wifely duties are over, baby – can you make it home for lunch today?'

'*Wifely* duties?' he growled down the phone, his excitement quickly turning into irritation. 'What's that supposed to mean? You trying to wind me up or something?'

'Course not, and I thought we talked about this a million times, baby . . .'

A million times or not, after that phone call, images of Priya rolling around in bed with Ash played out in his mind all morning and through most of Katie Gerou's funeral. At one point, he looked up from his shoes to discover the girl's devastated father scowling at him and he wanted to punch himself in the face.

He would have rollicked Stel for doing the same thing. Absolutely berated him. 'Always be present at a funeral, yeah?'

'Yes, boss.'

'Don't stand there like a slack-jaw in front of the grieving relatives.'

'Course not.'

'They need to see that you care about their loved one.'

'I got it, boss.'

He pulls the plug out of the sink and rinses the blobs of stubbly foam hiding behind the taps. What's next? he thinks, as he grabs his bottle of Old Spice out of the bathroom cabinet and slaps it onto his newly shorn cheeks. He wakes up tomorrow to find he's turned into Mike Sedaris? That he no longer gives a shit either?

The aftershave smells like a church service packed full of old men, but she likes it.

'Reminds me of my first boyfriend.'

'That a good thing?'

'Course,' she giggled. 'Girl's first time and all that.'

'As long as I don't smell like *him*.'

The problem with her boundaries, he thinks, padding barefoot into the bedroom to find a clean T-shirt for their date, is that the deeper he falls for her, the harder it is to ignore the spectre of the husband. To ignore her performing her wifely duties, as she puts it. To resist the temptation to park outside her house at midnight and imagine her giving Ash a blowjob in the negligee he bought her for Valentine's Day. On the other hand, would their affair even work if exposed to the light of day? Would he still feel the same about her if there was no workaholic husband to glamorise the cheating? No wine to steal from his expensive cabinet? If they were out with her friends? If he introduced her to his mother?

'An Indian girl, Angelo? *Really?*'

He tuts to himself as he pulls a navy designer T-shirt out of the drawer and decides his mother is actually to blame for all of it. If she hadn't spent his childhood arguing with Theo, if she hadn't dropped the bombshell that would blow his life apart, perhaps he would be more like his protégé, Stel. Indulging in one-night stands with girls called Gemma and then accidentally losing their numbers. All right, so the man was a bit of a Casanova, but at least he wasn't out there chasing ghosts.

He resists the urge to tell her. To drive round to her flat half dressed and scream it in her face.

'So now your love life's my fault, too?' He imagines her huffing into her fag. 'Take some responsibility for your own bloody shit, Angelo.'

The doorbell rings as he zips up his suit trousers. He never wears jeans or tracksuit bottoms, not even at home. It's easier to keep his emotions in check in smarter, tighter clothes. Much easier to stay in control.

He opens the window and calls out to her. 'Oi, stranger! Who are you, again?'

She blows him a kiss from the doorway and he jogs down the stairs like a lovesick school kid.

~

By the start of the eighties, Angelo was the *de facto* boss. His experience said so and his mug said so, too. He was the one who was holding the place together. The one they all came to with work-related troubles, most of which were related to Mike.

Mike Sedaris wasn't the same Mike any more. He wasn't the Mike who'd offered Angelo a job outside Sedaris & Smith. He wasn't the Mike who'd let him touch Mr Galano's body in the morgue. The Mike who'd taught him the valuable lessons that would promote him from scruffy, dope-suffused coffee-maker to the leader of the cortege.

Chief mourner at Sedaris & Smith was his career highlight, and Angelo loved everything about it. The showmanship, the ceremonial aspect of the last farewell, the suit, the tie, the top hat. He took immense pride in being part of something much bigger than his own existence. 'Funerals are for the living,' Mike would tell him in the days when he still cared. 'Look around you: the flowers, the music, the gravitas – this is all for those left behind.' The gratitude evident in their smiles and the sweaty handshakes afterwards. The relief that their loved one was resting peacefully and perhaps, somewhere, in the very back of Angelo's mind, he was trying to make things right with Theo.

'What's wrong with Mike?' It was the question on everyone's lips, but Angelo didn't have the answer. All he knew was that Sedaris & Smith, once filled with a respectful, carpeted hush, now reverberated with the sounds of the older man's frustrations. 'So! Where did the bastard delivery man leave my boxes?' His black moods. 'Why can't I hear the kettle boiling, hah? Where's the idiot new girl?'

More distressingly, his sales pitches, once packaged in care and solicitude, were now bordering on aggressive. 'You *must* hurry and make your decision in the next ten minutes, Mrs Rothstein. I know in my heart of hearts that this huge, expensive stone is what your husband would have wanted at the head of his grave.' Gloria would tut in disbelief as another client flounced past her lilies and Mike rushed off to play golf.

To Angelo, he appeared too old and world-weary for

the job. Well past the age of retirement but hanging on for the sake of it. He stopped living his own lessons, stopped caring for the bereaved of north London. Dead mothers? Oh well! Kids sobbing? Who cares! Father run over by a truck on his birthday? Shit happens and guess what? Mike no longer gives a shit!

Brian-John walked out and was replaced by an embalmer named Robert Hawking. Gloria went upstairs to powder her nose one morning and decided her chihuahua was depressed. 'How can I leave my baby like this? Mike will just have to cope without me!' Filip Sedaris reminded his father that he didn't want to touch dead people, by phone in order to avoid seeing his face, and the unfairly maligned idiot girl got a job at the estate agency across the road.

As if things could get any worse for Sedaris & Smith, the cards of gratitude that had once proudly decorated their doormat every morning stopped mentioning Mike, and then stopped coming at all. It was a wonder there were any customers left.

There was nowhere for Angelo to be promoted to except out of the window and, by then, he was feeling tempted. Sedaris & Smith was fast gaining a reputation that made him cringe to his brogues. He was embarrassed to be an undertaker – or rather, to be working at *this* undertaker. A business interested in profit and not in people, or, put another way, a place that preyed on misery. Everyone knew Mike, but not in a good way. 'Oh, *that* Mike!' became a familiar refrain. 'We used him because we didn't know anyone else.' Choice in their small community was limited and a seed was planted in Angelo's mind.

He made a promise to himself the day the cards stopped landing on their doormat. He would do right by the bereaved of north London and, as soon as he could get a bank loan approved, he would open his very own parlour. Put his lessons into practice and show his fading boss how a funeral director was supposed to behave.

Mike barged into Angelo Angelides Funerals late one night like a budget Marlon Brando. It was uncanny. Angelo almost expected to hear a violin whining the theme tune to *The Godfather*.

'Mike,' he grimaced. 'Lovely surprise.'

The old man reeked of booze. Angelo could smell it on him as he lurched towards the front desk and hammered on the service bell. Smacked his meaty hands together so that the incongruous sound of clapping ricocheted around the reception and made Angelo's hair stand on end.

'Well, well. If it isn't the new and improved funeral home I've been hearing so, so much about.' He shuffled the fur around his huge shoulders and smashed his boots into the newly laid pale pink carpets. 'What's this?' He picked up a pamphlet urging families to 'Plan Ahead' and tore it into little dead butterflies.

He'd read Angelo's interview in the *Foni*, he said, and he'd come to congratulate him in person. To see the 'Fresh New Face of Tomorrow's Funerals' for himself, although it was the same face Angelo always wore. 'Nothing fresh about it.'

'Well, you've seen my face and you're not here to lay a loved one to rest, so I'll say goodnight, Mike,' Angelo said, fiddling nervously with the collars of his shirt while squished in between his former boss and his new reception desk. Mike may have been old but he was still bloody big.

'Goodnight? Why, you in a hurry? The dead running off someplace? Let's shoot the breeze. Take a moment to remember.' A drive through the past where a generous Mike offered a depressed teenager an opportunity to turn his life around. 'All of this,' he waved his furry arms round the room. 'All of it, really, is because of me, and you don't even have the decency to call? I find out about your betrayal when I read a story in the local paper?'

Angelo opened his mouth to interject but Mike raised a hand to his face. He wasn't finished. In fact, he was just getting to the good part. The part where, like the Lord, he had given so much and Angelo had taken it away. 'Or stole it, to speak bluntly. Let's see what you took from me . . . My trust, my loyalty, my respect and, oh, all my bloody customers!'

'We're miles apart, Mike,' Angelo lied. 'No conflict of interest there.'

'Miles? Really? So, like, five or six?' he scoffed, while Angelo cleared a blob of shame from his throat.

'My reputation?'

'You did that by yourself,' Angelo retorted. 'That's why I left Sedaris & Smith in the first place.'

Hurt flickered like a shadow across the older man's face but there was no satisfaction in the blow. No real pleasure in offending him. 'Cocky little bastard, hah?' Angelo suddenly wondered if Mike might snap and hurl something. A pen, a coffin brochure, an empty urn. Smash up the shop with his bare hands.

'This about money, Mike? You want some sort of finder's fee, is that it?' Angelo turned his trouser pockets inside out in provocation, the elephant's ears holding their ground while Mike continued to desecrate his carpets with his soles.

'What?' He didn't need his money, he fumed. He owned two houses, a holiday home in Halkidiki and three cars – four if he counted the Porsche he'd just bought Gloria. He had a Bentley in his garage in Hadley Wood that he had no time to drive because he was too busy playing golf. This was about the future. About the legacy of Sedaris & Smith. 'Don't you get it, Angelo? It was all going to be yours one day soon. It was *always* going to be yours from the moment I laid eyes on you.'

Angelo's conscience made a bid for freedom, but he'd come too far to turn back.

'Like I said, you betrayed me, Angelo.'

He didn't want to be Mike's replacement son, despite the bond the two men had once shared. The memories they'd made. The years of training. His first brush with death, with Mr Galano's face poking out of its shroud to stare hopelessly at the ceiling. 'I'm sorry you feel that way, but I've got to make my own legacy, Mike,' he sighed regretfully. It was time for him to live the lessons he had learned. Bury the dead *his* way.

'Make your own legacy? Why? You think, because I'm an undertaker, I'm going to live forever? Sedaris & Smith would have been your legacy; there was no need for all this. For a rival bloody shop!'

'No thanks, Mike.' Angelo opened the door onto Holloway Road. He waited for Mike to brush menacingly past him but, in true Mike style, he had to rub it in one last time.

'No thanks?' Bourbon vapours drifted from his various orifices. 'You know what your real problem is?'

'I'm sure you're about to tell me, Mike.'

'You're so obsessed with what your life is missing, you refuse to see what's right in front of you.' Mike's spit flew into his eyeballs.

'What is it you think I can't see, Mike?'

But his answer was lost to the air.

~

He tosses his car keys onto the windowsill next to the dirty cups and piles of gossip magazines. Their colourful titles promise sexy, scandalous affairs with neighbours, teachers, babysitters and vicars. 'The filth you read, Mum, honestly.'

'It passes the time of day,' she sniffs. 'It's not like I

have anyone else to keep me company now poor Ev's gone, is it? I'm making coffee, you want one?'

'Yeah.'

She flounces into the kitchen, her grey curls trailing behind her, and he follows anxiously. For a few brief moments, they're dancing back to back, Angelo slamming the windows closed and turning off the radio while his mother opens little doors and drawers in search of hidden cutlery; today, the confines of the cluttered room are a mystery even to her.

It's Saturday, and he spent the entire morning swivelling in his wheezy office chair in anticipation of their conversation, trying to avoid answering the phone or making small talk with the perpetually upbeat Stel. 'All OK, boss? I'm popping to the deli – you want anything?' Down there, he was in charge. The master of the gloom and all he surveyed. His filing cabinets, his mounting newspaper clippings, his oak desk. Angelo's Underworld. While in the outside world, back in real life, his mother pulled all his strings.

He unfastened the top button of his shirt and brooded over the tasks blocking his path to her. To their talk, *the* most important one they would ever have, and only twenty years too late. Next week's funeral rota, delegating the day's duties to Stel, returning Mrs Elbida's call. The short drive along Seven Sisters Road in a stagnant queue of poisonous car exhausts. He imagined himself climbing over these things to get to her as if the morning was one giant physical obstacle.

He picked up the card propped up on his desk and

traced the outline of the silvery thank you. Inside, she'd simply signed her name, 'Melina', in small round letters that looked like balloons. They'd buried her father the week before Aunty Ev, and the man's funeral drifted back to him like smoke from a dying flame. The cawing of a crow as the pater recited the Trisagio prayer. The devastated daughter with the wavy brown hair and melancholy eyes. Stel's remarks in the Damsel over one too many Scotches. Perhaps that's why he opened her card in the privacy of his office instead of pinning it on the wall with all the others. Keep her away from the clutches of Casanova.

'You look like shit – you want a slice of toast or something?' His mother pushes a cup of coffee towards him and fumbles for a cigarette to squash her nerves.

Angelo's stomach rumbles. 'I'll grab something after.' He skipped breakfast. He woke up with an uneasy feeling in the pit of his belly, kicked at the slippery bedsheets and headed for the shower, enjoying the feel of the hot water feasting on his skin.

'Baths or showers, boss?' Stel once asked, during one of the many drunken conversations between the pair of them in the pub after work. 'Baths for me,' he said without waiting for a reply, his mouth full of bacon crisps. 'I like to relax and unwind after a long, hard day. Some bubble bath. Maybe a bit of "Unchained Melody".'

'What?' Angelo ribbed him mercilessly. 'You light scented candles as well, you big girl's blouse?' Showers for him. He liked to stand there and think of nothing as the water slapped and rinsed his arse. Telling him off for being dirty.

'Kinky, boss.'

Still wet, he reached for his black satin robe and muttered to himself as the girlish scent of apricots and cream teased its way into his nostrils. He wondered why Princess Priya didn't just buy her own things and leave them at his place instead of borrowing his stuff all the time. Why she insisted on taking her belongings home with her as if she were hiding a crime scene from the FBI.

He padded downstairs into the kitchen and opened the fridge. Slammed it shut as he twisted the lid off the milk to discover it stank. '*Gamoto!*' A side of him he didn't know he possessed, a superstitious side, told him it was a bad omen. That the out-of-date milk meant his mother was going to reveal something terrible. Something worthy of her gossip magazines. His real father was a murderer, the window cleaner, or, worst of all, someone he knew. Someone like Mike Sedaris.

'Mike Sedaris? Where'd you get that crazy idea from?' She tuts as she wipes her wet nose on the sleeve of her black cardigan. 'You know, I've still got this horrible cold and my head is banging like a drum.'

Her voice demands his pity and it was the same when Theo was alive – Emiliana inventing illnesses that began after their arguments and lingered until someone, preferably not her, apologised.

'I'm still mourning Aunty Ev, as well. I think I'm going to wear black for the whole forty-day memorial period. Do the Orthodox thing properly.'

'Why?' He frowns. 'She weren't remotely religious.'

'What's that got to do with anything?' she replies, blowing smoke into his face. 'It's called being respectful, Angelo.'

He drums his fingers on the table as she slurps her coffee.

His impatience irritates her. 'Oh, Angelo!' It's a name, she sighs, and it won't mean anything. Why would it? A random name after all these years, when Theo loved him like he was his own.

'So, tell me, then.'

'There's not much to tell, but I guess it's what your Aunty Ev wanted,' she concedes, smashing the remains of the cigarette into her green ashtray. 'She always thought you should know and she made me promise when she knew she was . . . well, you know, *dying* . . .' Another slurp of coffee. 'I dread to think what you've been imagining in that head of yours, but I met your biological father when I lived in Morphou. I was asked to star in the Orange Parade that year for, well, the obvious reasons.' She pauses to brush her hair off her shoulders. 'And that's how I met him. We used to meet in secret in the graveyard because it wasn't considered right for an unmarried girl to be seen out with a man. Not like *that*, anyway. Ridiculous, if you ask me. How are you supposed to know if you like someone until you actually spend time with them? He liked to read the inscriptions on the crosses in the cemetery and he talked about death *all* the time. He was a morbid one, like you, and it was all well and good until I found out

I was pregnant and then he wanted nothing to do with me. With either of us,' she adds quickly, for good measure.

'Why not? Was he already married?'

'Married! Is that what you think of me?' She pauses again, this time for his reassurance.

Angelo refuses to give her anything.

'He wasn't married,' she sulks, 'he still lived at home with his parents if you must know, and who cares what went through his mind, Angelo . . .'

'Morphou? What were you doing there. Aren't we from Limassol?'

'We moved there briefly after your grandfather died. He sold lemons at the market. Oranges as well, and sometimes grapefruits, but mainly lemons. He owned a small grove of trees with his father but he was always broke. *Your* father that is, not mine.'

'Lemons? And he definitely knew about me, this lemon famer from Morphou. That I existed, I mean?'

'Of course he did – I just said so, didn't I?' She begins to weep, squeezing her eyelids together until her dark eyes submit to her commands and slide a few token tears down her cheeks. Job well done, she reaches across the table for her packet of cigarettes.

'Anyway, when he refused to propose to me, I ran away. I drove back to Limassol where I was happiest, and I suppose where I felt more in control of things. I could think straight back home, you know? That's when I met my Theo.' She smiles fondly. 'He alone knew about you. He always knew the truth and he saw you as his own son even before you arrived. *He* was your real father, Angelo, don't you see? Pass me a tissue, would you, I've made a right mess of this cardigan . . .'

'What was his name?'

'I look like a bloody slug's attacked me. It's just a name and what does it matter, really, when he went back to his lemon grove without giving me – I mean *us* – a second thought?'

'It matters to me. Who was my real father?'

Exhausted by his craving to know, Emiliana finally deflates like a punctured tyre. Angelo can almost hear the air wheezing out of her. Her face sags into her shoulders and her shoulders collapse into her neck until, finally, there's nothing left of his mother but a pile of grey snot.

The sounds of peaceful birdsong mingle with the faint rumble of distant traffic; the familiar backdrop of a London cemetery. He's surprised to find himself beside this grave after all these years. Beneath a soupy, grey sky he kneels by the concrete cross, speckled in moss. By the cracked glass cabinet with the burnt-out tea light and the black and white photograph inside it.

'It's been a long time, Dad.' It feels good to call him that again. 'It's my fault. I'm sorry.'

He lifts the picture from the cabinet, carefully wiping away the dusting of dirt covering his face until it shines more brightly than any other part of him. The paper has grown hard and brittle and its edges are torn, but it's a great photo of his father. Theo, shot from below and looking even taller than his six feet and two inches. His light brown hair, combed to the side, and his polo neck accentuating his handsome jawline.

'He looks like Paul Whatsit,' his mother used to claim, usually while drunk and during their better times. 'Like a film star!'

'Quite.' Aunty Ev would nod along while her enthusiasm played catch-up with her loyalty.

A vague memory. They were celebrating something the day the picture was shot, a Christmas or a New Year's Eve. He can tell from Theo's smart clothes, the top tucked neatly into the waistband of his trousers. His posture. The smile that told the world he was used to being celebrated. That he enjoyed it.

His mother is right – words he never thought he would hear himself say, but she is. 'A name is a name, Angelo.' A sequence of arbitrary letters, but it's a name that has shaken loose the good times buried in his head. Theo jogging around the pond in Oaklands Park while he pedalled his red bike, his instructions scattered by the wind. Theo, lowering himself to a child's eye level to explain American politics. To tell him that JFK was dead. That someone had assassinated him. His own eyes wet with sadness and disbelief.

'Goodbye, Dad.' He replaces the photograph and closes the broken cabinet door, glad to have remembered how much Theo meant to him in the end.

In the newly dug-out section of the cemetery, not more than fifty yards away, he crunches through the gravel to place a bunch of pink carnations by his Aunty

Ev's headstone – the only stone among the small cluster of grey and black crosses. 'She wasn't religious,' Jimmy faltered, as he turned the pages of Angelo's catalogue with a heavy heart and trembling fingers. 'I don't even think she prayed.' He still couldn't believe he was there, in the arranging room of a funeral parlour, to choose his wife's gravestone. Not when there were so many years left to play out in his mind. Years of holidays, weddings and grandkids to look forward to.

'I don't think she would have wanted a cross but she thought the church thing was peaceful.'

'Of course.' This was Angelo's role in these sad, intimate moments: to nod and to listen.

'The chanting and things. She especially liked the chanting in ancient Greek.'

'I understand. Many do.' Nothing was too strange when people were drowning in their sorrow.

Take the grave next to his Aunty Ev: the man they buried the week before her, who now has seven piles of dead flowers obscuring his cross despite only having a handful of mourners in attendance at his funeral. Someone is still suffering from a broken heart, he thinks, surveying the rotting scene. Someone is still grieving his loss and he wonders if it is the girl with the balloon writing.

Life reasserts itself like a smack to the face. He's running late and it looks like rain again. She'll be standing on his doorstep with Ash's expensive bottle of wine peeking shamefully out of her handbag. 'Where you been?' Maybe he'll tell her about Theo. Maybe today will be the day they make an effort to understand each other.

'I was visiting my father's grave at New Southgate Cemetery. He died just before I turned fourteen but I've only just laid him to rest. You see, it took finding out about my biological father to realise that Theo was my dad all along.'

'Never mind all that! Let me in, I'm gagging for a glass of this wine . . .'

Maybe not, he thinks. Maybe they'll just carry on like they've always done, fulfilling each other's needs once a week with no hope of a meaningful relationship. He brushes the loose dirt from his trousers and searches for his car keys. On the neighbouring grave, the top bouquet wobbles loose from the pile and slides sadly onto the gravel.

Emiliana

May 1990

SHE TIPS THE coffee dregs into the sink and plonks the cup upside down next to the half-eaten Weetabix and last night's spaghetti bolognese. After all these years of living by herself, one might think she'd know exactly how much pasta to put in the pan for one, but the pile of desiccated leftovers tells a different story. She tuts at the wastefulness of it all.

She's glad Angelo's not here to judge; she imagines him surveying the little kitchen in disgust, barging her out of the way to stick on her pink Marigolds and squirt washing-up liquid over everything. There's no point in attempting housework, she's explained to him. Housework is circular. By the time she's finished one job, it's time to start another. Therefore, it's not worth bothering with in the first place.

'So that's it?' he mocked. 'You're just going to fester in your own filth?'

'Filth, says the man who pokes corpses all day?'

'Yeah? They're cleaner than your flat.'

She sparks up a fag and dissolves into her clapped-out sofa to enjoy it. Besides, she likes her broken things. Her so-called mess. Her clutter is a daily reminder of her life. Her framed photos, her magazines, her cups of coffee and variously branded packets of cigarettes stuffed into secret orifices. A reminder that *she* is still alive.

'Those things will kill you, you know.' One more thing for him to berate her about – as if he needs the excuse.

'Sons are worse, believe you me.'

They have allegedly discovered links between cigarettes and incurable illnesses. Cancers like the one that took Theo. 'Well, he never smoked a day in his life and he ate grapefruit every morning, so bang goes your great theory,' she said to Angelo once.

'It's called passive smoking,' he snapped in reply. Not that he would expect a narcissist like her to understand the concept of passive.

'So now you're saying I killed Theo?' She tutted in disbelief.

Her brand new friend, Flora Florides, is shocked when Emiliana recounts these conversations. 'The way you describe him, Lil! He sounds quite disrespectful,' she says from her childless perspective, her sapphire eyes shining.

'It's complicated, Flor,' says Emiliana, examining her unmanicured fingernails.

It's all too easy scrutinising other people's lives from an ivory tower, she thinks, sucking on her fag. Casting aspersions without knowing the full facts. Besides, while it's OK for her to insult her own son, it annoys her when Flora chimes in, 'Angelo has *daddy* issues.'

She gets up to turn on the telly and huffs loudly as

the same tired faces are beamed into her living space. A programme about stuffed pheasants hosted by an ugly slob of a chef. Indian women dancing around in floaty red dresses. Margaret Thatcher ranting while people throw flaming bottles in the street.

'So this is your great England, Theo?'

Mornings like these, mornings when there's nothing to watch and nothing to do, and Angelo's refusing to answer her telephone calls, she misses Ev. The woman who knew her best of all, and, if she's honest, probably loved her the most. It's only been four weeks since her funeral and the thought of spending an eternity without Evgenia by her side makes her want to open the window and throw herself in front of a car. Not that anyone would notice.

Thirty years they were the best of friends, almost to the day. She and Theo had just moved into their new house on Addison Avenue and he was tripping over boxes and she was shouting at him to change Angelo out of his pissed-in pants, and then, suddenly, there they were in the doorway. Evgenia and Jimmy. She thought for a moment that it was the English come to complain about all the commotion, Ev with her bleached hair and Jimmy with his big, gormless face. *He* looked especially native, but, when Evegnia offered to make everyone a cup of tea in broken Greek, Emiliana's heart leapt out of her bra.

A loud rapping at the window snaps her back into her present state and she extinguishes her fag in her frog-shaped ashtray. She can usually tell who's at her door by the way they announce themselves: Angelo uses his key and barges straight in without so much as a 'Hello, Mother,' while Ev used to ring the bell just the once and wait patiently for an answer.

'Lil? You in there?'

The intrusive knocking definitely sounds like Flor.

Emiliana mutters under her breath as she hunts beneath the sofa for her velvet slippers. Like the chef and the dancing, the woman is most definitely a Saturday morning pain in the backside. On the other hand, people are hardly flocking to hers for coffee these days, so Flora will just have to do.

'Flora Florides from Number 7 and it's a wonder we haven't met 'til now.'

'Isn't it just?' Emiliana's smile slid clean off her face the first time she clapped eyes on the silly woman. 'Then again, Missouri is a big close.'

'Yes, I suppose it is.' Flora peered curiously around the messy hallway. 'I hope I'm not intruding, only, Laura next door told me your friend just died so I've baked you an almond cake. You're not allergic to nuts?'

'Who?' Flora looked like a benevolent ghost from another century, standing in the doorway with her burnt cake and short red hair sticking up all over the place. Her translucent skin exposed a network of varicose veins running just beneath its surface. Emiliana had no idea who she was, let alone how this Laura supposedly knew about Ev. She let her in begrudgingly because she supposed it was the right thing to do, and Ev had *always* been on at her to be nicer.

And now she couldn't get rid of her. 'Lovely surprise, Flor,' Emiliana lies. 'Come in.'

'Thanks, Lil. I've come to check you're all right – what with, you know, your grief and everything . . .'

Flor waddles clumsily into her maisonette without relieving her duck feet of their shoes and Emiliana's blood bubbles at the sound of the ugly little heels clumping across her floors. It didn't cost much to kick them off, did it? Align them with the wall like her Ev used to do. Angelo was the same. Never took off his corpse-encrusted brogues, but heaven forbid she did the same when she visited his private mausoleum.

'Tea, Flor?'

'No, I'm not stopping, Lil. Things to do. Busy busy!'

The same charade every time, and the sight of the silly woman half sandwiched in her worn-out sofa because she is the total opposite of busy sparks a violent desire to chain-smoke. She rummages around for her cigarettes in the pockets of her cardigan before reluctantly extending one to Flor.

Flora chews the inside of her cheek. 'No thanks, I've decided to quit.'

'Really?' Emiliana's stylish eyebrows shoot up in surprise. 'Since when?'

'Since about two and a half hours ago.'

Emiliana mourns the last thing they had in common. 'I see.'

'It's vintage, by the way.' Flor's shiny blue eyes follow

Emiliana's glare across the room. 'The dress I'm wearing. I can see you're admiring it.'

'I am, and it's really . . . something.'

'Thank you – I got it from the charity shop on the high street last Wednesday. The heart place. I can take you next week if you like. They might have something for you, too?'

'Lovely.' It's the real reason she's come over, Emiliana thinks, flicking her lighter too close to her eye and almost cremating the pupil. To show off her tasteless outfit and moan about this Laura next door.

'Her kids are feral, Lil. Can hardly hear the telly with all their shrieking through the walls.'

Tell you what, Lil,' she continues from in between the folds of the carnivorous couch, 'if I was Laura next door, I'd pour myself a nice gin bath and quietly drown in it. Who'd have children these days? No offence,' she adds, sheepishly. 'I mean little sticky shouty ones, not grown-up, successful ones like your son.'

At the mention of gin, Emiliana's eyes flash mischievously. 'Shall we, Flor?' It's only eleven thirty but she can't possibly deal with the woman sober.

'Why not!'

She bounces into the kitchen to search for her best gin glasses with the alacrity of someone in her twenties. It's been a while since she's used them and she has to put her hands through a fair few cobwebs first, but, when she finally retrieves them from the back of the cupboard, Emiliana cries out in horror.

'Oh, Ev, my darling!'

The downside of never washing up is that Ev's pink lips are still all over her rims, and she promptly drops the glasses into the sink. They smash into smithereens and she's lost, suddenly. Lost in a little trickle of red memories and unsure what to do next.

She calls out weakly for her replacement friend. 'Flor . . .'

'You OK, Lil?' The woman extricates herself from the clapped-out couch and waddles to Emiliana's side, her face the colour of bleach. 'Oh dear, you've cut your finger. I'm not very good with blood, I'm afraid. Have you got one of them kits?'

'Kits?'

'A first aid thingy?'

'Do I look like a woman with a first aid kit in her kitchen cupboard, Flor?'

'I suppose not.' Flora bites the inside of her cheek again while Emiliana shouts at her to do something, anything, before she haemorrhages to death.

'Got any tissues?'

Evgenia would have had her finger all bandaged up by now. Bandaged up and kissed for good measure and instead, Emiliana is lumbered with bloody Flora Florides, a living reminder that life is laughing in her face.

She hasn't spoken to Angelo in weeks. Not since the conversation about his biological father – or 'the sperm donor', as Emiliana prefers to call him. She supposes it's the last she'll hear from him now, now that he's got what he wanted. 'That it, Angelo?' she asks the answering machine in his private mausoleum. 'You've buggered off now you've divested your mother of every last shred of her dignity? Charming.'

There's a clatter as she smashes the telephone into the receiver and hopes the racket will make his ears bleed. She dials again and with increasingly shaky fingers to tell him exactly that. 'I hope your ears are bleeding *right now*, Angelo!'

'Is that what you're worried about, my darling?' Ev whispered during one of their final, bedridden conversations. 'That's why you haven't told him the man's name yet – you're worried he'll fly to Cyprus and try and find him?'

The woman who knew her best was right again. Maybe she was afraid that her son would take the last ace from up her sleeve and disappear from her life for good. Worse still, that he would find Nico and invite him back. What then? A giant mountain of repercussions crashing down on her head as the lemon farmer sauntered back in to play pappa? Who would he be to her, then. A step-lover? Is that what the English called them?

'That won't happen, love,' Ev rasped.

'Why not?' Emiliana's frown lines were almost bone deep. 'Why won't it, Ev? Happens all the time in films.'

'Angelo would have to find him first and even if he did, is this man really going to want to jeopardise everything at his age? Upset his grown-up kids, share his estate with a stranger?'

'Estate? I would hardly call his lemon trees an estate.'

Ev's room already reeked of death. It was the same fleshy smell that had infected their bedroom in the last weeks of Theo's life. She knew it meant they didn't have much time together and Emiliana spoke more hurriedly than usual.

'I'll tell him, Ev,' she soothed. 'I'll tell him his father's name, but only for you.' She knew it was important to Evgenia and she said it to assuage her friend in her dying days more than anything else, but, once she'd flung the words from her mouth, she couldn't very well shove them back in.

'I know you will, my darling. I think it's high time, you know I do,' Ev replied, the last of her day's energy dissipating into her damp bedsheets and Emiliana's signal to get lost.

'Oh, Ev.' It's too soon to remember her best friend like that. Slowly leaking into her duvet. She pours herself a large glass of wine and heads down the hallway and into her bedroom to lick her wounds. Ten thirty, and she has no idea what her son is doing or who he's with. If he's out with someone special, or if he's at home by himself, contemplating his coffin empire. He may as well be a stranger off the street, she thinks, as she sprawls out in her bed like a bored queen. A stranger living across the road, because she knows more about Laura next door to Flora than she does about her own sprog.

She polishes off the wine in two impressive gulps and hopes that when it comes, her sleep will be dreamless.

~

They scuttled out of Limassol like a trio of guilty beetles the summer she turned twenty-three.

Her crazy brother was fit to strangle her as Louka's mother screamed threats through their blue shuttered windows. Promises of total moral humiliation for yet another broken engagement.

'How many men is that now, sister?'

'His breath stinks.'

Klito's dark eyes bored into her soul from the corner of the living room. 'So, buy the man a toothbrush.'

'His feet, too!'

'Throw a bucket of water over the filthy bastard, then.'

'*You* throw a bucket of water over him. I don't want to be near him any more – *that's* the whole point!'

Her brother picked at his teeth with a sharp fruit knife and rocked maniacally in their dead pappa's chair, swearing both under his breath and out loud. 'Selfish bitch. *You* are all you ever think about, that's the problem. Not his breath.' He flung the knife across the room in a fit of rage and stabbed their papery father in the eye.

'Mamma, tell him.' Emiliana ducked out of the way in the nick of time and flicked her delicious hair around to elicit the sympathy she deserved.

'Why should she get any sympathy?'

'I've lost a fiancé *and* nearly been blinded in the same wretched afternoon!'

'Lost him?' Klito mocked. 'You didn't lose him, you dumb cow. He's in the shower scrubbing his armpits where you left him an hour ago.'

'His parents built you a nice house in anticipation of marriage,' her mother chimed in. 'What's wrong with you that you couldn't have said something about this a year and a half ago?' She unravelled her headscarf and used it to mop her brow. 'Daughter?' Her own delicious dark hair tumbled over her shoulders and down her back to remind Emiliana of the single most important thing in life: whose ravishing looks she had inherited.

'If it's even true.' More sneers from Crazy Klito. 'She stinks worse than he does, I bet. All the men she's been to bed with.'

Her mother looked alarmed. 'Bed? You've been to *bed* with the young man? The mother is telling the truth out there about you being practically married to her son? Because God knows the entire marina can hear her shouting.'

'Of course not, Mamma,' Emiliana lied, but she hesitated and her brother threw a bigger knife into their pappa.

'Of course she's let him fuck her. Just like all the others. She can't help herself.'

'*Thkiaole*, this again!' Her mother's voice trembled as she dragged two leather suitcases out from beneath the bed and stuffed them full of despair.

Emiliana tutted at the unbelievable inconvenience of it all. 'What are you doing? Where are we going now? What about my nice things, Mamma?' she asked, dodging ornaments aimed at her head by her lazy, unemployed brother. A man of almost twenty-five having to drag his arse out of his chair and tag along with the women rather than earn his own living.

'Get a job, donkey brains.'

'Get a lock for your fanny and then maybe we could all live in peace.'

'Eiy!' Her mother silenced them both with the threat of a hard slap. 'We're going to Morphou. My late aunt's place is still empty. Just for a while, until people forget about you.'

'Forget about *me*?' It seemed an excessively severe punishment for a silly broken heart.

Nobody wanted to go. Tempers flared, more possessions grew wings and flew, and Emiliana cried at the unfairness of it all as her brother made dents in his knuckles.

'Whore! Slut!'

'So the options are to marry a man who doesn't make me happy, or run away in shame – is that it, Mamma?' she cried as the snot ran down her face. 'Are you going to let Klito speak to me like that, by the way? Call me those horrible names? Look at me, Mamma, I'm a complete mess. Will someone please pass me a cloth?'

A dirty flying rag smacked her in the face.

Still, she thought, as the lemony town of Morphou loomed into view a few days later and a peasant stopped in his tracks to cry 'Beautiful goddess!' at their passing car, there was always *that*.

~

The phone rings twice before Stelio picks it up.

"Ello, Mrs A.' His voice is like warm chocolate sauce, she thinks. A little bit naughty and very, very delicious.

'Is my idiot son there?'

An incredulous chortle. 'Like that is it, Mrs A?'

'I'm afraid so, Stelio.'

'Let me check.' She imagines him setting the phone down and breezing along Angelo's hideous pink corridors – or 'the bronchi', as the smart-arse liked to call them – his curly shoes facing outwards and his pert bum cheeks clenching in synchrony with the torso inside his shirt. A soft moan escapes from her lips and takes her by surprise.

There's a crackle as he returns from his errand. 'He's with a client right now, Mrs A, but I can take a message?'

She has two words for the ungrateful sod but she imprisons them behind gritted teeth. 'Oh, Em,' says Evgenia, shaking her ethereal golden halo at her from the ceiling. 'Leave the boy be.'

'Client?' she cries. 'Is that the best he can do? Well, just tell him his poor mother called *again*, OK?'

'I'll be sure to.' Another chuckle. She can tell he's about to hang up. That he's already turned his attention towards his paperwork and his client meetings. His lunch from the Italian deli across the street. She can hear it in his fading voice and she panics at the thought of being plunged back into the solitude of her flat so quickly after summoning another person.

She twists the telephone cord around her index

finger. She wishes she were twenty years younger or at least better at the vacuous conversation. Attractive men used to come on to her and not the other way around, and she doesn't know what to say. How to start. As for Theo, from what she could remember, theirs had mostly been a relationship of exclamation marks. 'Don't forget Angelo's hat!' 'Take the bins out!' 'Pass me my fags, they're next to the toaster!'

She supposes he saved the 'deep and meaningfuls' for Daphne.

'Angelo treating you well then, Stelio?'

That and his dick.

'Oh, he's the best, Mrs A. The very best.'

'The best?' Emiliana scoffs sarcastically. 'So everyone keeps telling me. Well, I guess I'll just have to read about him in the local paper, won't I?'

'Sorry again, Mrs A.'

She bangs the phone down and contemplates calling his house one more time. She even has a speech prepared for his answering machine but she abandons the idea in favour of a large glass of sparkling wine. Flora brought it round a few days ago. 'To toast the memory of your lovely late friend,' and she could have told her she didn't like fizzy drinks if the woman had bothered to ask. That the bubbles got on her nerves and up her nose and made her nauseous long before they made her drunk.

Ev would have known something like that, she thinks, twisting the cap off the bottle with a snake's hiss. Ev would never have brought round a bottle of fizzy plonk as a gift, but then, replacement Ev was definitely *not* her best friend.

She sparks a fag and spends a minute or two coughing up the contents of her lungs into her dishevelled living room. She fantasises about Stelio's bum while she's gasping for breath. His cheeky grin and lovely green eyes. 'They're like emeralds,' she exclaimed to Angelo, the first time he introduced them. 'So beautiful.' She wishes her eyes were bright green instead of carob brown.

'Not to mention he's exceptionally handsome.'

'Yeah? The ladies seem to think so,' her son admitted grudgingly. 'He's always got a girl on the go.'

Emiliana couldn't resist riling him; she never could. 'You know, Angelo, they say green is also the colour of envy?'

Another few gulps and she's fizzy enough to summon Flor. If it was any other day, any other day but Tuesday, she'd sink the bottle and take a long nap to while away the interminable hours. Today, though, she could use the company. She flicks through the paltry list of names in her address book with a damp finger; she hasn't spoken to most of them in decades and has no idea if they're alive or dead. 'Davos?' Was that a man or a business, she wonders, because they were never a friend, and by the time she arrives at 'F' she hopes the woman's out.

She sighs as her finger circles the Wheel of Doom.

'Lil? Is that you?' Flora sounds out of breath. 'I was just thinking about calling *you*!' As if she's been rushing to answer the telephone, and Emiliana is suddenly filled with revulsion for her. Disgust that the poor cow could need her friendship so badly that she might break her neck flying down the stairs.

'I've just opened your bottle of fizz, Flor – thought you might like to share?' She wants to laugh at her desperation. To ridicule her sad, pathetic life. To tell her she hopes she'll pour herself a gin bath and drown in it instead of this Laura next door.

'I'd love to, Lil.'

More's the pity, Emiliana thinks.

'I just have to feed Burt Reynolds first. Although I suspect Laura's been leaving food out for him, too,' she grumbles, 'because he's never hungry these days.'

'All right, you feed the cat and I'll see you in a bit, then.'

'I'll change my dress as well, put on the one you like from the charity?'

'Lovely, Flor.'

Emiliana finishes her cigarette and contemplates a new one. So, this is what it's finally come to? she thinks, trudging over to the window in her velvet slippers to wait for the ridiculous woman. A life of curtain-twitching? Waiting for a friend like Flora? It's all so bloody undignified.

～

The Mayor of Morphou's wife looked like a withered goat. Her face was covered in wispy white hair and her voice sounded goatish, too. 'I've come about your lovely daughter, Emili-aa-naa.'

Her mother's handsome face registered more emotions in a split second than a person experiences in a lifetime. Shock, surprise, confusion, acceptance and finally, the faintest sliver of pride. There they were, the three of them, cowering in shame in her dead aunt's house, when who should knock on their door to redeem them from despair?

'Mrs Mayor! Please, do come in from this infernal sun.' She ushered the expensively dressed woman into their shadowy front room and relieved her of her straw hat, hastily taming her own curls with her fingers and stuffing her shabby apron in the nearest domestic orifice. 'Emiliana, would you pour a glass of cold triantafyllo for our esteemed guest?'

Emiliana tutted in irritation. She'd been peeling penance potatoes over the sink for the past half an hour and wasn't in the mood for silly pleasantries. As the mountain of yellowish-brown carbohydrate rose in front of her, she fantasised about stabbing her little knife into the jugulars of her various tormentors. She would begin by murdering Louka's mother before lacerating the members of her disloyal clan with the same bloody blade. That would teach them to relegate her to scullery maid for daring to assert some independence.

'Emiliana! Will you pour the drink before the poor woman faints from heat exhaustion and we get sued?' The last bit slipped out by mistake.

What about Klito, she thought, as she rinsed the mud from her hands and untied her own unflattering apron from her waist. Why wasn't he being punished for calling her a whore? Come to think of it, why were men never punished for anything?

Mrs Goat accepted the glass gratefully. She gulped down the rose cordial before pulling a fan that cost more than their borrowed table out of her leather handbag. 'I'm ever so thankful for the refreshment. This awful heat! When will it end?'

Suitably un-shrivelled, she began to bleat to them about an orange festival. Every year, she explained between vigorous, lacy wafts, the residents of Morphou celebrated the citrus trees that held the town in their embrace by hosting a parade in their honour. It was a joyous event, with floats and basketfuls of fruit and, of course, a beautiful queen. This year, her husband the Mayor wondered if the lovely Emiliana might like to wear the crown. Mrs Goat paused to examine the effect of her words on the girl's bemused mother. 'At the parade, I mean.'

'He wants to crown Emiliana "Miss Portokalia"?'

'He most certainly does. She has been noticed around the town of Morphou, you see, and her good looks greatly remarked upon.'

'I bet they have.' Her mother inhaled the stale Cypriot air through her nostrils. Good looks, her arse. Trouble, more like. 'How very kind of the Mayor to think of us.'

'There will be several young ladies taking part in the event, but Emiliana will be the face of the parade. She will even have her own throne while the plainer ones . . .' Mrs Goat lowered her voice, 'will have to sit on the upturned crates.'

'Oh!' Emiliana pretended to gush proudly.

'We're a very private little family,' her mother lied through her smoker's teeth. In reality, she wondered what might happen if Louka's mother caught a whiff of the affair. Her daughter celebrating her son's heartbreak on top of a float full of oranges; it was surely akin to public gloating. In fact, it *was* public gloating, plain and simple. No other way to dress the thing up. On the other hand, it would be advantageous to befriend the rich and powerful Goats.

'Of course,' more bleating. 'But I can assure you that the parade is a wholesome family event and nothing at all to be concerned about. Emiliana's dress will be completely modest and not in the slightest bit transparent.' She lowered her voice to a soft bleat. 'Although I am sure there are some that might like it to be.'

'Will it be photographed, this event?' her mother interrupted nervously. 'I wouldn't want my Emiliana's picture to appear in any of the newspapers. It wouldn't be very becoming for an unmarried lady . . .'

'I give you my word.'

Her mother threw her own drink down her throat as if the answer to the orange dilemma might be hiding at the bottom of the glass. She told Mrs Goat she would think very hard about her kind offer. That usually preceded a capitulation and if Emiliana had been ten she would have twirled around the living-room table! Picked up her skirts and kicked her legs in the air! Maybe even kissed the wife's soft, furry cheeks. Instead, she flicked her delicious curls from side to side and beamed just like a queen might beam.

The scraping of wooden chair legs signalled the end of Mrs Goat's errand. 'I'll be in touch, then, Mrs . . . ?'

'Thank you very much for coming.'

For all the talk of her great beauty, she thought later, nobody paid her the slightest bit of attention that scorching August morning. Aside from a fleeting nod from the Goat for pouring her a cordial, Emiliana wasn't acknowledged at all.

~

Emiliana regards Flora Florides, now sprawled on her sofa, with a new contempt, and she blames the fizzy wine. She stares at the woman's anachronistic clothes and shoes, her wide-open legs in their laddered tights, her ridiculous red hairstyle and pink, breathless face.

'You been rushing around again, Flor?' she asks acidly.

'I didn't want to miss out on the wine, Lil.' At least she has the good grace to look ashamed. 'Seems I was a little late, though,' she adds sadly.

She was late. Emiliana grew bored of twitching by herself and polished off three-quarters of the bottle in revenge. The two women are forced to share the last few dribbles and she offers her guest a hollow 'Sorry, Flor,' that neither of them believe.

'Well, I'm here now. I can nip out and get us another from the offy if you're up for it, Lil?'

Emiliana lights her fortieth fag of the day and drags on it gratefully. Sometimes she likes to delude herself that she's doing the cigarette a favour by deigning to smoke it, and other times she can't deny the truth. That Angelo is right. That she needs the nicotine in the same way that she needs water or oxygen.

'Don't bother, Flor. I'll probably head to bed after this.' She's being deliberately snide, she knows she is, and it's because it's Card Tuesday and the woman sitting opposite her is *not* the Queen of Hearts.

'All right then, Lil, I'll sip slowly.' She's rambling on about bloody Laura next door again. How she took great pleasure in swanning past her and declaring that she was 'off to see a friend' because she can't imagine that mumsy Laura has any mates of her own.

She hardly knows a thing about Flora Florides, Emiliana thinks, continuing to scrutinise her coldly from across the living room, while she's heard far too much about this Laura. How she's blonde and willowy. How she ties her hair back most days and how it suits her because she's pretty but only in a plain way. How she has three stupid children whose names all begin with the same letter. How she drives them to school in her Ford Sierra and then rushes home to bake cookies. How her handsome husband is called Benjamin, but she affectionately refers to him as 'Bun'.

'How on earth did you find all this out?' Emiliana asked her once, her mouth open wider than Flor's legs. 'You been stalking her?'

'Oh, you know . . .' Emiliana did not know. As

someone with little interest in other people and their lives, she genuinely didn't have the foggiest. 'Snatched bits and bobs over the garden fence, mainly.'

'Mainly? And what about the other snatched bobs?'

Emiliana wonders, as the insufferable woman drones on, if her replacement friend might be a teensy bit jealous of this Laura next door. If the woman's kids were not feral brats but polite brats who played the piano after school and taught themselves little rhymes in French. The kind of brats she used to fantasise about when Angelo was hanging out with the druggies.

She decides to rattle Flora's cage. 'Trapped in the conservatory all day, Flor? I don't know about that; the life you describe sounds pretty idyllic to me.' She wonders, as she huffs and puffs on her cigarette, if this Bun has the same dreamy eyes as Stelio. The same tight arse cheeks. Another purr escapes from her lips. 'Isn't that what every woman wants at the end of the day? A nice-looking husband and two or three kids. Enough money to stay home and bake brownies while they're at school?'

Flora frowns into her smudged wine glass. 'Don't you think that a woman in her mid-thirties ought to have a little bit more going on than school runs and baking, though?' She lowers her voice to a loud whisper, as if this Laura next door might overhear them. 'All seems a bit *boring* to me.'

'Boring?' Emiliana shrieks in delight. She can see that she has annoyed the stupid woman and allows herself a victorious smirk. 'Really? So what is it that the childless do with their day that's so blooming wonderful? Do please enlighten me.'

Flora has passed the mildly annoyed phase and is now firmly flustered, but there isn't enough alcohol left in the bottle to continue Emiliana's cruel game. She takes her foot off the gas and cuts the woman some slack. 'Sorry, Flor. I guess what I'm trying to say is that you've no idea what her life is like and you probably shouldn't judge. Just like you wouldn't want Laura to think that the highlight of your day is a packet of reduced-to-clear custard creams and a jigsaw puzzle, I'm sure.'

There. The last part was a bit bitchy and she's not sure she believes any of it herself, but it sounded like something Evgenia might have said. Something that sounded like something kind . . .

In reality, she partly agrees with Flora. Laura's life sounds dull and suffocating. Emiliana hated mothering Angelo and couldn't imagine willingly having three of him. Still, there's something about hearing all this from the mouth of someone without kids of her own that incenses her in a way she can't explain, a way that's almost irrational, and she wants to prise herself out of her clapped-out sofa and wrap her hands around the woman's veiny throat. To scream, 'Shut up, Flor, what the hell would *you* know? How many sprogs have you squeezed out?' into her stupid face.

'Perhaps.' Flora looks as if she's swallowed a chilli seed that is in the process of over-heating her stomach. 'You're the expert on families, Lil,' she admits. 'I guess it all just seems a bit tedious from where I'm sitting. Like there should be more to life.'

'Well when you find out what it is, you be sure to let me know.' Emiliana wonders if Flor's other problem is that she likes this Laura a bit *too* much.

'Now what are you bloody on about?' She can hear Angelo spluttering in her ear after poor Ev's last Christmas party. 'What do you care if Aunty Ev invited Sarah?'

'I'm allowed my opinion, Angelo.'

'Not if it's offensive, you're not.' He almost threw her out of his Jag and into the cold that night without so much as a 'Merry Christmas'.

'Charming.'

If Flora is a lesbian, Emiliana concedes, she can't be a very popular one, seeing as all she does is sit on her neighbour's settee wearing her hideous dresses.

'What about you, Lil?' says Flora, dusting herself off bravely and rising from the ashes like a singed phoenix. 'Did you not want any more kids after your Angelo?'

Emiliana melts back into the couch, nursing her newest fag. 'Theo would have quite liked one of his own, I suppose, but to be honest with you, I didn't want any to begin with. Angelo was an accident. Well, "mistake" probably sums him up the best.'

Flora drains her glass of its condensation and shuffles around in her seat. *This* is more like it. This is what she pulled her best frock and torn tights on for. 'Oh?' The confrontations made her uncomfortable but the gossip she absolutely lived for. 'Did I hear right, Lil?'

'You did, Flor.' Oops. A drunken lapse in concentration brought about by the cheap bubbles up her nose, but in for a penny, Emiliana thinks – and what did it matter now, anyway, now that Ev was dead, Theo was even deader and Angelo had disappeared into one of his coffins?

There was nobody left to care. 'Angelo isn't Theo's son.'

Besides, Emiliana can't resist the mounting temptation to insert herself into another woman's life. With Evgenia newly buried, she needs to feel like the star of the show again, to be the centre of attention, and who better to pounce on, she thinks, than the impressionable, available Flor?

She pulls at the hairband restraining her long grey curls and shakes them loose the way her mother used to when she was serious. 'It's like this, Flor . . .'

Only this time, she'll try to tell it like it *really* happened.

~

'There is something I have to tell you, Nico.' Emiliana ran her fingers through her long, dark hair the way her mother used to. 'But first, I'd like to know what your intentions are towards me.'

That night in the cemetery, she was aware of her surroundings as if for the first time. How the stars were almost close enough to touch and shone like diamonds in the darkness and how, when she tilted her head as far back as it would go, she felt as though she was sailing among them. How the summer air was thick with the scent of the lemon trees, the same tangy scent she could smell on Nico's skin when they made love on top of the graves. How, when they were perfectly still, she could hear only the cicadas and the noise of her beating heart.

She was happy her float had stopped in front of him at Mrs Goat's orange festival the previous September. It was fortuitous. The parade where she was supposed to keep her eyes on her knees and definitely *not* look around for a new fiancé. Her mother's only rule and she'd broken it, but who could resist gazing at their sea of admirers? What kind of queen would begrudge them an orange and a smile?

She loved being pursued through the dusty streets of Morphou in the months that followed the encounter. Being told she was wonderful and beautiful and hearing Nico's obsession with her sizzling like the matches he struck against the tombstones, or her mother's rabbit stews. To feel him moaning against her neck because she was so delicious that he couldn't stop tasting her, not even for a second. For all her experience, Emiliana had never known a love as passionate as this one and she'd certainly never felt so desired.

'My *intentions*?' He sent his cigarette butt skidding into the darkness and instantly reached into his pack for another. She noticed that his hands shook nervously as he cupped them around his mouth.

He loved the cemetery behind St Angelo's Church.

Sitting among the old graves, he told her, was a life-affirming experience.

'What a strange thing to say.'

'Strange how?'

'Death pleases you?'

'I didn't say that. I said it makes me feel alive.'

'I don't understand.'

'Well, where better to be reminded that you exist than in a graveyard full of bones?' He gestured around the dark cemetery with his cigarette and the cicadas sniggered their response.

'I don't know – maybe somewhere where everyone else is alive, too. Like a party?'

'A party? You're very funny,' he chuckled. 'You know that?'

He was a real know-it-all. It was a wonder he didn't get bored plucking his father's lemon trees all day with his stupid ideas swirling around in his head.

Emiliana turned to face him. To study his small forehead and large crooked nose. His skin, tanned and creased from the hours spent toiling in the sun. This mysterious Nico. Too short to be considered handsome, but too attractive to be entirely dismissed. Too clever to sell lemons at the market, but too lazy to do anything to change that.

She felt confident in her future as he lit his trembling cigarette and smothered the match beneath his sandal. Confident in the crushed diamonds that sparkled above them, the emblems of fidelity and marriage. In the eyes that said they couldn't live without her. Which was just as well, because her eyes were as wide as saucers, and shone not with diamonds, but with fear.

She was pregnant.

Two, maybe more months along, and she knew the signs because she'd been pregnant once before. Only last time, the baby had oozed from her womb in a river of black, lumpy blood. So much blood that she'd gasped at her stained hands in astonishment. She'd been relieved, really, when the bleeding slowed down and she was well enough to get out of bed. When she'd finally stopped imagining what the child might have looked like if he had lived long enough to be born.

What he might have smelled like.

This time, there was no blood in her underwear or on her shaking hands, but there was the lemon farmer from Morphou. This time would be different because he was crazy about her and he'd declared his love many times.

'Well, Nico?'

The problem was that he was too busy smoking. 'Well what?'

'Do you ever plan on asking me to marry you, or are we to carry on like this forever? As secret lovers in a graveyard?'

There was only his silence as he exhaled smoke into her lovely diamonds and examined his tar-stained fingers. As if the salient thing that night was not her question or even her fears, but the fact that he hadn't scrubbed his hands well enough.

Her eyes brimmed with tears of disbelief and she was

afraid that if she sat next to him any longer, they would spill down her cheeks and betray her childish fantasies. That he would sneer at her the way her brother had when she'd broken off her engagement to Louka. Call her the hateful things men flung at the women they didn't value or respect. Women who drank spirits and smoked cigarettes in graveyards. Women who gave birth to babies out of wedlock. How could he do this horrible thing to his supposedly sizzling Emiliana?

She stood to her feet, her cheeks stinging with his rejection and her humiliation. 'You're unbelievable, Nico, you know that?' How could she have been so deluded?

'Me?' he croaked weakly. 'What did I do?'

He sounded like a frog, she thought, as she shook her dusty skirts into his upturned face and melted into the darkness with her secret. A stupid, pathetic frog.

~

'A frog?' Well and truly out of booze, the two women migrate into the tiny kitchen to watch the kettle boil. 'Oh, Lil, how awful for you! You must have been so terrified, in those strict times as well . . .'

Emiliana searches her consolation friend's eyes for sympathy and decides that, at least for the time being, she likes who she sees reflected there. The *real* Emiliana. Not Angelo's moody mother or Theo's ungrateful wife, but someone who's endured a lifetime of injustice and deserves all the condolences she can collect.

It's not turning out to be a bad Card Tuesday after all, she concedes. 'A bloody frog, Flor.' She looks around for her favourite ashtray to desecrate as the kettle completes its climactic whistle and spews water all over the counter. 'And I think "petrified" is the word you're looking for.'

'After all that crooning about how gorgeous you were, too. Blooming cheek of the man to turn his back on you like that.'

'Wasn't it?'

'So, what happened next?' Flora's eyes beg her for more narrative, and the upside of having a friend with no discernible personality, she thinks, is that there's more time to talk about herself.

'Pass me a couple of mugs, Flor.' Emiliana pours the tea into the proffered cups and blows ripples over the top. She enjoys watching her reflection split into a million distorted pieces before the fragments still to a whole.

'And grab the biscuit tin while you're at it. It's on the top shelf next to the new first aid kit.' She flicks her hair around proudly. 'Now, where were we?'

~

It was after midnight by the time she'd wheezed her way back to the dead aunt's home, maybe even later – Emiliana didn't know or care any more. She'd lost all sense of perspective, along with her pride and a litre of sweat. She'd half hoped Nico would pursue her through the lemon trees and half hoped that he wouldn't. It was too late anyway. Too late to make amends for his deathly silence by telling her he was sorry *now*.

Careful not to wake up her mother and brother, Emiliana orbited the furniture in contemplation, fearing death by dehydration and grateful for only one thing: the bare white walls of their temporary accommodation. The absence of disapproving, papery predecessors frowning from their various hanging spaces. Her pappa's bushy, living-room moustache; her grandmother's spidery, kitchen eyebrows.

'What am I supposed to do now, Yiayia?' she cried in desperation. 'Now that he's gone and left me with a baby?'

She considered an apocalyptic event. Running a hot bath and sinking into it with a bottle of her brother's strongest spirit. Taking a coat hanger and shoving it up her whatsit to end the nightmare and salvage her fragile reputation. Knowing *her* unlucky stars, though, she'd probably kill herself along with it. 'Dying for Nico in a bath full of ouzo?' Self-preservation kicked in like a mule with rabies. 'Not a bloody chance.'

There was only one thing for it. She dragged her mother's suitcase of despair out from the cupboard and filled it with yet more despair. She would return home. Back to the familiar landscape of Limassol where she could think straight, not in circles that made her head spin. Put some distance between herself and her brother's fruit knife. Maybe even make an appointment with a doctor to confirm what she already suspected.

She heaved her bulging case into the back of Klito's pick-up truck and decided that, as she was already concealing a baby, taking her brother's vehicle was negligible in comparison. Emiliana turned the keys in the ignition with trembling fingers and sighed with relief as the old Chevrolet spluttered to life. Finally, some bloody luck. Women weren't supposed to drive cars. It was improper, along with anything else that was any fun, so she felt powerful executing her three-point-no-return and heading back to the south of the island. So powerful that she even wound down the window as she left the shadows behind, and made waves with her hand in the half-light.

~

Emiliana sinks back into the sofa to admire her effect on Flora. 'That's it, Flor.'

'So . . .' Flora twitches in satisfaction. 'Theo was the handsome gynaecologist in Limassol who confirmed that you were expecting?'

'He was indeed. Paul Newman married me warts and all, Flor – and by warts I do mean Angelo.'

Flora's tea claims another chocolate finger as it slips from her grasp. 'Wow, Lil. You're so brave.' She reaches into the tin for a new one, bypassing the teacup and shovelling it straight into the back of her mouth. 'What a story – especially the part where you drove off into the sunrise with your hand waving out of the window. Gave me chills!'

'Thanks, Flor.'

'Well, how marvellous.'

It won't last, Emiliana thinks, sadly. Her replacement friend's adulation won't survive the night, but she basks in the glow of it anyway. In a few minutes' time, Flora will want to know what happened to the lemon farmer, just like Ev did all those years ago.

She recalls it well. They were in her old house on Addison Avenue, sitting beneath the jellyfish lampshade, a bowl of spicy crackers nestled between them, and Emiliana couldn't bring herself to tell her. 'How could you do such a terrible thing, Em?' she imagined her tutting. 'Honestly?'

She couldn't tell the handsome doctor who offered to save her future and hand it back to her all giftwrapped, either. She flung her arms around him that day and sobbed into his delicious neck for all she was worth. The lemon father had abandoned her with a baby, she cried, dabbing at the corners of her eyes with her knuckles, and she had nobody else to turn to.

She was lucky she was so beautiful. It was something her mother would scream at her in the midst of an argument. That an uglier woman would have begged twice as hard to be rescued from anything and especially moral oblivion.

'Who is this *garo*?' Paul Newman asked as he stroked her luscious curls, his face creased with astonishment. 'This unscrupulous donkey who could do this to a woman like you?' She wished he'd taken his rubber gloves off first.

'What does it matter, doctor?' she sniffed, fearful of those hands going in her lovely hair. 'What does it matter now?'

Emiliana plonks her cup next to the piles of well-thumbed magazines and sparks up a cigarette. 'Lil?' Flora prompts. 'So, what did this lemon farmer say when you told him you were pregnant?'

Emiliana sighs. *This* part definitely calls for a smoke. 'I never did tell Nico about the baby, Flor.'

'You what, Lil?'

'As I just said, Flor.' Emiliana can see the admiration emptying from Flora's eyes like bathwater glugging out of a tub.

'What do you mean, you never told him?' the silly woman blusters into her teacup. 'You're saying you kept the baby a secret from him in an act of revenge?'

'Exactly, Flor.' Emiliana drops her cigarette butt into her frog-shaped ashtray because there's no point in rubbing it in any more. 'Don't you think he deserved it, though, for what he did to me in the graveyard?'

'But you've told your Angelo the truth?' The chocolate fingers have given Flora a faint moustache, which now wiggles up and down in agitation. 'He knows what happened?'

'Not yet. Just you, actually, Flor. I will tell him, though. I'm just waiting for the right time.'

Wasn't she always?

'Goodness! I don't quite know what to say.' Her consolation friend executes a strangulated half-gasp as a cold and uncomfortable silence shrouds the living room.

Emiliana gets up to switch the telly on for a bit of light relief. It's been a long evening. There's a repeat of the baking show on BBC2. The ugly chef with the fat nose is unveiling a chocolate soufflé sprinkled with icing sugar. He seems particularly pleased with himself, she thinks. 'It looks nice, don't you think, Flor?' The two women stare in silence at the screen as he brings a spoonful of the dessert to his mouth. 'The chocolate soufflé, I mean?'

Emiliana dislodges her wedding ring from her finger and places it on the draining board with a clink. She fills the sink with warm, soapy water and dunks the dirty cups into it one by one. Living alone is exhausting, she thinks, careful not to let Angelo's favourite Arsenal mug slide out of her grasp and break. The sequence of small, mind-numbing tasks she has to execute daily, and she's still on her own at the end of it all. She pulls the plug out of the sink and hopes that the satisfied gurgle of a clean kitchen will rouse Angelo from his coffins. She holds her breath, counting to five and then ten and, finally, fifteen, waiting for the telephone to ring.

Saturday afternoon. He's most likely at home, doing whatever it is that death-obsessed people do in their spare time. Flicking through cremation catalogues or cleaning bits of corpse from his fingernails. Keeping up with the latest deadly trends. She smirks as she remembers his stupid toy skeleton. What kind of kid plays with bones?

She'll ring *him*, she thinks, circling the infernal Wheel

of Doom with still-damp fingers. She'll be the bigger person yet again.

'Hello?' A groggy voice takes her by surprise. She wasn't expecting anyone to answer the phone, especially not a woman. She's the first real person Emiliana has spoken to all week. Unless she counts the meaningless exchanges with the postman, or the grumpy old git who lives upstairs. Their conversations are always the same.

'Good morning, Mr Milosovich.'

'A good morning, is it? Tell it to my hip!'

As if she has time for other people's problems.

'Who is this?' Emiliana attempts to prevent her curiosity from compromising her casual tone.

'Priya. Who is *this*?' The strange woman sounds like she might be drunk. As if she's drowning in a soup of garbled, muffled words and she can hear Angelo mumbling in the background about spilling wine on the bedsheets.

Emiliana sighs for the millionth time that day. 'I'm Angelo's mother. Is he there?'

'Hang on a minute.' There's sniggering on the other end of the line, followed by a series of rancorous whispers. She's annoyed now, more than anything else, and by the time the connection is severed, she's feeling almost relieved. Pair of idiots, she thinks. Rolling around in bed in the middle of the day like teenagers. Doesn't he supposedly have an empire to run? And what sort of name is 'Priya', anyway? She narrows her eyes. Sounds suspiciously *Indian* to her.

She decides to try Flora again and she's dialled her that many times this week there's no need for the address book. She hasn't heard from her since the revelation about Nico and she wonders if this is what truth tastes like. Like silence and dust. She tilts her head up to the ceiling to taunt Evgenia. 'Seems a bit overrated to me?'

'Flor?'

When Flora eventually deigns to answer the telephone, her voice isn't particularly pleased to hear hers. 'Hello, Emiliana.'

Nobody ever calls her 'Emiliana'. It sounds strange. Accusatory, even.

'Took you long enough, Flor.' Her own voice is sharper than glass. 'Fancy a cuppa over at mine?'

There's a brief moment's hesitation before Flora tells her she's with Laura, and the cheek of it, the sheer, bloody cheek of the thing propels Emiliana's tongue down her throat.

'You're with Laura next door?'

'She's just popped round to get Xander's ball,' the stupid woman stammers. 'He kicked it over the garden fence and I was making coffee for myself anyway. Milk, Laura? Or I have double cream if you prefer something a bit more special?'

'You could have just thrown it back,' Emiliana interrupts, rudely. 'And it's "Xander", now, is it? What happened to "brat"? Well, suit yourself, then . . .' she continues, when Flora doesn't respond to her gibe. 'I only had ten minutes to spare. I have plans of my own tonight.' Flora blusters a bit but doesn't argue and it's just as well, because Emiliana wouldn't know what to say.

She slams the phone down into its cradle in irritation and trudges over to the window in her velvet slippers to twitch the curtains some more. 'Plans?' She makes herself laugh sometimes, she really does. She hasn't had any social plans since her Ev died. She sparks another fag, not because she particularly feels like one this time, but because it gives her something to do with her hands.

The world beyond her living-room curtain is bustling with young people celebrating their energy. A fresh-faced mother in tight, shiny leggings runs after a toddler. A teenage boy walks a sausage dog with tiny little legs. They make her feel tired, these youngsters with their whole lives ahead of them. Tired and lonely, as though the gap between what they are still capable of and what she has become has squeezed her out of the world.

She wonders where she would be today if Theo were still alive. Certainly not staring out between lacy curtains and watching kettles boiling. Scraping the bottom of the friendship barrel with the likes of Flora Florides. They would have proper friends, lots of them, and prestigious functions to attend in tuxedos and ball-gowns. Awards and galas, places where they would shine and be gossiped about.

'Don't they make a beautiful couple?'

'He's a senior consultant at Queen Charlotte's and she's gorgeous, even at her age.'

'Don't they look lovely together?'

'I love the dress. Is it real velvet?'

She brings her bare ring finger up to her face. He died twenty years ago in February and it strikes her, with a rare stab of sadness, that he's been gone for longer than she knew him. She thinks back to his funeral. Angelo in one of his sulks and the graveside packed with his handsome doctor friends. The 'genetically blessed', Ev used to call them when Theo was out of earshot. 'Strutting about at the top of the food chain, flaunting their brains and good looks. I don't know how you cope with it, Em, I really don't!'

She was at the funeral, of course. Daphne. Camouflaged among their colleagues for safety, her tears concealed behind huge sunglasses and dressed for the entire world like a budget Jackie Onassis. He never once introduced them. Never even confessed to loving her, but a wife knows these things and she said as much to Evgenia. 'A woman knows when her love rival is in the vicinity, Ev.' Emiliana could sense her in the surrounding air. As though there wasn't enough oxygen in the cemetery that day for the two of them to breathe.

Besides, Theo didn't need to admit to the affair. The woman *leaked* out of him. Daphne said this, Daphne did that, Daphne pass the salt. On the rare occasions when he was home early enough to join them for dinner she suspects, like most men who cheat on their wives, he wasn't even aware he was shedding her.

'What if you're wrong, Em?' Ev cautioned over her Tuesday night card-fan. 'What if this Daphne woman is just a colleague and not a lover at all?'

'Please! Who wouldn't want to sleep with Dr Theo?'

She suspected this Daphne was the reason Theo was so desperate to move them all to St Wherever. He wanted to buy a place near her house to facilitate their affair. Nothing to do with private schools and streets lined with trees. He wanted to close the miles between his family and his mistress and make his love life easier.

She refused, of course, and there were arguments. So many that she lost count, but she still remembers the night he knelt in front of the cracked fireplace mirror and accused *her* of being the home-wrecker.

~

'So *I'm* supposed to be the home-wrecker?' They bought a couple of return train tickets to Brighton and spent the whole day by the sea, just the two of them. 'Says the man who's never home to the wife who never goes anywhere. Maybe I should pack my bags and disappear – then he'd know what a home-wrecker looks like.'

They rented stripy deckchairs and plonked them next to the West Pier to enjoy strawberry ice-cream cones. Ev didn't believe her, she could tell. 'An affair?' She shook her head. 'Theo's crazy about you, Em. Anyone can see that.'

'Doesn't mean a thing, Ev. So he loves us both, so what?' Emiliana licked her ice cream to a point. 'Anyway,' she shook her cone at the sky, 'it's the sixties, they're all at it. Your Jimmy too, most probably.'

'Jimmy?' Evgenia chuckled good-naturedly, slipping off her shoes to sift pebbles beneath fat, inelegant feet. Her toenails sparkled pink, the same pink as her fingernails and her short checked dress. 'I guarantee you, my darling, the only side dish my Jimmy's indulging in is a dollop of taramasalata from Zeus.' She polished off the last of her ice cream and tossed the cone into the pebbles for the ants.

'If you say so, Ev.' Emiliana rubbed at her bare arms with a sigh as the cool breeze brushed over her skin and left goosebumps in its wake. 'Brighton Beach is hardly the Mediterranean, is it?' and as if to further illustrate the point, a lame dog urinated in front of them. 'Charming.'

'No, my darling, but think of all the advantages England has to offer.' Ev slipped her shoes back on and rummaged around for her matching pink cardigan.

'Like what?' Emiliana was now shivering uncontrollably but was too lazy to prop herself up. 'Can you pass me mine while you're down there, darling?'

'The politics, for one.' Ev pulled her best friend's cardigan out before going back in for her own. 'Not sure if you've been following what's going on over there, but Jimmy thinks Cyprus is heading for a civil war.'

'A civil war?' Emiliana could barely follow the trajectory of a finger without losing interest, never mind the path to a battle. 'Theo's never said.'

'Not to mention, there are plenty more opportunities here,' Ev pointed out. 'For the kids, I mean.'

'What opportunities? James-Dean is two and

Angelo's nine so I don't think we need to worry about medical school.' She shoved the last of her ice-cream cone into her gob with a loud crunch.

'Don't forget my Dezzy,' Ev chuckled. 'She's going to be twenty this year. I can hardly believe it myself.'

'Oops!' Emiliana always forgot about the forgettable Dezzy.

'She's just been offered a secretarial placement, as a matter of fact,' Ev declared proudly. 'In one of them posh law firms in Holborn. The ones with three surnames above the front door.'

'Secretary?' Emiliana's stylishly plucked eyebrows shot up in genuine surprise. Dezzy as someone's sexy assistant? Whatever next! 'She'll have to buy herself some new girly clothes, then,' she remarked helpfully, reaching into the pebbles for her packet of cigarettes. 'Men like their secretaries in tight skirts. Like on the telly.'

'I see.' A flock of seagulls swooped over silver waters and punctured the ensuing silence with their squawking. 'I'll be sure to tell her,' Ev replied finally, and her best friend's lack of pride was one of the things Emiliana loved most about her. While other women pretended that everything was perfect beneath their roofs, Ev was the first to admit that hers leaked.

'You're very welcome. Ciggy?'

An eruption of childish laughter reminded Ev that they were due some fun of their own and she bent over to pull a secret bottle of gin out of her handbag and wave it jubilantly in the air. 'Surprise! You up for a drink?'

'Always, Ev.'

She shoved a paper cup into Emiliana's hand and they raised them to husbands watching their own children and to wives enjoying some peace.

'First time I've left my little monkey, actually.' Ev hid her misty eyes behind an engraved lighter from Jimmy. 'For a whole day, I mean.'

James-Dean certainly was a monkey, Emiliana thought snidely. Forever hanging off his mother's tits. On the other hand, she was a bit envious of her friend's maternal inclinations. Her willingness to spend hours feeding ducks or pushing the little snot-monster on the swings. Sitting in a café with a plate of iced buns when she could have been watching *Double Your Money* with her feet up.

'You should come with us next Saturday,' Ev suggested. 'To the place we go to on the high street. They do lovely cakes. Bring your Angelo?'

Emiliana mumbled vaguely and in the direction of the water. She couldn't think of anything worse. Her son didn't want to spend any time with her, in a café or anywhere else. Angelo belonged to Angelo and he didn't need anyone to love him.

'Though . . . Saturday is his special day with Theo.' He certainly didn't need a mother, and that suited Emiliana just fine because she'd never asked to be one in the first place. 'He takes him to the park to ride his bicycle, although you'd think it was a Cadillac the way Theo goes on about it.'

'I see.' And Evgenia did, so there was no need to say any more.

They reclined in their flimsy chairs for hours, drinking neat gin out of paper cups and scoffing cheese and salami sandwiches to soak up the slosh. Gossiping about their husbands as the sea breeze lifted their hair clean off their shoulders and gently let it down again. Sauntering around the Lanes, afterwards, smiling shyly at the gangs of Rocker boys gathered for trouble in the alleys.

'All right, ladies?' And while their leather jackets and bushy sideburns did nothing for Emiliana, it did feel good to be admired by other men.

'Been a lovely day, my darling.' Ev leaned across to plant a drunken kiss on her friend's powdery cheek. 'Thanks for coming with me to Brighton.'

'Of course – where else would I rather be than with you?'

Just before half past eight, Ev looped her arm through hers and the pair of them bobbed happily back up the hill to the train station. Breathing in the last of the salty air as the sun sank beneath the candyfloss houses.

It was after ten when she waved goodnight to Ev. Stuck her key in the lock of her own front door and twisted it twice. She imagined her best friend doing the same thing two doors down. Jimmy ambushing her in the hallway with a glass of wine as she slipped her shoes off and aligned them carefully with the telephone table in their hallway. 'Thanks, my love. Been a very long day. You haven't seen my furry slippers by any chance?'

Stupid Jim would be fussing over her like he always

did – fetching her slippers, muttering that she was late, that he'd been getting worried. So worried that he'd almost rung the station in Brighton for the train times because he was so lost without her. Ev would hush him with a pink manicured finger, point to the ceiling and tiptoe up the stairs to coo at their sleeping child while Jimmy followed behind like an obedient dog. She would peer into the cot and stroke his curls, careful not to tip wine all over him. Brighton had been a real tonic, she would whisper to nobody in particular, but nothing beat the smell of home.

Standing in her own hallway two doors up, Emiliana tried hard to summon her own inner motherliness so she could experience the same welcome as her best friend. She slipped her shoes off and arranged them on the welcome mat, creeping barefoot up the stairs with the intention of stroking Angelo's hair, maybe even planting a kiss or two on his damp forehead. She held her finger to her lips as she surveyed the gloom for Theo, only to discover him sleeping in Angelo's bed. They seemed so content, the pair of them, snuggled up like hot dogs beneath Angelo's blue duvet, that Emiliana was thrust backwards by the scene.

She held on to the bannister while she regained her breath, retracing her earlier steps in an effort to stop her head from spinning. Flicking on the lights for a bit of clarity but finding more remnants of their day. The remains of a fried egg sandwich on the dining-room table, homework books scattered across the floor. The Cadillac, propped against the wall. A half-completed jigsaw puzzle on the rug in front of the television, a wooden tower balancing by the door. All signs that they'd enjoyed themselves without her, and no doubt Theo had left them there on purpose.

He held all the cards. That was their main problem. Everything revolved around Theo. The hospital, their bank accounts, whose barbecue invitations they accepted and whose they ignored. Consultants at the top of the pile, juniors at the bottom.

Even her Angelo revolved around him, to a certain extent.

Did she belong to him, too? she wondered. 'Who am I, Ev, if I'm not Theo's grateful wife?'

'You need to find yourself a little part-time role, my darling,' Ev told her, commiserating from behind her smoky card-fan. 'Maro from two doors down has just landed a receptionist job at Oaklands Primary. I mean, heaven help the parent who crosses her first thing on a Monday, but at least it gets her out of the house for a few hours.'

Emiliana sighed. She didn't want a stupid job. She craved independence and the two were not the same. If anything, one thing compromised the other. 'Is it too much to ask, Ev? A bit of independence while Angelo is at school. Accomplishing something besides peeling potatoes and sticking chickens in the oven?'

'Of course not, my darling,' Ev soothed. 'My mother was just the same before she lost her whatnots. She hated being stuck in the house all day while my father dithered around pretending he had the faintest clue, but the question is, what are you going to *do* about it?'

Emiliana knew exactly what she was going to do. She'd threatened to go through with it enough times and there was no time like the present. Theo was at the park with Angelo and the Cadillac and they wouldn't be back for hours. She would pack a few things and steal his beloved Merc. Drive to the nearest hotel via an off-licence and buy a basketful of life's essentials: gin and fags. Check in and barricade herself in the cheapest room she could find. Pay up front for a week, or until he realised that she'd left him and begged her to come home. 'Emi, please. I'm *sorry*.' She didn't know what she was supposed to do in this hotel room for an entire week other than ignore Theo's calls, but she would definitely enjoy thinking of him roasting chickens and ironing Angelo's school shirts while she glugged gin and toasted Evgenia.

She would have to telephone her, of course; let Ev know she was safe and ask her to phone Theo, but not until much later. She wanted him to stew a bit first. Stomp around their empty house and consider his loss. Maybe even ring this Daphne woman and call it all off. 'I'm sorry, darling, I've just realised I can't do this to Emi any more . . .' She tore dresses and tops from hangers and heaped them into a pile on the bed in a frenzy of wild excitement. She grabbed shoes, too, although she doubted there would be many occasions to show off the high heels if she was spending the week reclining on her back.

He would tell her she was unappreciative. Accuse

her of dismissing his many sacrifices. Accuse her of forgetting the past.

'Remember what, Theo? What is it that you want me to remember all the bloody time?'

'You know what I did for you, Emi. God knows, I love you both, but it hurt me to lie to my own mother.'

She was forgetting that he was her saviour for a whole minute, and that was their other main problem. Theo Angelides felt he could have done better.

'Did I actually say that, Emi? Did say I could have done better than you?'

He didn't need to *actually* say it. He was sleeping with Daphne and that was enough proof. She stuffed her clothes into bags and dragged them down the stairs behind her, probing the porcelain bowl on the cabinet next to the door with agitated fingers, only to discover it empty. He'd taken the car keys to the bloody park with him. Was there anything Dr Theo Angelides didn't control?

The only sane thing left to do was to rip the telephone out of the wall and hurl it, cord and all, against the mirror above the fireplace. Emiliana shrieked as it cracked into nice even pieces. The mirror wobbled precariously but it clung to its hook, spawning six tear-stained versions of her face. Each reflection looked a lot like the one next to it, but there were also subtle differences. An ear bent slightly out of shape; a dark eye, slanting downwards. Teeth not quite aligning and a crooked, deformed nose.

She was glad that the mirror had broken in such a

way. Glad that Theo would come home from his precious park to bear witness to her many surfaces.

~

The ringing of the telephone slices through the memories. The sound is shrill, insistent. Funny how life works: it's been ages since anyone's summoned her and now they're desperate for her attention. It sounds more like Flora Florides than Angelo, she decides, the way it's ringing like that, but then it could be someone else entirely. A long lost contact from her address book. Davos, maybe? She relinquishes the curtain to its fluttery fate and roots around for her slippers.

When she resurrects the receiver, she sounds out of breath, despite herself. 'Hello?' Like ridiculous Flor, running down the stairs and nearly tripping over the cat, her joy childish and unbridled. 'Flor, is that you?' Emiliana plays a little guessing game with herself to prolong the anticipation. If it is Flora, she'll make a nice cup of coffee afterwards. A proper one in her cafetiere with cream and sugar. If it's Angelo, she'll open a chilled bottle of white and indulge in some daytime drinking.

'It's me.' His voice sounds like the rumble of distant thunder over her picnic blanket. Wine it is, then. Her heart rate accelerates at the thought.

'Angelo?' It's been God knows how long since she's heard from the ungrateful little sod and now he's interrupting her perfectly fine Saturday? Her curtain-twitching? Her baking programme? The big-nosed chef whisking egg whites in a bowl and making them a lovely pavlova? Her excitement gives way to surprise and then mists of indignation. 'Where the hell have you been all these weeks?'

'Something's happened.' He tells her that he found something out and needed time to think.

'What? What's happened?' She fishes about her person for an emergency cigarette and finds one marooned in the pocket of her cardigan. She waves it around in the air, enjoying the promising feel of it nestled between her fingers; something to enjoy with the wine, later. 'This about the secret Indian woman? Because if it is, you know I can't give this thing my blessing.'

'Yeah, I figured as much,' he sneers sarcastically, as though this telephone conversation with his mother is all he has come to expect from life.

'Good, well as long as we both know where we stand with whatsherface.'

He chuckles humourlessly. 'I've always known where to stand, Mum. You stuck me in enough corners growing up. This ain't about Priya, though.'

'That's charming,' she tuts. 'Well, if it isn't about the secret Indian, what is it . . . ?'

The cloud releases its angry torrent over her blanket as he tells her that he's found him.

'Found who?' she laughs. 'God?' Because the idea of her son worshipping anyone but himself is completely inconceivable.

'Who do you think I'm talking about?' he snarls. '*Him*.'

Emiliana stretches the phone cord to within an inch of its life so she can collapse into the clapped-out sofa. 'You mean *Nico*?' She shoves her unlit cigarette into her gob to chew on its bitter end. 'You been to Cyprus and tracked Nico down?' Memories of lemon-scented grave-yards materialise in her front room. Crushed diamond skies and ancient bones rotting in the stifling heat. The croak of a flaky, unreliable frog.

She's always known it would come to this, and she told Ev as much. 'My last ace,' she warned her, 'and then he'll disappear – that's what telling him about the sperm donor is going to achieve.'

'Cyprus?' His laugh sounds even more distant now, as though it's moved on from her blanket to spoil someone else's lunch. She exhales in a momentary relief. 'You'd like that, wouldn't you, Mum?' She can hear him shuffling papers, spinning around in his Count Dracula chair. 'Turns out I didn't have to travel to the motherland after all. He lived right round the corner actually.' Tapping his obsessively organised desk with a ridiculously expensive pen. 'Lancaster Gardens, it says here. Number 22.'

'You said he *lived*?'

'Man's dead. I have a copy of the certificate. I've just realised who the hell he was, although how could I have possibly known until you told me his name . . .'

'You have a copy of his death certificate?' she asks, in a near hysterical high pitch. 'What on earth for?'

'Why do you think a funeral director would have a copy of someone's death certificate, Mum?' His anger crackles in her ear. 'What do I do for a bloody living?'

'Oh.' It dawns on her like a slow sunrise and she's glad she's stuck in the jaws of her flesh-eating sofa because her legs have started to tremble. Only very slightly because none of this is her fault, but it's a tremble that precludes standing up. 'How was I supposed to know where he lived, Angelo? I haven't heard from the man in thirty-five years.' The last part is barely a whisper.

'It's never your fault, though, is it?' he snarls. 'You never do anything wrong. How about if you'd just told me his name in the first place instead of tormenting me with it for twenty years? How about if I knew who I was burying? How about if I knew *anything* at all?'

Emiliana feels a bit queasy. She wishes her Ev was here to comfort her, or at the very least to pass her the ashtray.

'That's not all.'

'No?' What now, she thinks.

'I have a sister. Her name is Melina.'

'You have a *what*?' For some reason, this news is infinitely worse than the thought of her undertaker son unknowingly burying his father. It sneaks up behind her like an assassin and grabs her by the throat. Strangles her until she sees stars. Lemon-coloured ones that explode behind her eyes. Nico skulking out of the cemetery after breaking her heart and carrying on with his life? Marrying someone else? Having more kids? How could he?

'I haven't decided what to do about the girl yet . . .'

It's too much to bear.

'If I should make contact. Introduce myself and tell her that her father denied my existence, or if I should leave her to mourn the man in peace. To remember the good times, cos that's important, too . . .'

A long, weary sigh escapes from Emiliana's lips and hangs in the air like the future. If she reaches up, she can pop it with her fingers.

'She did write me this card. She left it with Stel. Course, I didn't think much of it at the time.'

'Angelo?' The past has finally staggered up to Missouri Close with an armful of suitcases. 'There's something you should know first.' It's time to confess the truth. 'Are you sitting down?' Not the truth she told her best friend to win her admiration, or the version she told Theo to save her skin. The truth that tasted like leftover spaghetti suppers and sunless afternoons by the window.

Melina

June 1990

SHE TAKES THE morning off so they can pack up Pappa together. Noni's line was engaged for ages and by the time she walks over to her mamma's house, the sitting room is full of paper towers.

She manoeuvres around them to slip an Aretha Franklin album out of its sleeve and arrange it on her treasured turntable. 'I've *really* missed this.' She releases the needle and the room erupts into soothing soul music. She sways from side to side, rubbing at the tops of her arms. She's been working in a salon for too long and can't think without a song in her head.

'I've made a start,' Aliki calls out breathlessly. 'Here, grab a box.'

It looks like more than a start to Melina.

She sits cross-legged between piles of his things. Boots, belts, bills. Her pappa's possessions seem more alive without him. As though his death has exposed them to the light. She picks up a shoe and holds it in the air. The black top has been polished to perfection but the heel is flat and worn. 'Remember how he used to wear these to march up and down Green Lanes looking for the freshest tomatoes, Mamma?' she asks sadly. 'The shiniest?'

Her mother wipes her brow with the back of her hand and leaves a faint grubby smear behind. 'He spent more time lecturing the shopkeepers on Thatcher than he did buying the tomatoes, I think. He never came home with anything except a newspaper. Stick them in the box on the left, will you?'

Next to the shoe is a file bulging with papers and a date scribbled on the front. 'He kept all these bills and letters?' Documents going back in time and well beyond the year on the flap. 'Why?' She opens the file and runs her fingers over his name. Seeing it in full and in bold print feels like a paper cut to her heart.

'He thought the taxman was going to knock on the door and send him to prison for not keeping cigarette receipts. He wanted to be prepared,' Aliki snorts. 'Those can go in the bin bag, along with his underwear.'

A half-empty bottle of brandy rolls out of nowhere and makes its way slowly, ominously, towards her. Melina twists the lid off with a 'pop' and sniffs the amber-coloured liquid. She closes her eyes. It smells like Christmas breath.

'Bin, too, please.'

'The fags?'

'Well, I'm not going to smoke them.'

She seems in a hurry to erase him, Melina thinks. Throwing his things into bags and boxes. To wipe the house clean of him with her dusty cloth and start a new life by herself. A life where she can pull her hair back into a bun and fasten it with a colourful grip. Where her bra-less boobs can flop freely beneath her top and she can wear the Sellotape roll as a bangle.

She's glowing, too. While nobody would ever describe her mamma as attractive, this morning she is definitely glowing. 'You look nice with your hair up. It suits you.'

'Do I, *agabi*?' Aliki chuckles, continuing her upward spin. 'Pass me that box over there – I have a few more bits to put in.'

A black and white framed photograph catches Melina's eye. She picks it up and runs her hand over the sticky glass. It feels grimy beneath her fingertips, some kind of ancient residue.

'The face looks familiar.' The photo unsettles her in a way she can't explain. Like a moth fluttering too close in the darkness or the chill escaping from an open freezer.

'It's because it's your father's face,' Aliki smiles.

'I mean, it looks . . . I don't know. Like someone else's face.'

It shows her parents standing in front of a beach. Her pappa's frown tells the world that his life is depressing while her mother's big teeth edge shyly out of her lips despite her efforts to conceal them. She notices that although they're standing next to each other they're not actually touching. In the background, the sea shines happily.

'Have I seen it before?'

Aliki looks up from her armful of possessions. 'It was on your pappa's bedside cabinet. He liked to stare at it before he went to sleep, although God knows why. Probably because he thought *he* looked handsome.'

'He does, though, don't you think?'

Her mamma mumbles her reply from the inside of a bag.

'You both seem so young. How old were you here?'

'Mid-thirties, maybe. I've always hated myself in it. I look like Bugs Bunny. Stick it in the loft box with the old bedsheets.'

At lunchtime, her mother releases her armload over the sofa and wipes her hands on her leggings. 'Chai?' She waltzes into the kitchen to make sandwiches like it's any other day and they're not burying her pappa's possessions. Melina reluctantly traces her steps, filling the kettle with water while Aliki cuts slices of sesame bread and slathers them in a thick layer of butter. She dumps chunky layers of cheese over the top.

'Remember his rants about how much marge you used in your sandwiches, Mamma? Said you were trying to give him a heart attack?'

Aliki frowns as she tosses the dirty knife into the sink with a loud clang. 'He liked to eat them well enough. Besides, your pappa was always moaning about something.' She kisses a blob of margarine from her thumbnail. 'Here, sit and eat. You look like you've lost weight.'

Melina coaxes a black sesame seed from its crusty bed while her mother plunges her teeth into her sandwich. 'I've been thinking . . .' There's a short silence while she chews, swallows and then contemplates her next bite. 'Maybe you should move back in here. Hassan, too. It's silly to throw your money away on rent at Irini's when your old room is empty.' Tomato juice fires out from the sides of the bread to stain her purple T-shirt.

Melina pushes her own plate away. She slumps back into the chair as flashes of their last argument replace the happier memories from this table. Memories of eggy breakfasts and fish and chip suppers. His silly stories about the English man apologising to the lamp-post. He was furious that night, the night he marched up to her room to confront her about Hass. 'This what I deserve, Melina?'

'It's too soon.' It's what she wanted to tell her mamma yesterday when she asked her to come over and help. 'I'm not ready to come home yet.'

'Just think about it, agabi.' She gets up to make herself another cheese sandwich and refill the kettle. 'That's all.'

From the sitting room, Melina can make out the tentative first notes of her favourite Aretha track.

'How'd it go today?'

They sweep aside newly discarded kebab wrappers to lie next to each other on the bed with their bare feet propped up against the wall. Hass passes her his after-dinner joint and she puffs on it gratefully. She's happiest when she's hazy. In the background, Whitney Houston belts out 'One Moment in Time.'

She ran up to her old room after lunch and grabbed as many of her cassette tapes as she could find. Her make-up, too. She moved out in such a hurry that she abandoned beloved possessions. Her music, her lipsticks, her colourful nail varnishes. It feels like only half of her is living at Irini's, but at least that half is with Hass.

Melina passes the joint back to him and exhales the smoke towards the ceiling, which is painted in the same creamy colour as her skin. 'It was weird. Like being at another funeral, only this time for all his things.'

'Yeah? Sorry, Mel.'

'You should have seen my mamma. She couldn't wait to chuck everything into a bin bag.'

'She's just trying to move on with her life, I guess.'

'He only died in April.' Melina sighs. 'I don't get it.'

'People grieve in different ways.'

In the hallway, a series of noises signals the end of another day at Irini's house. Mr Ibrahim, shuffling wearily into his bedroom. Pete Pelecano, slamming doors because his wife won't return his calls. Vincent, jogging up the stairs to use the toilet before someone else locks themselves inside.

'That bloke's always on the bog. Needs to get his bowels checked, seriously.'

'What if it's *her* lurking out there?' Melina sits upright, suddenly fuelled by paranoia. 'Irini?'

'Relax,' Hass croons in her ear. 'She's not gonna burst in here and report us to the police for smoking a bit of dope. Besides, ain't she, like, a mate of your mum's?'

'More like an acquaintance,' Melina admits, biting her bottom lip. Although all she really knows about the creepy landlady is that she likes to dress in black. 'If that.'

Hass smashes his dying butt on the cover of his magazine before tossing it into an ashtray on the floor. He burps proudly. 'I think your mum's right, for what it's worth. We need somewhere proper to live. Somewhere we can save up for a place of our own. This house is full of losers as well. No offence to the geezers, but we can do better. Especially with your dad and that . . .'

He was going to say 'gone'.

Melina picks up his magazine. 'Navid isn't a loser.' She holds it at arm's length. On the cover, a girl with bleached blonde hair and dark eye make-up offers up her boobs in the palms of her hands. They're yours, she's saying to the reader. Here, take them.

'Who?'

'The Iranian guy in the room downstairs. I think he's a student. Plus, I'm not ready to go home.' She wonders how old the girl on the magazine is. Nineteen? Twenty? Younger? How much she's been paid to pose like that. Topless and in her knickers.

'Just saying.' He leans over to grab the magazine from her hands and plant his lips on hers. He still tastes of garlic and chilli sauce.

She recoils in mild disgust. 'I'm not really in the mood tonight, babe.'

It's the last thing she feels like doing after spending the morning shoving the remains of her pappa into boxes. Containers marked either 'Charity', 'Loft' or 'Rubbish'. The sum of his life, she thinks. Three different ways of being expelled from his home. Was the end this undignified for everyone, or was this a special kind of punishment for him?

'S'OK, Mel, I get it.' He sighs as he rolls off the bed and lands on his feet. He leaves the bedroom door wide open for everyone to see her shame as he thuds down the hallway to queue for his piss.

Melina opens a single, sticky eye to squint at the clock next to the bed. It's ten past nine.

'Shit!' She pokes Hass in the ribs with a frantic elbow. 'Babe! Why didn't you wake me up?'

Hass groans. Readjusts his balls and flip-flops onto his belly. 'I'm not going in 'til later, innit?'

She rolls her eyes. There's no need to set an alarm when you work in your father's shop. She flings back a corner of the duvet and looks around for her dressing gown and make-up bag. 'I'm so effing late . . .'

She flies down the hallway towards the bathroom with her gown flapping behind her to discover the door once again locked. 'Hello?' She raps irritably on the frosted glass. 'You gonna be long in there?' The sound of hissing water is disorientating. It reminds her that her world has changed. That she has to dance round the routines of four strangers every morning because she can't face going home to her memories.

She nibbles the skin around her fingernails thinking that Noni is going to kill her. She's *really* going to kill her. She's been in trouble with the boss twice this week already. The first time for accidentally nicking Mrs Webster's ear with her scissors and inflicting a bloody little cut, and the second for over-processing Mrs Papadakis.

'It looks a bit bleached, my darling,' the older woman said, fingering her botched hair sadly. 'I was hoping for something a bit more subtle than this.'

Afterwards, Noni ushered her into the staffroom that was actually a glorified cupboard for 'a word'. 'You sure you're OK, Mel?' Her cola gum cracked cold, hard bubbles in her face.

'Yeah, course,' Melina lied. 'I just got a bit trigger-happy with the new accelerant. Won't happen again, Nons.'

'Good, cos I was thinking of leaving you in charge when this little one arrives.' Noni cradled her baby belly protectively. 'Just until next March, but only if you can handle it?'

'Course.' Melina dragged her lips into a reluctant smile. More responsibility. That's exactly what she needs when all she can think about is her pappa. When she can just about cope with rolling out of bed on time and catching the bus to work.

The door clicks open and a semi-naked Vincent emerges triumphantly from the steam. 'Mornin', Mel.' He pulls his shower cap from his head and shakes his short dreadlocks loose. 'Sorry about that – it's all yours now.' The colourful beads on the end of each braid clink together as he jogs down the stairs to his bedroom.

Is she the only one in a hurry today? she thinks. 'Shit, shit, *shit!*'

She locks the door behind her and wipes the condensation from the mirror above the sink with a squeaky sleeve. Then she takes a few deep breaths to steady herself and unzips her stripy make-up bag. She arranges her products in order. Her moisturiser, her foundation, her eyebrow pencil, her eyeshadows, a tube of mascara, her favourite blusher, lip gloss, her silver eyelash curlers. By the time she's finished organising her little pots and jars on the windowsill, she feels calmer and more relaxed.

She enjoys doing her make-up. Watching her face come alive. If she's honest, she's more interested in make-up than hair and, if it wasn't for the stink her pappa kicked up when he found out about Noni's, she would have switched vocations by now. Instead, she dug her little heels in and clung on for dear life, afraid to have caused so much hurt for nothing.

'It's not too late, you know,' her best friend Rainey has told her. Rainey is a successful make-up artist to the stars. She owns an upmarket studio in Covent Garden and is always trying to offer her a job. 'I'll pay for the conversion courses and you can share the flat upstairs with me. Come on, Mel, be *such* a laugh . . .'

'Don't tempt me, Ray, seriously.'

'What's stopping you?'

Their phone calls were always rushed and breathy. As if Rainey's new life was so fabulous, she couldn't bear to tear herself away.

Melina turns her own head to the side and thinks that her mamma is right. She's lost too much weight and her newly sunken cheeks emphasise her nose. She looks more like her pappa with her nose sticking out like that. More Greek.

She flips the lid of the eyeshadow palette and regards each of the colours in turn. She chooses a light grey one and dusts her brush gently over its shimmery surface, then blows the excess powder into her reflection.

Her pappa hated Rainey, who when Melina was growing up was the blonde-haired, blue-eyed embodiment of Otherness and everything that was wrong with the English. Nico blamed Rainey for every bad day, power cut or expensive phone bill. Every hair that sprouted on his daughter's pubescent body. It was Rainey's fault that his daughter fancied David Bowie to the point of frenzy and lost interest in the snails and the slugs. *Everything* was Rainey's fault.

Melina showed him her picture a few months before he died. She was profiled in a glossy magazine and it wasn't the first time, either. She told him that Rainey had done well for herself. That she ran a studio in Covent Garden and worked with famous celebrities and models. That despite having a mother who drank too much and a boyfriend before the age of sixteen, she didn't turn out like he'd hoped.

'Like I hoped?' he tutted, tossing the magazine back in her face. 'That what you think of me? I was afraid for *you*, Melina. I'm still afraid for you.'

She carefully coats her lashes in gloopy mascara,

flicking her wrist like a pro. She likes to imagine an alternative life for herself, a life where she wakes up not in Irini's house next to Hass, but in the flat above Rainey's studio. A flat where the rich, bluesy voice of Etta James rouses her from her sleep and her friend pops her head round the door to tell her that Madonna is in a cab. 'Coffee, Mel?' She's even bought them a new espresso machine for the kitchen.

Dream on, she thinks miserably.

Her eyes perfectly accentuated, she runs her fluffiest brush over her pot of Crazy Coral blusher and puckers her lips to expose her cheekbones.

'Mel?' The rattling of the bathroom door handle startles her and she drops the brush into the damp sink. Hass's voice is groggy and confused.

'What, babe?' She sounds more pissed off than she means to.

'Get a move on, yeah? I've just had your boss moaning in my ear.'

~

The new girl marched across the school cafeteria and plonked her tray opposite hers. 'Hi. Can I sit here?'

Melina shrugged nonchalantly, but she couldn't help staring as the girl removed pots and plates from her lunch tray and arranged them in a line. Sausages, jelly, carton of milk, apple.

'There we go.'

'What you doing?'

'It's the order in which they go into my mouth,' the new girl explained. 'Left to right. Saves *loads* of time.' She scraped her chair back and flung herself into it, plunging her fork into her sausage and bringing it up to her nose. Her eyes crossed in the middle. 'Eurgh . . . smells like a knob!'

Melina sniggered into her jelly spoon. She had no idea what a knob was supposed to smell like. Sitting next to Kevin Jones in Geography was the closest she'd ever been to a boy.

The new girl squeezed her sausage in between two rows of metal-lined teeth and talked with her mouth half full. 'I'm Rainey May, by the way.'

She was the new girl in Mrs Sellar's class. Melina had noticed her stomping confidently along the ugly, lino-leum-lined corridors that connected their school blocks, and she admired her guts. Braving Manor High at fourteen in a face plastered with make-up. Melina would be wetting her knickers in her position. Puking up in the girls' loos.

'Is that your real name?' Melina narrowed her eyes in suspicion. 'Rainey May?'

'Unfortunately.' The new girl rolled her own eyes melodramatically. She was pretty, Melina thought. Pretty in a quirky kind of way. Her lips, nose and chin were all exaggerated but they somehow flattered her face. 'Mum's a pagan, hence "Rainey", but she's also an alky, which is why she stuck an "e" in it.' She waved her fork around in Melina's face. 'Welcome to my *amazing* life.'

Melina didn't know what a pagan was but she was familiar with the term 'alcoholic'. Her mamma accused her pappa of being one when he poured himself a brandy in the middle of the day. 'Metaxa before lunch, Nico? What's next, ouzo before breakfast?'

'My dad drinks, too,' Melina sighed.

The new girl extricated bits of sausage from her train tracks and, after a brief examination, shoved them into the back of her gob. 'Yeah, but there's drinking and then there's *drinking*. I mean, Mum's usually passed out on the sofa with an ashtray on her tits before I've even made it home from school.' She paused to hiccup loudly. 'Not that it's a competition or anything, but she's going to burn the house down one day and you heard it in this cafeteria first.'

'Sad.' Melina didn't know how else to respond. She changed the subject. 'I'm Melina, by the way. It means "honey" in Greek.'

'Greek honey?' The new girl slid her plate of bangers and mash to the side and started on her jelly. 'I thought my name was lame. Do you come with a blob of yoghurt, then?'

There was a brief, uncertain silence before both girls burst out laughing. 'Argh!' Melina rummaged around for a clean tissue. 'You've made milk come out of my nose! That really hurt!'

'Seriously,' Rainey wiped her leaky blue eyes on the back of her hand, 'I wish I was called Honey. Or Summer, or Skylark – or anything but Rainey May.'

'What about April May?' Melina giggled.

'Ha ha. You're so funny, Greek honey!'

'Why don't you like your name, though?'

'Nobody likes the rain . . .' Rainey shrugged.

'I like the rain.'

'Why?' The new girl slurped green jelly off her spoon and her stretched lips made cute little kissing noises. 'All it does is ruin your mascara and wash out your hairspray.'

She did use a *lot* of hairspray. Melina wondered if that was why her blonde bob stayed glued to her ears despite all the animated head thrusts.

Fresh out of Geography class with Kevin Jones, Melina knew all about the importance of rain. 'Cos rain is vital to life on earth.' She could hear Mrs Roper's voice in her head, egging her on. 'So in a way, you're like, a life-saver.'

'Get you, swot-face. "Vital to life on earth?" Did you actually swallow the textbook?' The new girl smiled a silver smile. 'Life-saver? Nobody's ever called me that before. I think I like it.'

Melina picked up her apple, polished it on her school sweater and took an enthusiastic bite. Apple juice squirted everywhere.

'Eurgh! Greek honey, that went in my eyes!'

Melina smiled. Sitting opposite Rainey May, life seemed sweeter, more promising, and, when Pamela Plater sauntered past their table and snorted spitefully in their direction, it didn't matter so much anymore.

'Snobby bitch.' Rainey stuck her middle finger high

up in the air for the dinner ladies to report later. 'What's her problem?'

Melina shrugged stoically. 'I guess we're losers cos we're not sitting with the cool girls. Cecilia Reddington and them lot.'

'Losers? Next time I'll punch her stuck-up face in. See who's lost then.' Rainey fumbled with the straw on her carton of milk, pleased to have boasted herself into a brand new friendship. 'Hey, you wanna come to the cinema with me next Friday?'

'The cinema?' Melina's palms grew warm and sticky. She could imagine how that would go down with her pappa. Like a ton of sick, most probably.

'Yeah. *The Deer Hunter*'s playing at the Odeon. It's an eighteen but if I do your make-up we'll *definitely* get in. Trust me, Mum taught me how to do it during one of her sober weekends. That and how to get the ticket guy who needs new specs.'

'I guess,' Melina mumbled.

'Guess what?'

'I mean, I'd love to come but I'd have to ask my dad first.'

Melina shuffled nervously up the steps and rang the old-fashioned doorbell. It chimed like a church bell. She tilted her head all the way back to admire the two-storey white building. She wondered if she'd come to the right place until Rainey appeared at the door dressed like a glitter ball in a silvery blouse, white polo neck and short, shimmery skirt. She rolled her eyes in her typical Rainey way. 'Welcome to May Towers . . .'

'You live *here*?' Melina wiped her feet on the hairy doormat and allowed the huge house to swallow her up.

'Why's that weird? You thought we'd be living in a tent cos I told you Mum's an alky?' Rainey winked mischievously and Melina blushed. She was embarrassed for imagining dusty windowsills and empty wine bottles after only a handful of conversations.

'Through here.' The hallway was long and tiled like a chessboard. Melina's trainers squeaked shamefully over the shiny squares and reminded her that she needed a new pair. The hall suddenly curved to the right and exploded into a room filled with fancy furniture and long velvet curtains. It looked like a picture you might find in a magazine someone left at the dentist.

'Course I didn't think you lived in a tent.' The lie shivered like a skinny, naked person. 'I'm just impressed, that's all. It's so nice in here, seriously.'

Rainey shrugged. 'I guess.' She threw her friend's coat on the sofa while Melina glanced around for the notorious Mrs May. The pagan alcoholic who didn't know how to spell 'rainy' but liked to buy velvet drapes. 'Oh, Mum's gone out with her boyfriend, in case you're wondering. She met him at a support group and shoved him off the wagon. Poor guy had been sober for like, five years, as well. Like I said, welcome to my fabulous life.'

'Where's your dad?' Melina asked with the naivety of someone who didn't know anything other than a mother, a father, boiled eggs around the breakfast table.

'He moved in with a woman named Kitty two years ago. But it's OK,' Rainey continued mockingly, 'cos now he's marrying a cat and Mum has Rupert to get smashed with. Hey, do you like music?' Before Melina could answer her question, Rainey skipped along the chessboard hallway to retrieve an armful of open boxes. 'Mum's record collection.' Her excited voice pingponged off the impressive ceilings. 'Have you heard of a singer called Etta James?'

Melina shrugged.

Rainey looked around the room in mock confusion. 'Er . . . you know what soul music is, though, right?'

If it wasn't featured in *Smash Hits* magazine Melina probably hadn't heard of it. 'Course.'

Rainey slid a record onto her mother's player and the deep, gravelly sound of Etta James smacked Melina in the face.

'You like it?'

'Yeah, a lot. Sounds like she's crying.'

'She kind of is.' Rainey put on her grown-up voice for the next bit. 'Soul is a form of expression.'

She lowered Melina onto the sofa by her wrists and began rummaging through another one of the boxes. 'Let's see. We'll start with a nice, creamy base. Cover your spots, no offence or anything, and then we'll do the eyes. Your eyes are amazing, by the way . . .'

Melina sighed contentedly as her friend arranged her pots and palettes like she lined up her lunch at school. She felt as though she'd crawled into someone else's skin for the night. A skin that buzzed, tingled and pulsed, and fitted her much better than her own.

'Hold still for this bit. So, your dad was cool about tonight?'

Melina tried to nod without moving her head as her friend's hot breath tickled her skin. She could hardly admit that her pappa had stood in the doorway shouting, 'Over my dead body!' at the top of his voice until Mr Barnaby next door knocked on their adjoining wall.

'Please, Pappa!'

He'd been wearing his work clothes. His blue tank top with his white shirt poking out over the top, and although she hated him more than anything in that moment, a part of her felt sad that he'd put on his smart things just so he could haul boxes for Sonny.

'Move out of the way,' she'd begged, 'she'll be waiting for me.'

'She? Who is this "she", and why have I not heard of her before?'

'She's called Rainey May and she's new at school.'

'She's called *what*?' he'd yelled, his frothy spit flying everywhere. 'Are you bloody joking me, Melina?'

Her mamma had run down the stairs to intercede. 'Nico, give her the key – the girls are only going to the cinema in Turnpike Lane.'

'You knew?' He turned to glare at his fresh victim.

'You knew about this secret cinema with Rainy Spain or whatever the bloody hell her name is?'

'What secret, Nico? You're being paranoid.'

Melina had spied the perfect moment to untangle the door key from his sweaty palm. Squeezing through the door and sprinting down Lancaster Gardens while her mamma did her best to cling onto his tank top. After all, she reasoned, as she huffed and puffed, her mamma had chosen to live with him. To marry him. She hadn't chosen to be his daughter.

'Yeah. He was fine with it.'

Rainey looked cute when she was concentrating. She worked with her mouth half open and her tongue poking out, her blonde head bobbing along to Etta. Occasionally, she forgot herself and sang a line or two out loud. Melina thought she sounded much older than her fourteen years.

'See,' she smiled, 'you had nothing to be nervous about.'

Melina blushed. 'I wasn't *that* nervous.'

When she'd broken free of the geranium borders of Lancaster Gardens, she slowed down to a brisk walk and began to enjoy her illicit adventure. The surrounding dusk, brimming with a swirl of oranges, reds and pinks. Buses glowing brightly on their way to somewhere special, and yellow shop fronts lighting the high street like birthday candles. She was glad she'd defied her pappa if it meant she could see the world coming alive like this.

'There. All done.'

Rainey handed her a mirror and Melina gasped at her new reflection. Her friend had magically transformed her from a pale, spotty teenager to a young woman on the verge of winning her freedom. 'You like it?'

Melina grabbed the mirror from her hands and waltzed around the sitting room, staring at her new face. 'Ray, I *love* it!' The yellows in her irises her pappa admired so much whirled round and round like fireworks. 'It's like you've switched the lights on inside my head or something.'

'It's cos I used a dark brown on your lids,' Rainey explained knowingly. 'Brings out the gold speckles.' She pretended to bow. 'You're welcome. My turn now.'

She sat cross-legged on the carpet and pulled another box towards her. Melina lay back on her friend's giant sofa and closed her newly decorated eyelids. She was exhausted from all the tingling. She wondered if this was how taking drugs might feel. Or letting Kevin Jones touch her after class. In the background, Etta's voice faded to silence before a new track burst into life. 'At last . . .'

Rainey chatted to herself as she slipped a clip into her short blonde hair and rubbed foundation into her cheeks. Her excited stream of consciousness sounded like someone tuning a radio. 'I hope we get Mr Specs at the ticket counter after all this flippin' effort.'

'Me too.' Melina could feel herself drifting into a sweet sleep. She wasn't thinking about the cinema. She didn't care whether they saw *The Deer Hunter* at the Odeon. She was too busy counting her lucky Rainey stars and wondering what she'd done to deserve them.

They walked back to Rainey's munching rank hot dogs from Bob's Burger Van.

'It's not fair,' Rainey whined. 'I *really* wanted to see that film.'

'I know, me too.' Melina sounded less convincing. She wondered, as she bit her way up the stale bun, why hot dogs always smelled so good but tasted like rubber.

'Rotten luck not getting Mr Specs. Sucks like a leech.'

'Yeah, sucks.' Someone called Russell had served them instead. He told Rainey that he wasn't going to sell them tickets no matter how much make-up they were wearing. 'Go home, girls, this is a big boys' film.'

'He could talk – how old was he, then?' Rainey looked hurt despite her brave, glittery face. 'My nanna can grow a more convincing tash.'

Melina gulped down the last bit of hot dog and shoved the evidence, a ketchup-stained handkerchief, into her pocket. Her pappa didn't approve of Bob's Burgers, or anyone else's burgers for that matter. 'They're all the same. Dirty crooks. They take your money and sell you cat meat' was his expert opinion on the subject.

'Eaten many cats, Nico?' Over the years, her mother

had developed a way of making her sarcastic words sound completely genuine. 'Or dogs?'

Rainey burped onion breath in her ear. 'So, there's meant to be this crazy scene in the film where Christopher Walken and Robert De Niro stick a bullet in a gun and take turns firing it into their heads.'

'Why would they do that?'

'Dunno. See who dies first, I guess. Rupert says it's called the Russian roulette cos he's seen it five times already.'

Melina was relieved to have missed it. The night was turning into one of the greatest of her life, if not *the* greatest, and she was glad not to have wasted it watching men playing with guns. 'Sounds bloody horrible.' She felt so grown up that she even snuck in a 'bloody' for good measure.

She wondered, with a sneaky smile, what her pappa would say if he could see her now, walking along in the dark, her face plastered in Rainey's make-up, discussing Russian roulettes. Talking to Russell the Cinema Boy and eating forbidden dog meat. She found out at about half past nine when she arrived home. He was waiting for her on the stairs, still overdressed for his workday. He was preparing to deliver a speech as she dumped her coat and untied her trainers.

'I'm tired, Pappa.' She rolled her eyes the way Rainey had showed her. 'Please move out of my way.'

Her pappa liked lectures. He had lots of them up his shirtsleeves. Lectures about Melina failing school and winding up on benefits like Ricky Smith. Speeches about Melina marrying a Turkish man and spending the rest of her life wallowing in regret like a pig. In this particular scenario, she would often sob, 'my pappa was so right about everything, why didn't I listen to him?' into her pillow.

Then there was his favourite: the Immigrant Arse speech.

The Immigrant Arse speech was about a cold and weary arse that travelled all the way to London to give its ungrateful daughter a better life. The immigrant arse didn't mind skivvying for Sonny Smith if it meant Melina would one day be a doctor, but if she wasted her chances or pissed them up the wall with Rainy Spain, the arse would die miserable and blistered. Sometimes he would throw in a 'hairy' too.

She knew her pappa was about to confront her with the Immigrant Arse speech because his eyes bulged out of his face and his nose twitched like a bumblebee had just flown up it.

'After everything I've done for you . . .' The large nose began to buzz beneath the frame of his glasses.

She didn't want to hear it, especially not tonight. Not after *the* best night ever. 'Please, Pappa, I just want to go to my room.'

He moved aside grudgingly. 'Go to the bathroom first. Wash that shit off your face.'

Looking back, secret cinema night is when it all started. Melina, trampling all over the geranium boundaries of Lancaster Gardens in an attempt to recapture those first illicit moments of freedom. Spending all her time with Rainey May because her pappa didn't like her. Making choices that didn't always suit her because she knew they would piss him off.

~

Noni and her husband, Taz, have been busy. Overnight, they've filled the salon with England flags, banners and balloons. Melina wades through the World Cup decorations, wondering if her boss has developed amnesia. If she's forgotten that most of their clients are women in their eighties. She doubts Mrs Karagianni will be drinking lager and cheering for Paul Gascoigne to score the winning penalty.

'How nice of you to join us, Mel.'

Melina mouths a 'So sorry' on her way to the glorified cupboard to ditch her bag while the boss shoots her a narrow-eyed smile to let her know she's still seething.

Candace-the-Junior has shampooed her first client of the day and plonked her in the chair. Everyone's been waiting for her. Melina sighs as she rolls up her sleeves and unwraps the woman's towel, soaking up the excess drips as if she were a little wet dog. Mrs Miltiades smiles feebly at her own reflection. She's expecting conversation. She's almost ninety and having her hair done at Noni's is a Tuesday morning highlight. She wants Melina to entertain her. To ask after her son and her grandchildren and to offer endless cups of sugary tea.

Melina dodges the woman's mirrored gaze. She

switches on the powerful hairdryer, relieved of the brief distraction. She used to be good at the chit-chat, even over the constant whooshing. Remembering first names and birthdays and baby due dates. 'How's your pregnant daughter doing, Mrs K?' 'Lovely, and how was little Mikey's birthday party?' Now, all she can think about is her mamma. How she floated around the house yesterday as if her grief were as light as a bubble. She wishes she was mourning the same, forgettable Nico as her mother was. Carrying bubbles around in her heart instead of tombstones.

Melina places the hairdryer back in its bracket and squeezes Mrs Miltiades' silky shoulders. 'All OK, Mrs M?' They feel bony and fragile beneath her fingers, as if they might snap under the slightest pressure.

'It's my grandson's wedding this Sunday.' Mrs Miltiades speaks slowly, uncertainly. 'So I just want half an inch off to thicken it up a bit, no more than that, my darling.' She wags her finger in the air as if she's trying to burst her own words.

'Ah, bless.' Melina stole the non-committal 'bless' from Noni a few years ago and uses it when she's not really listening. She reaches across Mrs Miltiades for her comb and scissors, straightening the woman's damp, grey hair down the length of her back and sliding the sharp blade across it. The sound of it is satisfying. Like gas hissing from a hob.

She's fond of Mrs Miltiades. She's fond of all her senior clients. She enjoys styling their hair and helping them put on their flowery shawls while they rummage around for their loose change. Popping their tips into her glass jar and watching the silver mountain grow into the future. There's nothing wrong with the mature market, she thinks, but there's nothing that exciting about it, either.

She misses the early years of her hairdressing career when there was a buzz in the salon and Noni let her play her own music. Aretha, Nina, Otis, Etta. Music that reminded her of college and nights out with Rainey May. When younger clients spilled through the door asking for bold colours and funky, punky haircuts. Bleach blondes, bottle reds and deep plums. Fuzzy fringes and huge perms that caught people's attention in the street.

'Where's this wedding, then, Mrs M?' She may as well indulge the poor woman while she slices through the paper-thin hair.

Mrs Miltiades beams proudly. Small talk at last. 'My son's hired The Poseidon in Barnet, have you heard of it?'

'Don't think so.' She can barely remember what a party feels like.

'They've invited over eight hundred people. Not too much off please, my darling, I've been growing it, you see.'

'Seriously?' Melina barely knew ten people, never mind a whole school's worth of guests.

'Only the best for our lovely Andrew.' Mrs Miltiades claps her hands together in the mirror. 'He's such a kind young man. Do you maybe know him?'

Eight hundred guests? Melina imagines a typical

Greek mamma's boy drowning in an expensive suit. A spoilt brat whose parents already bought him his first house because he's too special to work for it himself. Was this who her pappa so desperately wanted her to marry? Skinny, spoilt little Andrew in his stupid baggy suit? 'Afraid I don't, Mrs M . . .'

She spins Mrs Miltiades around in her chair a little too quickly and catches the old woman off guard. 'Oops! Sorry!'

The good times were fun but they didn't last long. The fashion changed and Noni refused to change with it. 'Eighties bold' evolved into 'nineties chic' and the style-conscious went to Kool Kutz round the corner. Kem, the owner there, was fresh out of college and knew how to handle a pair of scissors. Noni popped her gum and shrugged her shoulders, welcoming the grannies of Turnpike Lane with open arms and cheesy pop music. There was no need to top up their training for trims, blue rinses and root tints.

Melina stifles a yawn of boredom as she finishes layering the woman's fringe and unfastens the hairy gown from the bony shoulders.

Rainey thought it was hilarious that Melina worked in a granny salon when she was painting celebrities in Covent Garden. 'What time you finishing your shift at the graveyard this evening? Come and meet me for a cocktail afterwards!'

'Piss off, Ray.'

'All done for you now, Mrs M.'

'Oh!' Mrs Miltiades gasps at the mirror. 'It's very

short, darling. I only wanted a trim. Did I not say? I thought I had?'

'I think it suits you.' Melina squeezes the frail shoulders again. She can't remember what the woman asked for. She was miles away. 'It's edgy.' She was always miles away.

'Edgy?' Mrs Miltiades regards herself from all angles, trying her best to make peace with the bad hair. 'I was hoping to show it off in the wedding pictures but I suppose I shall just have to buy a hat. Oh dear, this is disappointing.' She bites her quivering lip as she flicks the mistakenly shorn hair off her lap and onto the floor.

Melina looks around for Candace-the-Junior and finds her gawping by the sinks. 'I'm done. Come and sweep up my station, please?' The teenager shoots Noni a knowing look and Melina's blood runs colder than the freezer. A trainee wouldn't dare disrespect an experienced stylist unless it was approved by the boss.

'Mel, you got a sec actually?' Noni puts Mrs Miltiades' reluctantly proffered fiver in the till and separates her bum from her stool. She waddles into the glorified cupboard like a woman used to being followed, then lowers herself into a wooden chair opposite Melina and exhales dramatically. 'Is it me, or is everything round here getting smaller and hotter?'

It was definitely her.

'I'm sorry about this morning. There was a queue for the bathroom at the new place we're renting.'

Noni pulls a piece of bubble gum out of her trouser

pocket, unwraps it, and swaps the brain-like wad in her mouth with the fresh one. There's a brief silence while she chews the square into an acceptable texture. 'Mel . . .'

Melina's heart sinks.

'There's no easy way of saying this, but I think you need some time away to sort your head out.'

'I'm fine, thanks, Noni.'

Noni smiles at her regretfully. 'Thing is . . .' She's not making suggestions. 'I've had loads of complaints about your work recently, Mel. I mean, I get it. He was your father and God knows what I would do if I lost my pappali, but I've only got a small client base. If ten Mrs Ms cancel their appointments in a row, I'm in serious financial trouble.'

The air in the little cupboard feels hot and suffocating and Melina wishes she'd worn her hair up and away from her sticky neck. 'How long we talking?' She notices, as she tries to avoid Noni's stare, that the shelf behind her is crammed full of Wagon Wheels. She wonders if they're a new pregnancy craving. 'Like, a few weeks?'

Noni shuffles her bloated bum around in her chair. 'I was thinking 'til I'm back from maternity leave, and then maybe we could meet up for a coffee.'

'Next year?' Melina stutters. 'You mean you're firing me?'

'I'm going to pay you until the end of July, Mel. I think that's plenty fair and Taz agrees. We think you should take the summer off and spend it with your mum.'

'Who's gonna cover me?' she butts in. 'My client appointments?' How she chooses to spend her looming unemployment is none of Noni and the Tasmanian Devil's business.

'I called my cousin Vi this morning. You remember her – tall girl with the weird lisp thingy? She did her training here a few years ago?'

'I don't remember her at all, as it goes.' Melina doesn't feel like being polite about Noni's extended family. 'So she couldn't have been all that.'

'Oh, Mel.' Noni leans back in her seat and rubs her belly like the woman who won it all at the fair. 'I'm sorry it's come to this.' She pities her, Melina can tell. 'I would've loved to have made you acting manager but it just ain't working out.' She blows a bubble as big as her bump and bursts it with her front teeth. 'We had some laughs in here though, didn't we? Especially in them early days?'

She was just like her mamma. Just like Hass. The three of them acting like her guilt should have a use by date.

'Good luck with the baby, Noni.'

Like her grief for her pappa was an inconvenience.

'Same to you, Mel.'

Melina stumbles to her feet and looks around for the handbag she dumped earlier. She's in a hurry to go. She can feel her eyes welling up with tears of humiliation and she doesn't want to give Noni the satisfaction.

'You should sue her disrespectful arse.' Hass smokes his after-dinner joint before dinner to calm himself down. Melina leans across the bed and extracts it from his fingers. Tonight, she's really craving the high.

'Sue her for what?' She inhales deeply, holding her breath until the first, satisfying head rush kicks in before blowing the smoke towards the skin-coloured ceiling.

'For sacking you over a stupid mistake when you've been there for what?' He pauses to count on his fingers. 'Seven years. Where's her effing loyalty?'

Melina leans back on the bed and closes her eyes as the events of the day melt into a blur. A blur is manageable. She can control a blur. 'I guess there was more than one incident.' She pictures Mrs Miltiades in a flamingo pink fascinator and stifles a guilty giggle.

'Yeah, how many we talking, then?'

'Dunno, two.' There was no point getting into it now. 'Maybe three.'

Hass reclaims his joint and sucks on it irritably. 'We need to move into your mum's, Mel. We can't afford to stay here, chucking money down Irini's drains.'

Melina imagines her mamma floating around the kitchen in her colourful top, offering to boil eggs for breakfast as her boobs flopped around unrestrained. She winces as if the thought literally scratched her skin. 'We've got a few months.'

Downstairs, Vincent and Pete Pelecano are watching the football and they've turned the volume up to anti-social levels. Whistles, claps and cheers fill the flesh-coloured bedroom and contrast with her melancholy mood. 'Who's playing?'

'Spain and Uruguay.'

Melina wonders if Navid is watching the game with them. She can't imagine him drinking lager and jumping up and down on the sofas. He seems sophisticated. More sophisticated than Vincent, Pete and Hass, for that matter. Their paths crossed on the front step earlier. She was coming in as he was leaving; his long arm made an arch with the doorway and she ducked beneath it and, as his eyes briefly acknowledged hers, she noticed that they were coloured like conkers. She thought they were beautiful. That *he* was beautiful. Afterwards, she could feel herself blushing as she jogged up the stairs.

Loud roars erupt from the living room and burst Melina's bubble. 'You can go and join them if you like.' She can see that he's tempted to ditch her and it hurts. 'I won't mind.' What was another loss when she'd lost so much already?

She sighs a little too loudly. 'He never liked me being a hairdresser. He thought it was a waste of his years at the cash and carry. He's probably laughing at me from up there, or down there, or wherever the hell he's stuck.' Somehow, he's always stuck.

Hass offers her his dying joint and she grabs at her consolation prize. He rolls off the bed and tucks his T-shirt into the waistband of his jeans. Runs his fingers through his black spiky hair. He's looking forward to their impromptu evening apart, she can tell. Lately, she's been dragging him down.

'He wanted me to become a doctor like Mr Patel's daughter.'

'Who?'

'The man who owned the sweet shop at the bottom of our road.'

'Well, from what I hear, your dad didn't like a lot of things, Mel. You sure about me watching the end of the game with the lads?'

'Course, babe.'

'I'll go down Green Lanes and grab some kebabs after.'

They were 'the lads' tonight. The other day they were all a bunch of losers and tossers. He leans across the bed to plant a kiss on her lips.

'Shut the door on your way out.'

She folds herself beneath the covers and fantasises about Navid. How, when he looked at her in Irini's doorway, his eyes were as beautifully blameless as hers were guilt-ridden.

~

It was supposed to be a celebration dinner. She bought fish and chips from the English place her mamma preferred and they arranged themselves around the table to hear her news. 'It's a salon called Noni's in Turnpike Lane. It's really trendy, *everybody* goes there and . . .' to emphasise just how cool and trendy the place actually was, 'instead of a dot over the letter "i" on the sign, there's a little pair of scissors hovering in the air. Get it?'

Her mamma got it, while her pappa sighed and swore.

'Scissors in my eye?' He reached for the salt and poured a small mountain over his chips.

'Careful, Nico,' Aliki warned from behind her stripy hair-hat. 'You'll give yourself that heart attack you've been promising us for years.'

Her pappa muttered something inaudible under his breath.

'What was that, Nico?'

'I said, it's not the salt that's going to kill me, wife, it's my own bloody daughter!'

'Me?' Melina pushed her supper away. She wasn't so hungry any more. 'What did I do?'

'A career in a salon – *really*, Melina?'

'Well, where did you expect her to end up?' Her mamma shook her head at her husband's stupidity. 'In a rocket? She's just finished a hairdressing course.'

To be fair, Melina had only enrolled on the course in the first place so she could spend more time with Rainey. She had applied to do Cosmetology at Haringey College and the timetables were conveniently similar.

'Cosmetology?' Melina had pulled a silly face to make her friend smile. 'Is that, like, studying the planets and stuff?'

It meant they could walk to the chippy together at lunchtimes. Sit on the little wall outside the entrance and gossip about the other students in their classes. The girl who dressed head to toe in tin foil, the boy with six hoops through his tongue.

'Very funny, Greek honey! Actually, it's about learning how to apply different beauty treatments, and you'll be sorry when I'm *the* make-up artist to the slebs.'

Melina didn't doubt it for a single second. Rainey even looked the part since she'd had her braces removed, her pink, pouty lips now framing lovely straight teeth instead of the horrible silver train tracks.

Her pappa exhaled slowly and stroked his unshaved chin. Melina could hear the stubble bristling beneath his calloused fingers. 'Melina . . .' He spoke more kindly, hoping to rekindle some common sense within her. 'Is this really what you want to do with your life? You want to sweep up hair and make cups of tea all day. Think of your future,' he urged. 'Think of where you'll be when I'm long gone and you're not trying to make a silly point, hah?'

'I won't be sweeping up the hair, though, Pappa. They have a junior to do all that. I'm going to be working as a stylist.'

Nice Nico routine over, her pappa smashed his fist down onto the table and made them all jump, including himself. 'Is this what I busted my immigrant arse off for? For split ends and dandruff?' Soggy chips flew everywhere but at least the speech was short.

It was her mamma's turn to sigh, and she did it like a person who was sick to death, not just of her husband, but of her life as well.

'*She* put you up to this?' Ah, there it was. Melina had been wondering when he would remember that everything was Rainey's fault. 'Rainy Spain?'

'What? No!'

'You know Mr Patel's daughter is studying medicine

at university? She's in her second year – he told me so when I went in to buy . . .' He couldn't bring himself to say 'fags'. 'When I went in to buy chewing gum the other day. He looked like the cat who ate all the fish.'

'Cream, Pappa. The cat that got the cream.'

'Fish? Cream? Same difference. Point is, he was *proud*.'

'Good for Mr Patel's daughter.' Aliki squished a bit of cod between her fingers, examining it for fish bones before poking it into her small mouth. 'Who cares, Nico? Some people are doctors, some people are hairdressers and some people fix leaking taps for a living.'

'I care, because she'll be a nice oncologist living in a nice house, thank you very much, and my daughter will be sweeping up hair. What did Mr Patel do so right, hah? Did I not carry enough boxes or something?'

'Pappa, I won't be sweeping up the hair . . .' But he wasn't listening any more. He wasn't listening to her and he wasn't listening to her mamma. He dumped his fish and chip wrappers in the bin and huffed into the sitting room to search for his secret cigarettes.

Melina fled to her room in floods of tears. He had ruined her celebration meal. They were supposed to be having a nice night toasting her new job and he had ruined everything. She switched on her stereo and blasted 'Respect' at full volume, singing at the top of her voice just to piss him off.

Her mamma cleaned up the last of their takeaway dinner and shuffled up the stairs to comfort her. 'Can I come in, agabi?' She looked like a worn-out geisha, standing in the doorway with a cup of chai nestled in her palms.

'I don't want to be a stupid doctor, Mamma.' Melina sat up on her bed and wiped a snot worm on the back of her hand. 'Or a lawyer or a barrister, or anything that *he* wants me to be.'

'I know, agabi.' Her mamma stroked her hair and dabbed at her mascara-stained tears with the tips of her thumbs. 'He'll come around, you'll see,' although they both knew he wouldn't.

Melina didn't want to be a doctor but she didn't necessarily want to be a hairdresser, either. She didn't know what she wanted to do with the rest of her life because she was only eighteen. Happiness was soul music. Drinking cheap lager with Rainey May in the Manor Arms while Aretha blared from the jukebox. Walking to her friend's house as the sun set behind the rooftops and the world bled in oranges and mauves.

'What's next, Melina?' Remembering their unfinished business, her pappa climbed out of his brown sofa to shout at her some more from the bottom of the stairs. 'A Turkish husband? Is that what's coming for me next?'

~

She's become preoccupied with people's routines. She's turned into her pappa, spying on the neighbours through the bedroom window because she has too much time on her hands. Mr Ibrahim, trudging out of the house at six thirty every morning. Pete Pelecano, stomping along the hallway to take the world's loudest piss. Vincent, bouncing happily up the stairs to lock himself in the loo until Hass knocks on the door an hour later. 'Bro, you gonna be in the bog much longer?' Irini, shuffling around in her loft room until lunchtime in an attempt to minimise her imprint on the house.

The footsteps are like a series of clocks. They let Melina know when it's safe to surface from her own room and when it's not. When to sneak into the upstairs kitchen in marshmallow-pink pyjamas to enjoy some peace and quiet.

Navid is always the last to leave. His footsteps are different. They're considerate, like Mr Ibrahim's, but they're also filled with a confidence that the older man's lack. They tell the world that he's fit and handsome. That he likes to boil Turkish coffee in his dressing gown and drink it by the window. She imagines him standing where she is now, sipping his coffee and gazing out at the rooftops. Since their brief doorway encounter, she can't unglue him from her mind. His olive skin and his brown, blameless eyes. She wonders what Hass would say if he could open her head and fish these thoughts out with a net.

'The Arab?' he'd sneer. 'You're well out of order, Mel.'

'Why? It's no different to you fantasising about the topless girls,' she'd reply

'Course it is. Girls in magazines ain't real. Everyone knows that. The geezer downstairs is.'

Navid wasn't real, either.

She fills the crusty kettle in the corner and flicks the switch. It looks like it's been rescued from an ancient shipwreck and she's surprised when it roars into life. It's a relief to be alone in the house. Like bunking off school to watch crap daytime telly when everyone else is out.

She knows next to nothing about the other lodgers, although she enjoys making up stories about them. Mr Ibrahim is a barista in a coffee shop but the tips are rubbish so he plays the violin outside Selfridges. Vincent owns a million pairs of trainers because he's running away from his girlfriend. He also has an irritable bowel. Pete Pelecano is trying to win his wife back but her orgasms are better with the lover. He's also secretly gay. Navid is studying to become a civil engineer although he would much rather be in Iran.

She knows this last part is true because Irini dropped it into a conversation once – although she sprinkled her words with a dose of xenophobia. 'Well, he should turn around and go back there, then, shouldn't he? If England is such a terrible place.'

Melina wonders why anyone would choose to stay in a place like this. In a sad, worn-out house that stinks of burnt cheese on toast with a landlady who doesn't like people.

Why is *she* still here, come to that?

An afternoon at the beginning of April flashes in her mind. She was standing by the very same window, looking out over the sea of chimneys and thinking that they looked like hands. Life felt ripe for a change. A hazy sun was peeking out from behind the clouds and her mamma had been to see her. To reassure her that she was doing the right thing by moving out with Hass. 'You're twenty-five years old, agabi. Live your life *your* way.' Those were her exact words. 'Your life.' Her mamma's encouragement filled her with confidence and she was happier than she had been in ages.

The telephone in the downstairs hallway rang too loudly, shattering her peace. Irini answered it and called out her name. Everything was too loud, all of a sudden. The ringing of the phone, Irini's voice, the anxiety swooshing in her ears. She knew. She saw it in the changing colours of Irini's face. The yellow skin fading to grey and then white.

Her mamma blurted it into her ear. 'Melina. I've just got in and found Pappa on the stairs.'

'Call for an ambulance?'

'It's too late. He's cold. I think he's gone, Melina.'

'What? No! Mamma? Are you still there? Hang up and call an ambulance now!'

'I said he's already gone.' She sounded defeated, deflated, but strangely calm.

Melina's body grew limp and she let go of the phone. It made a clunking noise as it hit the floor. She bent over to pick it up because it felt important, suddenly. Replacing the receiver. Her mamma might try to call again and tell her it was all a mistake.

When she was a little girl, her pappa used to take her to Broomfield House to look at the displays. The mysterious stuffed animals with the sad, glassy eyes. Aged eight, it was her favourite thing to do.

'Who says they're dead, hah?' he teased.

'Of course they're dead!' she would squeal. 'They're stuffed, Pappa. They have to die before they get filled with feathers and things otherwise it would hurt them too much.'

'Really? That what you think?' He would lower his voice to a whisper. 'Look again, but more closely this time. I think they're just pretending.'

~

Rainey was a true vision of colour that night. She wore a bright green jumper accessorised with a string of giant yellow beads and an apricot shade of lipstick. She looked amazing as she crooned 'A Natural Woman' into her bottle of lager and the crusty regulars of the Manor Arms were enjoying the spontaneous show. Melina waited for Aretha to fade before motioning for her to come back. Rainey executed a tipsy little bow in front of the jukebox and her admirers congratulated her with sparse claps. 'Well done, gorgeous, that was cracking! Got any more of them tunes?'

A fan fixed Rainey in his blurry sights and stalked her all the way back to their table. 'Um. Can I get you a drink?' His forearms were inked with Betty Boop tattoos and he was wearing Freddie Mercury's moustache. Melina's heart sank. She was sick of waiting. Sick of sharing. She had an exciting secret to blurt out and she wished the world would piss off and leave them alone.

Rainey made him stand there like a tattooed lemon while she took three long glugs of her lager. 'I got one already, ta.'

'Can I have your, um, number, then?'

'I'm with someone. Sorry.'

Melina smirked into her drink.

'What about your mate?' He nodded reluctantly towards the runner-up but his eyes were still boring into Rainey.

'I dunno. Why don't you ask her yourself?'

'I've got a boyfriend, too.'

Rainey's head jerked up from the top of her bottle. It was the way Melina said it. Like she actually wasn't joking. 'Can you get lost now, please?' She brushed Freddie off as if he were a worm-laying fly and reached across the table for Melina's hands.

'Really?'

'Really! I've been trying to tell you all night.'

The next five minutes were entirely filled with Rainey's yelling and shrieking. 'So? Spill! I gotta hear this!'

Melina was glad to be back in the spotlight. This was why she'd invited her to the pub. *This* was her big news. 'His name is Hassan but his friends call him Hass.'

'Hass!' More indecipherable shrieking. 'I love it! Did you tell him that your name is Greek Honey?'

'Very funny!'

The joke never aged.

'Where'd you meet him?'

'In his dad's grocery shop. He works there. Well . . .

when he feels like it.' Melina was pleased with that last part. It made it sound like they were already a couple. Like she knew him intimately.

'So ...' Rainey was still holding on to her hands. 'You just walked into his grocery shop and there he was, like, thank you God?'

Actually, her mamma had bought her a denim mini-skirt and a pair of pink leg warmers from the market to cheer her up after the argument with her pappa. 'Skirt suits you, agabi.' She'd watched her getting dressed from the doorway of her room and then sent her on a pointless errand to buy anari. 'Go to Ozil's further down the Lanes, OK? His cheeses are always the best.' Her instructions were very specific.

'Get your mum, the matchmaker.'

'My mum?' Melina frowned in confusion. 'My mum's oblivious to anything like that, seriously. I'm surprised she's even had sex.'

'Doesn't sound like it to me,' Rainey teased. 'New skirt and leg warmers? Sounds like she set you up.'

'No way.' Melina shook her head. 'How would she even know he would be there?'

Rainey shrugged. 'You been on a date with him yet? This Hass?' She hissed his name on purpose.

'Yeah,' Melina admitted, proudly. 'We went to Ally Pally.' He'd picked her up after work and surprised her with a drive to Alexandra Palace. He'd parked next to the balustrade and they'd climbed the grassy hill to admire the blanket of rooftops stretching all the way out to east London.

'Now *this* is a view.'

It really was, and it was the first time Melina had seen the city like that. From up high. There were so many houses crammed into such a small space, she hadn't realised how many. She felt privileged, presiding over everything from the balustrade. Like she was Queen Alexandra and the world was hers.

'Wow!'

'Innit wicked?'

She felt giddy with happiness.

Afterwards, Hass spread his jacket on the grass and they lay side by side, staring up at the orange sky. It had been criss-crossed with fluffy condensation trails that promised them new adventures.

'Are we together, then?' he'd finally asked, stubbing his joint out behind her and leaning over to kiss her on the mouth. 'Like, properly?'

'I guess,' she'd giggled.

'You guess?' His lips had tasted like marijuana as his hand wandered beneath her jumper to trace the outline of her bra. More first times. 'What sort of lame answer is that?'

Rainey swooned. 'Sounds like the best night ever.'

Melina was suddenly thrust back into the Manor Arms. 'It was definitely the second best.'

'Why second?'

'Cos walking to yours that first time was better. The night we didn't get into the cinema.'

'Awww . . .' Rainey put her hand over her heart. 'Tell it to your face then. Looks like it's been slapped.'

Melina leaned back in her chair and pulled at the edges of the sticker on her bottle. She liked to pick at things when she was concentrating too hard. Her spots, mostly, and the bits of skin around her nails.

'You nervous about the shagging part? You want Rainey May to tell you where the guy sticks it?'

'Shut up!' Melina blushed as Rainey pointed up her skirt. 'I'm worried because, well . . . he's Turkish.'

'So?' Rainey, who had been dating a Pakistani boy on and off since school, suddenly grew defensive. 'He's Turkish and Ahmad is from Pakistan – who cares?'

'Not me.' Melina set her straight. 'I mean, my father wouldn't like it.'

'Why? He a racist or something?'

Melina hesitated. How could she explain her pappa to someone as liberal and free-spirited as Rainey? Someone whose parents were born into the English culture and let her forge her own path? Especially when Melina had hidden so much from her already. The arguments that preceded their nights out and the fights that followed their phone calls. His silly names for her. 'Rainy Spain!'; 'Rain Again?' His speeches on the stairs. She didn't want Rainey to patronise her or to think of her as sheltered and ignorant.

'Look . . .' Rainey leaned across the table to squeeze her hands again. Melina noticed that her fingernails were painted in different colours. 'If it makes life easier, you can use me as an alibi.' Pinks, oranges, greens, yellows. She wondered if they practised it in class.

'Alibi? You make it sound like I'm planning to murder him.'

'I guess you could?' Rainey's eyes shone wickedly. 'Or, I could just cover for you. You can say you're with me whenever your dad asks and if he calls me, I'll lie.'

'You'd do that?'

'Course.' Rainey blew her a rainbow kiss over the top of her bottle. 'What are life-savers for?'

~

England are playing Belgium in the last round of the tournament before the quarter finals. Vincent, Pete and Hass sit around the television downstairs with their packets of crisps and cans of lager. The house smells of boozy expectation and she supposes it's better than the burnt cheese on toast. She likes the idea of football. It's what redeems it, she thinks – the idea. The camaraderie. People drinking in beer gardens. Everyone on the same side for ninety minutes, willing the same thing to happen.

He was happy to be joining 'the lads' again tonight, she could tell. He didn't even ask her permission this time. 'It's a big game. Don't wait up, babe.' Despite his kisses, she can tell she is losing him to his life.

She thinks back to that night in the Manor Arms. Rainey posing in front of the jukebox in her eighties clothes and giant yellow beads. Shrieking with excitement because Melina finally met a boy. He told her something else on their first date, although she didn't share it with Rainey. It felt too private, too personal. He told her that his mum walked out before he could walk to be with another man. He never saw her again. Nobody did, not even his father. She could tell that the story bothered him although he shrugged it off in his macho Hass way. That it was on the tip of his tongue all the time and the slightest tickle, push or squeeze and the words would come pouring out.

'I'm sorry,' she told him as they stared up at the cotton-wool sky, although the word felt light and insubstantial. Like a feather floating in between them, nothing more than that. 'I'm so sorry.'

She wonders now, sitting on the windowsill and staring out at the street while the television blares loudly downstairs, why he told her about Mrs Ozil in the first place. Was it so that she would pity him? So that she would fall in love? Would she still be with him if he wasn't Turkish, or if she'd met someone like Navid first?

Lately, she's been wondering a lot of things.

For instance, why her grief doesn't feel like an explosion but like a series of painful sensations. This afternoon, when she walked to her mamma's house, she was even resentful of the trees. The way they rustled happily in the summer breeze while in her heart, it's winter. She feels other things, too. Anger, mostly. She's angry with the football fans for having something to celebrate and with her mamma for ditching her bra. Making cheese sandwiches like nothing matters. Like *he* never mattered at all.

'Don't wait up, babe.' She can feel him slipping away. She can feel it all slipping away. Like grains of sand through her open fingers.

'Goal!' The redbrick houses of Harringay erupt into life. Lights flicker on and off across the road and, in the background, car horns blare their disbelief into the summer air. England are in the lead.

'You're supposed to be going places, Melina. I thought you were my bright shining star.' He used to say this to her whenever she disappointed him. When her exam results were below average or when Rainey called the house on a school night. When the news about Hassan leaked into his life and his re-runs of *On the Buses*.

'Go on!' Downstairs, the lions raise the roof while she carries on sitting on the windowsill.

She disentangles Hassan's hands from around her waist and rolls out from beneath the duvet.

'Aww, Mel,' he grumbles. 'I was enjoying my morning snuggle.'

'It's a Saturday, babe. I've gotta go . . .'

'Can't your mum do it?'

'Mamma?' Melina tuts in irritation. 'She hasn't been to see him since April.'

He buries his head beneath the pillow to muffle the intrusive sounds of slamming doors and banging drawers. 'I won't be long.' She throws on a black top and a pair of black jeans and scoops her hair up into a messy bun. She contemplates make-up. Something to disguise her sunken eyes and sallow skin, and decides there's no point. She hasn't worn it since she lost her job and she's not about to put it on for this. 'The point is to make you feel better.' She can hear Rainey's disapproving voice in her ear, telling her that browns bring out the flecks in her eyes. 'That's the point of wearing make-up.'

She pulls the bedroom door closed behind her and hurries down the stairs. She hunts for her bag beneath the piles of jackets and when she finds it hidden behind Navid's, she smiles to herself. Hass thinks her too trusting for leaving her things lying around. 'We don't really know the geezers, do we?' When he was trying to score a point, the other men were losers again. 'Any one of them could nick a fiver from your purse.'

She jogs down the street to the nearest bus stop. Saturday mornings are busy and there's only one seat left. She climbs over a sweaty man wearing a pair of giant headphones to fold herself tightly into the space. The man's fleshy arm sticks to the top of hers in the heat and she cringes at the intimate sensation. She turns her body towards the window and surveys the passing scenes.

Beyond the pane, city life goes on as usual. A mother in a hijab pushes a baby in a pram. A woman flicks a red sari over her shoulder and struggles with a million bags. A middle-aged man in traditional Islamic clothing marches purposefully into a mini market called Mustafa's. The shop sign is red and white.

'Is this what you want? For your son to be called Mustafa instead of Nico?'

'What's wrong with naming my son Mustafa?'

The bus stops opposite the cemetery gates and the doors hiss open as though they're glad to be rid of her.

'Where are your principles, Melina?'

'Prejudices are not principles, Pappa.' She was so tired by then. Tired of all the pleading and the arguing.

She crosses the street and buys a bouquet of roses from the flower seller outside the entrance. He recognises her but there's no small talk. There never is. People don't come here to chit-chat. Her trainers crunch along the gravel path as she heads towards the new section where he's buried; the sound of feet on gravel is satisfying and reminds her of childhood trips to the beach. Brighton, Southend, Margate, Blackpool, although he refused to go back to Morphou. He told them he was scared of flying but, looking back, she wonders if there might have been more to his reluctance.

Melina sighs as she picks over the past. The voice in her head, the one that tells her there's no point in anything any more, asks her what she thinks she's doing. What she's trying to prove by visiting his grave. Laying down more bouquets and watering them with her apologies. 'What for?' the voice sneers. 'It's too late. The flowers won't grow now!'

When she's within sight of the black cross with the swirly gold inscription, the crunching stops. There's somebody else there, standing over the grave with his hands crossed in front of him. Despite the heat, the stranger is wearing a dark blazer. Melina looks around, wondering if he's with an entourage or if he's lost his way. Who is he? She thought she knew everyone in her pappa's life, that there was nobody left to mourn him.

Intrigue conquers fear and she walks slowly towards the grave. The man looks up from his hands. 'I hoped I'd run into you here, Melina.'

His voice resurrects the hair on the back of her arms. Everything about him is familiar. The way he looks, the way he sounds, the way he smells. Even the way he is stooping over the cross, his head bent below his shoulders. He's so familiar that she forgets herself and drops the roses into the gravel.

'I'm Angelo Angelides, by the way.' He extends a palm and she shakes it, firmly, a sudden burst of confidence taking her by surprise. 'You wrote me a thank you card.'

The undertaker? 'You're the funeral director?' Is that why she recognised him? Why he knew her name?

'Yeah. We buried your father a few months back. Me and my apprentice, Stel.'

She picks up the bouquet and lays it down on top of the others. Most of them have rotted into corpse-flowers but she can't bear to throw them in the bin. She straightens up slowly and absorbs him in flashes. His shiny black brogues. His suit trousers, leather belt and Rolex. His big nose and small dark eyes. He's well dressed. Rich, even. The business of death must be booming.

'I've been staring at your card for a while, now, and wondering if I should get in touch.'

'OK . . .' Anticipation creeps into her voice uninvited.

'Yeah, see, I recently found something out. Something my mother admitted after many years of secrets and it concerns you, as well.' He points towards a nearby wooden bench surrounded by a small grove of cypress trees. He clears his throat and the gold watch on his wrist glints in the sunlight. 'Shall we?'

He attempts polite conversation as she follows him through the graves. 'The woman buried just there was my aunty. I miss her very much.'

'I'm sorry.' The inscription reads '*Evgenia Theocaris*' and there's a bunch of pink carnations propped up against her headstone.

'Thanks. She was a very special lady. That one just over there?' She follows the direction of his finger. 'She was one of mine as well. Twenty-four. Died in her sleep.'

'People die in their sleep?' Melina flinches at life's apparent fragility as she surveys the carpet of flowers. So many flowers that they spill out onto the little path, blurring the lines between life and death. '*Katarina "Katie" Gerou*'.

'Not generally. I mean, that's what the family put out there but I bet the inquest said something different.'

'Why would they want people to think she died in her sleep?'

'Shame, usually. Let's just say that the Church still frowns on certain ways of dying.'

Melina has no idea what he's talking about.

'You religious?'

She shakes her head.

'Neither am I. Doing this job, you see far too much to believe in the rainbows and the fairy tales. It's a nice idea, though.'

He sits down on the bench and she takes a seat beside him. She notices that his trouser leg is almost touching hers. Almost, but not quite.

'There were no rainbows the day we buried Katie.'

'I can't believe people actually search for rainbows at funerals.' The idea seemed so sad to her. So pitiful. Looking up at the sky, despite everything. 'Makes me want to cry, to be honest.'

'Yeah. You'd be surprised what gets the families through a funeral. Rainbows, shapes in the clouds, a clear droplet on a leaf.' Angelo sighs. 'Other times, it's as simple as knowing the truth about their loved one. Who they *really* were.' She can feel him staring at her, but she can't bring herself to face him. Not yet. 'It's brought me some peace, anyway. Knowing.'

They listen in silence to the sound of birdsong until he's ready to tell her.

Melina waits for her outside Covent Garden station, her bags arranged carefully at her feet, smallest to largest. It's been so long since she's taken the bus into town that she feels like a tourist. A disorientated tourist soaking things up for the first time. The crowds, the colours, the parks, the pubs. Everything seems too big, too loud and too bright.

It's the afternoon of the World Cup final and the streets are throbbing with excitement. Men tie T-shirts around their waists to expose hairy bellies to the sun. Women wear silly blue and white wigs and press radios to their ears. Their squeaky voices float around Melina like bubbles in gold champagne.

'Why is everyone cheering for Argentina?' she asked Hass during their final kebab supper at Irini's. It was a greasy celebration. A proper one this time, because he couldn't wait to pack his stuff and go home.

'West Germany knocked us out, so now we want their enemy to win. That's how it works.' He explained football ethics to her with his mouth full of lamb souvlaki.

'I don't get it.' She liked the way it sounded, though. 'England sings for Argentina.' Like a poem or the title of a film. It sounded hopeful.

Afterwards, she left him gathering up his many pairs of trainers and called Rainey from the telephone in the hallway. She was the last to know and she was upset, Melina could tell from the tone of her voice. The long, unpunctuated silences. 'I'm your best friend, Mel. I could at least have come to his funeral.'

'I'm sorry, Ray.' The truth was, telling her would have made everything too raw, too real. 'I guess I just wasn't ready.'

A man struts past her in a shirt and tie. The over-stressed, overdressed City worker among the drunken football fans. Today, he's the one who doesn't belong. Melina's mind drifts back to Angelo. She wonders if he'll be watching the game on an expensive television or if he's too busy minding his dead. His Evgenias and his Katie Gerous. She doesn't know how he can stomach it, doing what he does, but she's glad he was the one who buried him. It seems fitting, somehow.

She figured it out. In the short interval between listening to the birdsong and the words that would change the course of her life, she knew why she recognised him. He looked just like the face in the black and white photograph. The one her mamma hated and her pappa kept by his bed. The faces were so alike that there could be no other explanation.

'He was my father, too.'

Still, there was something about hearing the words.

'I'm sorry, Melina, but I don't believe there's any bliss in ignorance.'

Knowing that her pappa had his secrets; that he, too, made mistakes. That he was fallible after all. 'Don't be. I'm glad you told me.'

'Yeah?'

'I think so. I will be.'

He was grateful for her exoneration.

Afterwards, she let him ink his telephone number onto the back of her hand and she even managed a smile. 'When you feel ready, Melina.' She liked the way he spoke her name, the syllables dancing on his tongue. As if she had waited her whole life for someone to say her name properly and finally, here was Angelo.

Melina spots her in the crowd and waves her arm like a windscreen wiper. She's dressed like sunshine in July. 'Oh, Mel!' Rainey swims through the sea of boozy breath and salty skin to reach her. 'You should have called me sooner.' She pulls her large sunglasses onto her head to scan her friend's new face. 'Where does Hass think you are?'

'He thinks I've gone back to my mum's for a while.'

'And your mum?'

'That I'm staying at Mr Ozil's. I'll phone in a couple of days. I just need some time to figure things out.'

'They can wait.' Rainey clicks her tongue against the roof of her mouth as she links her long arm through hers. 'You gotta do what's best for you now, Mel.'

It's what Angelo said, too. 'When you feel ready, come and find me.'

They weave in and out of the football fans on their way to Rainey's flat. 'Stay as long as you like – *mi casa* and all that. I've even bought a new record player for Etta . . .' Her voice dissolves in the summer breeze as the anticipated match finally kicks off. Melina can no longer make out what she is saying over the sounds of cheering and chanting.

Acknowledgements

I would like to thank my parents whose memories of Cyprus during the fifties and sixties breathed colour and authenticity into Nico and Emiliana's Orange Parade. I hope I was able to do justice to our many conversations.

Thanks to my husband, Jim. The fount of all historical knowledge. I'd also like to mention a wonderful video called Harvey's Soho which I came across during my research into a pre-war London childhood.*

I would like to express my gratitude to funeral director, Gary Valentine-Fuller Dip FAA, DipFD. Thank you for taking the time to discuss matters of the afterlife with me.

Finally, with special thanks to my editor, Abigail Scruby, to Charlotte Robathan, Amber Burlinson, Eleanor Birne and Lisa Highton.

* This Is Soho, 'Harvey's Soho', 16 November 2014, www.youtube.com/watch?v=T8FlkoIq8NA